SO WILD THE WIND

So Wild the Wind

Bonnie Hobbs

FIVE STAR
A part of Gale, a Cengage Company

GALE
A Cengage Company

Farmington Hills, Mich • San Francisco • New York • Waterville, Maine
Meriden, Conn • Mason, Ohio • Chicago

GALE
A Cengage Company

Copyright 2018 by Bonnie Hobbs
Five Star™ Publishing, a part of Gale, a Cengage Company

LIBRARY OF CONGRESS CATALOGING-IN-PUBLICATION DATA

Names: Hobbs, Bonnie author.
Title: So wild the wind / Bonnie Hobbs.
Description: First edition. | Farmington Hills, Mich. : Five Star, 2018. | Identifiers: LCCN 2017055252 (print) | LCCN 2018001149 (ebook) | ISBN 9781432838546 (ebook) | ISBN 9781432838539 (ebook) | ISBN 9781432838522 (hardcover)
Subjects: LCSH: Widows—Fiction. | Triangles (Interpersonal relations)—Fiction. | GSAFD: Western stories | Historical fiction
Classification: LCC PS3608.O233 (ebook) | LCC PS3608.O233 S63 2018 (print) | DDC 813/.6—dc23
LC record available at https://lccn.loc.gov/2017055252

First Edition. First Printing: July 2018
Find us on Facebook–https://www.facebook.com/FiveStarCengage
Visit our website–http://www.gale.cengage.com/fivestar/
Contact Five Star™ Publishing at FiveStar@cengage.com

Printed in Mexico
1 2 3 4 5 6 7 22 21 20 19 18

So Wild the Wind

PROLOGUE

The Texas Gulf Coast
1866

Just before sunset, the wind began shrieking, whipping the sea into froth. Martin Cooper lingered at his library window, entranced. Beneath the wind's licking tongue, the sea had gone mad.

"Fa-Father?"

He turned his head. The child had materialized beyond the library's open door. "William? You should not be here."

"But the wind and, and the th-thunder."

"Find Cora. Stay with her." He furrowed his brow and turned his gaze back to the sea, digging two fingers into his temple to stop the onset of pain before again glancing toward the boy. "You are how old, William?"

"You know, Father." He lifted his hand and splayed his fingers. "I'm five."

Cooper smoothed his features. "Yes. Five. Yet afraid of wind like a baby. Go now. Shut the door."

After the door clicked quietly closed, Cooper studied the storm. The wind shrieked like a—no, it was the sea, roaring, as changeable as a woman, yet different. The sea could burst with passion or with rage, take hold and move on—it might forget. A woman, though, would carry rage inside forever. Experience had taught him so.

He nearly smiled. This was good, very good. A clever analogy.

7

The sea was like a woman, yet more reasonable. He must write it down. He snatched a pen from the desk nearby. But where was the inkstand? While he searched, his thoughts stirred, wafting away like morning mist. He stood tapping the window with the useless pen.

He squinted. Was that a light along the shore? He reached for his spyglass.

Yes, a light, but it was only the new shopkeeper lurching along with a lantern. A nosy man, scuttling here and there, dragging his useless leg. What *was* his name? Yes. Bishop. Rafe Bishop. The man's display of impairment was disgusting. He didn't know enough to keep out of sight, yet might be excused for he was, after all, a Yankee. Likely had little breeding. Cooper swung his glass beyond the cripple to the sea.

The storm had blown inland across the bluff and past his house. The wind had run ahead of the sun that now eased into a fiery sunset beyond the town. So the sun herded the wind? Surely it should be the other way—the wind, so wild, should be whipping the sun—but which made more sense?

The sea calmed now that the wind had gone. It darkened beneath a starlit sky. If only he could stroke the sea like he would a lover's body. "There," he whispered. "There now, hush." He lowered the spyglass and leaned his throbbing head against the cool windowpane, closing his eyes. Remembering *her* and yearning for lost love—her eyes as blue as the sea, her dark hair loose and floating around her, undulating in the crystal water. He couldn't save her. Cruel waves carried her away.

What had William said? Five years old. Five years had passed. He sighed, fogging the glass. If only the sea would give her up. If only she would come back to him, even for one day. He would make her understand how wrong she was, how cruel for leaving. He would have a chance to defend what she called his evil obsession. What would he do for one more day with her? He would do anything.

CHAPTER ONE

Off the Texas Gulf Coast
1867—one year later

Alida Garrison's linen skirt, seawater sodden, tried to drag her deeper. She fought to think with clarity, to stay afloat. Rain pelted her, wind howled, but roaring thunder and the greater part of sizzling lightning had passed over and away. Toward the eastern horizon, bright flashes lit a gray-green sky. She struggled for a better grip on the splintered door and stared at the eerie light.

Something brushed her legs. She kicked it away, her heart pounding as she fought to inch herself further onto this pitiful raft. She had only strength enough to haul her chest and belly up, leaving her legs dangling, skirts ballooning about them. Anything peering from the murky depths would see white legs wriggling like worms on a hook.

Would a creature be curious? Would it be hungry? Fear chilled her as this tepid sea never could. When something grazed her thigh, she screamed and thrashed water to foam, then took a breath and willed herself into a semblance of composure, squinting into the water. Better to know the horror than imagine worse.

The storm had churned the sea into murky soup, dusky at its depths. A ghostly form drifted just below the surface. Alida squinted, leaning closer. Ropes trailed from her bit of wood and tangled around—around what?

11

Sarah. Her sister, Sarah.

Wisps of cloud scattered in a sudden gust of wind. A setting sun thrust spindly fingers through them and back into the sea it had left behind. Sarah's white face shimmered up through the water in the faint light. Raven-black hair, so like Alida's own, swirled around it. Blue eyes, wide and empty, stared from just below the surface and Sarah's arm undulated as if beckoning her sister to follow. Alida tugged at a loop of rope, frantic to draw her sister to the surface, but when Sarah's body broke free it glided down and away. Alida plunged after her, but Sarah sank lower and lower, one arm still reaching, eyes staring, drifting on a deeper tide.

Alida kicked back to the surface and burst from it, gasping and retching. The door—where was it? She flailed, desperate. One arm struck something hard, caught hold. Her dress, so heavy. She tore at sparkling glass buttons down the front of her bodice, then shrugged out of the dress, kicking it and the petticoats away. A tight-laced corset still hampered her breath. She couldn't make her fingers work to unhook it, so she reached behind and clawed at the lacing. Though these waters were not cold, her fingers were frozen stiff as talons from gripping the slab of wood. The knots held. She abandoned the effort, taking slower, shallower breaths and coughing her throat free of frothing seawater.

Barrels and boxes bobbed around her. Fallen sails slapped the surface and sank. Rigging tangled around her legs and things she feared to know nudged her. As she kicked free, waves rose around her like hills, like mountains. At the top of each swell she scanned the water. "Seth! James!" she screamed. Where was Seth, her Seth? And Sarah's husband, James, and Sarah's infant. Horror set her trembling. Where had she last seen them? Where were they when the ship smashed into the rocks? It had groaned and then shrieked as it split apart. Panicked sailors shouted.

Sarah had screamed and screamed. Alida remembered the baby squalling, maybe too young to know what to fear, but shrieking just the same at the chaos she sensed all around. Her own Seth, little Seth, had stared wide-eyed at Alida, trusting her to save him.

Now the water rose and fell in a silence broken only by her ragged breathing and the wildly whistling wind. Had everyone left her alone to suffer in this pitiless sea?

Her sister's accusations were justified, then. If this journey was Alida's folly, their deaths were Alida's fault.

The setting sun's last light showed men floating face down on or just beneath the water. She caught her lower lip between her teeth and bit down hard, drawing blood, determined to hold in the screams she longed to loose on the wind. She was the practical one, after all, telling her sister screaming never helped. But Sarah was gone. Alida wanted to take every patronizing word back and scream forever. When she parted her lips, a swell of murky brine washed up and filled her mouth. She gagged it out, then rested her head on the splintered wood, both hands numb from hanging on, her nails torn, fingertips bloody. Saltwater stung the scrapes along her forearms. The pain kept her conscious.

Darkness crept nearer. Numb and exhausted, she wondered— why not let the sea take her? Why not slip quietly beneath the water, join Sarah and help with the baby who was surely lost? Sarah was not strong enough to be on her own. But no. Seth could still be alive just as she was, hanging on to some bit of wood, alone and terrified. This desperate hope drove her to raise her head and shout his name over and over until her voice deserted her.

Something bumped her raft. Thoughts of surrender fled. She would fight. She spun to face it, but saw only another body. She pushed it gently with her foot. The man rolled onto his back. It was James, Sarah's husband. So pale. Alida caught her breath in a sob and nudged him away with the next swell. Any hope she had for the infant's survival went with him. Again she shouted for Seth, her voice a croak. She held herself upright on trembling arms, praying for an answer.

When none came she turned to face westward, closer to shore now for all her thrashing. The sun had dipped behind a line of distant hills, leaving a band of gray-green clouds hanging beneath star-stippled blackness high above. To her left, jagged rocks thrust into the gloom, the rocks that killed the ship. To her right, she could just make out the sandy spit of land they had sailed by just one day before. Now the sea rolled gently, though wind still gusted and swirled it into little water spouts that danced around her. She watched them, mesmerized, nearly letting go.

Then, cutting through a rumble of thunder, came human voices, shouting, screaming. She roused to the sound. "Here," she cried. "I'm here!" She pushed up on her forearms. "Seth?"

When the shouts faded, she fell back onto her belly, taking a tighter grip on the floating door and kicking hard. The memory of her family played in her mind like a magic lantern show. She had clutched Sarah's baby in the crook of one arm as the sea flooded the cabin. Seth stumbled to her and climbed up her body like a squirrel does a tree, silent in his terror. James held Sarah, her face pressed to his chest, her screams muffled. James's eyes showed calm resignation, as if he had been waiting for horror to befall and end his life since the war had failed to do so.

Something had struck Alida's head. She could remember nothing from then until waking in the surging water, holding on tight to the splintered door. She touched her scalp just above her temple. Pain knifed through and lodged just behind her eyes. Breathing hard, she stopped kicking and raised her head,

14

struggling to think despite the pounding in her skull.

The sound of heavy, rhythmic breathing confounded her. Then she recognized it. Waves against the shore. She kicked toward the sound, toward the hissing of water as it pulled back from a sandy beach. Again she heard men's voices pleading for help. She stopped kicking and fought for breath, to join her cries to the others, but their plaintive begging changed abruptly to screams of terror and pain. What on land could be more terrifying than drowning?

The screams carrying on the wind made this even more like a nightmare, yet she knew it was no dream. Not even in the worst of the war, fleeing cannon fire with Seth clutched to her breast, all of them burrowing like moles in the caves above Vicksburg, had she ever had a dream this horrifying. The sea plastered her hair to her face. The wind howled and tore away the fading cries. She licked brine and blood away from where her teeth had pierced her lip.

At least Sarah and James weren't among those who screamed so horribly. But what if Seth reached land without her to protect him? What kind of land made grown men scream in fear?

"Seth, I'm coming," she whispered, kicking harder. Soon pounding waves delivered her to shore. Their force tore her from her bit of wood and flung her onto wet sand, grinding her skin against it, washing her up onto a beach set gleaming by a rising full moon. Spent, she fought to raise her head, fought to stay alive for Seth. Sand filled her mouth, clogged her ears, nose and eyes. She spat it out and tried to push up on her arms and roll over, but couldn't fight free of the sucking sand. She flopped back on her belly, coughing.

Strong hands grasped her shoulders and heaved her over. Wind pebbled her skin. She shivered and spat. "My boy," she whispered. "Save him."

CHAPTER TWO

"Bring water. Quickly!" A man's voice cut through the wind. "Damn it, she's sucking in sand with every breath. We need to sluice her free."

Alida lifted her head. Pain slashed from temple to temple. The world went dark and from the darkness came Sarah's baby girl, newly born and nameless, bobbing in her cradle on a quiet sea. Seth, too. He held onto the cradle's side and smiled. "Hello, Mama," he said. Alida reached out, happy to see them, but her arm fell onto sand sharp as ground glass that flayed her skin and pulled her back.

"Pobrecita." Pitying words washed to her over the crashing of the waves. A wavering voice, an old woman's voice. "Rafael, you are losing her."

"No," Alida whispered. She took a ragged breath, choked and coughed. "I sold that cradle," she murmured. Memory jerked her back to reality. She struggled to sit up and gagged, trying to suck in another breath.

"Don't speak. Just breathe." The deep voice rumbled with quiet authority. It soothed her. She wanted to obey. Hands slipped beneath her, lifting her, carrying her away from the sand. Determined fingers brushed grit from her face, swiped at crusted lashes.

"She said Rafael. Are you an angel?" she whispered. "Such strong hands. Am I dying then? Are you the angel?"

"Not hardly." Again, a voice so deep. He set her down,

16

someplace mercifully dry, but kept hold of her.

"Do not let her talk, Rafael. You! You there. Bring fresh water." The old woman's voice climbed higher, hovering above them.

"Something's slammed her there at her temple, *Señora.* See? Blood's still oozing."

Alida lifted her hand to touch the bleeding place, but touched her rescuer's worried face instead. She had to see if he was real. Light, a lantern or torch, shone from behind her and illuminated his eyes. Amber eyes, paler than brown with flecks of gold and brimming with pity.

"So I am alive," she whispered.

"Hush," he said.

"Sarah and James are gone."

He took her hand. "Shh."

"They grieved . . . for the old life. I wanted . . . be free of it." She closed her eyes and slipped her hand from his. Her arm hit the ground. He stepped away. Seconds later something heavy fell across her, scratching her skin and smelling of horses. She opened her eyes and tried to focus. He had carried her to a quiet place behind a rock wall, out of wind and spray. An old woman hovered, smoothing Alida's stiffening, salt-soaked hair, murmuring gentle words in a melodic tongue. The man with gentle eyes returned and knelt, holding a cup of fresh water to her lips. She stared into his eyes, fearing but demanding truth. "Did you find—was there a boy?"

He shook his head, his gaze holding hers.

"Only you are saved," the old woman murmured. "A lost child? Ah, no."

Sorrow in her voice pried open a door in Alida. She shook her head, pushing the cup away, spilling the water as she spilled her grief. "No," she said. "Not Seth. We've come through so much and . . ." She wept then, adding tears to skin already brine-soaked.

The old woman's voice came winging from above. *"Aí, Dios mío!"*

"The baby too," Alida said. "I let them go." Tears flooded her eyes and sluiced away the last of the sand. She coughed and the man's strong arm curved around her, tightening across her chest and bending her to one side as she heaved up everything in her belly. His other hand pressed her forehead, holding her steady. When the retching quieted, he again held a cup to her lips. She drank, swallowing sand and all.

The light behind her illuminated the man's face again. She stared, using him as a touchstone to keep herself in the world. A scar began just below the inside corner of his right eye and cut down to a strong, square jaw shadowed with stubble, a rugged, somber face, lips pressed into a stern line. His nose was aquiline, just large enough to be—what? Sarah, who cared about such things, would say aristocratic. But Sarah was dead. The recollection sucked Alida's breath from her and stirred another storm of tears.

Rafe Bishop tried to give this poor woman over to *Señora* Rivera, but she gripped his shirt and heaved herself up tight against his chest. He pried her fingers from his shirt and eased her down. Eyelashes beaded with seawater and sand fluttered closed against pale, sculpted cheeks. When the *señora* nudged closer, he stood and stepped away.

Such anguish. So delicate to have survived what had killed everyone else on that ship. He'd seen bloody corpses, poor devils, broken along the shore. They must have been thrown against the rocks, for how else could they have been so battered? So she was lucky. More strength in those pale-skinned, delicate limbs than he would've imagined. Her eyes were clouded and tear-filled, but he'd wager determination usually

18

simmered behind them, though she spoke with a cultured Southern drawl that set his teeth on edge. The sound made him feel he'd been given a mouth full of sugar.

"Rafael! Your knife. Cut this string. No wonder she has no breath."

He sliced the corset strings and the young woman sucked in air, ending in a wheezing, barking cough. He winced.

"Turn away, Rafael. She shivers in this wet rag and I must remove it. *Aí*, the bruises," the *señora* murmured. "Her fingers, so bloody."

"She had a strangling grip on that bit of wood," Rafe said, turning his back.

Señora Rivera sucked at her teeth. "Here, *niñita*, my shawl will cover you," she murmured, then yelped.

Rafe spun. The strange woman's wide-eyed glare jerked from *Señora* Rivera to him, then back. She struck out with both fists, her teeth bloodying her lip as she grunted and thrashed.

"Stop now." Rafe gripped her wrists.

"I must find him. Let me go!" She batted him away, snarling like a cornered dog, then froze. "James?" she whispered, bringing arched brows together and touching the bloody swelling at her temple. "But you drowned." She struggled up on one elbow, reaching toward him. "I saw you."

Rafe knelt and cradled her hand, a hand hardly larger than a child's. If he hadn't already glimpsed the swell of breasts and a woman's hips beneath her sodden chemise, he might have thought she was indeed a child. "James? Your husband, ma'am? So far we've seen none but you. Lie back, now. Be calm if you can."

"Oh." She closed her wide blue eyes. "You are much like Sarah's James, but I saw him—and Sarah. But not the baby." She winced and squinted into his face. "I held her, then I—I . . ." She fell back and sucked in rattling breaths. "Why them?

Them and not me."

The cadence of her voice made him lift his lip in a sneer as his prejudice took hold. A knee-jerk reaction. Though he wished himself to be a better man, since the war he'd not been able to quell intolerance. "Hush. That kind of thinking won't help." He sounded too gruff and knew it. "Who are you, ma'am?" he said, gentling his voice.

"You saved me?"

"I pulled you off the sand. I believe you got there all by yourself."

She closed her eyes. "Could my boy be alive?"

Rafe didn't want to strip her of hope. He hesitated. "How old is he?"

"Six. Big for six. He's a scrapper, and survived so much." Her lips trembled.

"Maybe he's like you and fought to live." He raised his gaze to the sea. "Men have launched a boat, taken lanterns. It's late now and dark . . ."

"Oh, no! Dark? He'll be so frightened." She grasped his hand.

Rafe pressed her fingers. "Your name, ma'am?"

"Alida," she whispered. "Garrison—Mrs."

Rafe stood when the *señora* pushed closer. She patted Mrs. Garrison, peeling away the wet corset, leaving the chemise and winding the black shawl around her. Rafe eased into shadow. Mrs. Garrison coughed long and hard, her chest rattling. This time the spasm didn't pass. He pushed close again, knelt and lifted her across his arm, pounding her back until she caught a breath.

"You," she whispered when she could.

"Yes, me."

"The lights disappeared."

"No lights here, ma'am. Just stars and moon."

She blinked from beneath tangled hair and coughed again.

Señora Rivera scowled, her deeply lined face a mask of worry as she caught Rafe's eye.

"I know," he said. "It's bad."

"*Sí.* She has breathed in the sea and also sand. The sea longs to claim her yet."

"Should we take her to your house? Use my room. I'll stay at my store." He smiled at the old woman. "You can manage?"

"You are a good boy to worry, Rafael. But God gives strength enough to those who desire to help."

Rafe shook his head. "I fear I've seen things that make those words ring false, good lady."

She narrowed her eyes and her smile faded, but she said nothing more as she chafed Alida Garrison's cold hands.

"I'll bring what you need from the store if I have it."

Señora Rivera closed her eyes, as if thinking. "Sugar I will need, in chocolate and tea to strengthen her. You get us another blanket, yes? She needs something softer than what a horse wears. A gown or dress? She would be lost in a dress of mine. So small, poor thing."

As Rafe shrugged into his coat he remembered to curve his shoulders forward and make his chest look sunken. He'd fashioned the coat especially to remind him. "I'll carry her to your house."

"No! Another can carry her, Rafael. You would not be strong enough. Not all the way up the hill." She patted his hand.

Rafe ducked his head and rounded his shoulders even more. "She's no bigger than a child. I can manage."

"All right, if you must play the hero. Carry her home, then go. Can you bring medicine? Something to quiet her cough and calm her. She needs something quickly. My herbs take time to do their work."

He nodded. "Laudanum and brandy. I have a tonic that boasts of curing coughs, but I suspect it's just more laudanum."

He stared at Mrs. Garrison, sensing she needed protection, though she'd survived this horror and therefore, contrary to her appearance and quiet drawl, was likely no delicate flower. Succumbing to the wiles of a belle in distress had been his undoing before. He'd not fall for it again.

"Rafael?" The *señora* stared, tilting her head to one side. "A moment ago you were different." She shrugged. "Somehow you seemed much taller."

The observation rattled him. He'd forgotten himself in the thrill of finding the woman and saving her. Years had passed since he'd been at all heroic. He gathered Alida into his arms. As he carried her up the hill, he feigned a limp, breathing heavily, though in truth she was no burden.

Light from torches carried by the townsfolk showed a scattering of debris and bodies along the shore. Rafe's heart lurched and he spat out a sudden rise of bile, for the beach looked too much like a battlefield. He'd hoped never again to see such carnage. But at least they'd saved one, a grief-stricken, bedraggled beauty. He forgot to play his part and moved along smartly until his landlady gave him a curious, sidelong frown. He pretended to stumble and hung back. "More slowly, good lady. I can't keep up," he called.

She slowed. Pity took the place of suspicion. "I see Father Sebastian up ahead," the *señora* said. "He must pray for this poor little woman. He has much to do. So many souls sent to God this night."

"But not this one."

She crossed herself. "Not yet, Rafael. Not yet."

CHAPTER THREE

"Put her down just there, Rafael. *Con calma,* carefully."

Rafe smiled. The old woman fussed like a broody hen. He eased past her into his rented room. "Not your bed, good lady. We'll get her settled in mine."

"Your bed—a man's bed? I don't think . . ."

Rafe smiled at his landlady's quandary. "I won't be in it."

She shot a scathing scowl his way, then shrugged, nodding like she'd won an argument. She turned, lifted the lid off a chest and pulled out a blanket, then bent to build up the fire in the main room and set a kettle to boil. "Chocolate. I will make chocolate to warm her."

Rafe laid his bedraggled burden on the bed, smiling at the *señora*'s answer to almost every ill: chocolate. Mrs. Garrison stirred and gripped his shirt, pressing against him. "Here, now," he whispered. "Easy, ma'am. Rest easy."

The *señora* bustled in. "Pull that stinking horse blanket away, but with care. It is rough enough to take off her skin. *Pobrecita, angelita.*"

Rafe tugged at the white-knuckled fingers twined in his shirt. "Little angel? Nothing angelic about this grip." He stepped back to let the *señora* lean in closer.

"Turn your eyes, Rafael. I must peel away this wet rag. Oh, her poor young body." *Señora* Rivera sucked her teeth and shook her head.

Mrs. Garrison roused and gripped her chemise closed. Her

23

confused gaze searched the room. She glared at Rafe before she stilled.

Moving cautiously, he perched on the edge of the bed. "I'm Rafe Bishop. Do you remember? We pulled you from the sea. Now we've brought you to this kind lady's home."

"Yes—yes." Her eyes focused. "They're gone. My Seth. I had him, then . . ." Her words rasped from deep in her throat. "I let go—and the tiny baby. I let *her* go."

The sound of such anguish, even coming as it did in an accent he despised, drew him to recall his own, though he'd worked hard to bury it. "Where were you bound?" he said. His own voice sounded as hoarse as hers. It rattled like gravel in a pan.

"Bound for nowhere," she whispered.

"But you were going somewhere, surely."

"Captain York was—he was . . ." She stopped and bit her lip, shuddered, and went on. "He was taking us to a new life in Mexico." Her voice rose with every word. "To start anew. Our house on the river, only rubble."

"You didn't get far."

Her features twisted. "I called it an adventure, making them come." She caught her breath in a sob. "Now I've killed them all."

Rafe stood, inviting *Señora* Rivera to take his place.

"The water boils," she said. "I will bring chocolate." She left the room.

Rafe lingered, backing beyond the circle of lamplight. "What cargo did the ship carry?" he asked.

"What? Why—machinery, I think. And us, of course," she whispered. "Precious cargo."

"This captain. Did he have strong feelings about the war?"

She closed her eyes. "The war is over, sir."

"Not for everyone."

"The captain lost a son. He—"

"So he was bitter?"

Her eyes flew open, flashing. A blush of pink washed ashen cheeks. "No more than most," she said.

"Was he thinking to stir it up again?"

"What? He wasn't insane." She sucked in a rattling breath and shook her head. "Why do you ask such things? He's dead. A good man is dead."

Rafe had no easy answer. He stood like a fool in the shadows, listening to her weeping as she forced out every breath.

When finally she spoke again, words trickled from her. "Life was once mighty easy, grand ol' days." A cough tore through her. "Mama sits in black, mourning Papa. She wouldn't come. Lucky Mama." Her hand dropped to the blanket as if it were as heavy as lead.

Rafe backed from the room and into the small kitchen. He sank to a stool by the table that always wobbled. He'd meant to repair it, but never got to it. Now he made it rock back and forth, thinking the rhythm might soothe him while he thought about this.

Playing hero to a castaway was not part of his task. Though put off by the life she represented—clearly she'd been part of a pampered aristocracy—he was still moved by her grief and admired her determination to survive.

He looked up, wincing at her wracking cough. *Señora* Rivera turned slowly from the stove, the cup of hot chocolate steaming in her hand. She scowled at it. "She cannot drink this, or anything, I think."

"She's very ill, isn't she?"

"*Sí*." The old woman moved to the table, her black skirt sweeping the floor. She put down the cup and clutched her shawl at her throat with one gnarled hand as if she were cold, and sank down to balance on a stool.

"Did you see lights on the rocks, *Señora*? The woman spoke of lights."

She shook her head impatiently. "On some nights, yes, then no. Here and there. Who knows about these lights? You sometimes take a light to the shore, don't you? I have seen this, but I do not ask why." She jerked her chin at the window facing the rocky bluff by the sea and the stone house rising from it. "Sometimes on stormy nights, *Señor* Cooper's house shows a lamp in every window. You've seen them."

He nodded.

"Maybe the ship saw his house and was puzzled." She crossed herself. "The man tries to call her home."

Rafe looked out the window at Cooper's brooding house. As the *señora* had said, its windows blazed with light. He'd seen it before over the months he'd been here, and his suspicions had been aroused, though he could never find anything. "Calling who, *Señora*? I've asked around. No one will speak of it, but . . ."

"He is a man apart." She sighed. "Such a sad tale. A rich but friendless man. I am too weary for such sadness. I will tell it another time."

"Can you manage Mrs. Garrison's care? Should we . . ."

"Should we what? Throw her back?" She pushed to her feet, smiled and cupped his face with knotted fingers as she passed. "You are a good boy to worry, Rafael."

Rafe stood. "I'll get on down to the store and bring what you need."

"You have prayers there? That is what I mostly need, I think."

"You likely have plenty of those, you and Father Sebastian."

"Did carrying her hurt your back, Rafael?"

"No, ma'am. I'm fine."

"I think you are not, but do not complain."

He shrugged. "Does no good." He gave the old woman a

sloppy smile, guilty for deceiving her, then left the small house and moved away down the hill toward the village, being sure to drag one leg. As he neared the store he remembered he'd left customers there, having taken off like everyone else when word of the shipwreck came. Surely they'd left by now.

For a year he had played the part of a cripple, known as a genial storekeeper and fiddle player. He moved about the village, a threat to no one. There had been talk of a suspected die-hard rebel in these parts, dangerous enough to worry Washington. The army had placed Rafe in the store. He heard all the gossip as he catered to the needs and whims of villagers and rawboned farmers from inland. One old rancher stood out, and Rafe passed on his report, but he couldn't decide about the mysterious Martin Cooper. Had he done enough to find out? He had much to make up for.

As he neared the store he saw four slow-talking but quick-moving men loading the goods they'd bought on wagons. Inside, their wives moved from bin to barrel, fingering every item. The youngest of them, her face long, gaunt and weathered beyond her years, was encumbered by a child a-straddle one hip. Texas sun burned fiercely on the land beyond the inland hills and gave no pity to the pale skins of these ragged settlers.

She fingered every bolt of cloth, every ribbon. The women never bought, and Rafe was inclined to give her a length of ribbon to get her moving, for he chafed to get back to *Señora* Rivera's house.

The young mother lingered at a pile of woolen blankets. Her child watched Rafe with wary eyes, sucking its thumb. Rafe waggled his eyebrows and pulled a face, but the child only stared at him with grave curiosity. Rafe shrugged and gathered two blankets to take to his landlady, then climbed two rungs of a ladder to reach the highest shelf.

Children were perplexing creatures. A man never knew where

27

he stood with them . . . or with a woman, for that matter, a good reason to stand alone. Before he knew it, his thoughts flew to Alida Garrison. Heat flushed his face. No. She was not for him. He'd been burned by her kind before.

"This here is mighty purty. This'n here."

The customer's voice jerked him back. "Shall I take it from the case, ma'am?" He had just brought down a jug of cough elixir and was about to pour some into a smaller flask. He adjusted the funnel and uncorked the bottle. It smelled of pungent cherries.

She was eyeing a silver locket, but shook her head, her face flaming. She knew, as he did, she could never buy such a thing. As always, Rafe was grateful he didn't have to rely on this store's income. Glad to be on the army's payroll while he tried to dig out embers of a possibly rekindled rebellion.

His back ached from hunching over behind his counter, but he assumed his limping gait, shambling to the front window, wiping his hands on the dingy apron he'd tied around his waist. Usually he could shed the uncomfortable posture by sundown. Tonight the muscles in his neck and along his spine screamed, begging him to ease the strain, to lift his chin and square his shoulders. Not yet, not if he meant to keep in character. The scar slicing his cheek helped. That puckered ridge was no sham, a souvenir from Gettysburg where his regiment fought off Pickett's gallant, hopeless charge. No pretense in that wound, nor the ones he kept hidden inside.

He squinted out the window, fighting impatience. The sun had slipped below the low hills to the west, and Rafe watched clouds gather around the risen moon, forgetting the women still in the store. One spoke and the harsh twang jarred him from his thoughts. He started to turn, but lightning flashed like a second sun in the east over the sea, illuminating fat-bellied clouds herded together by a foul wind. Was there any other kind in this godforsaken place? Lightning's brilliance showed him treacherous rocks at the entrance to the little cove, rocks that had claimed the unlucky ship. It had happened before, and he wondered how ships could have been lured in. By what—or whom?

He eased open the door, but the wind had worked itself into a fit again and tried to wrench it from his hand. He held tight. Just as he stepped out onto the sagging porch, a cloud opened and he took a face full of rain. He blinked it away and clawed straggling hair from his eyes. The cloudburst ended as suddenly as it began.

"Mister. Hey, Mister."

Rafe backed into the store, pulled the door closed and turned with an insincere smile, blotting rain from his face with his shopkeeper's apron. "Yes, ma'am?"

The woman with the child pointed to a jar of boiled sweets. "How much are them things there?" She narrowed her gaze, a hard bargainer, nobody's fool, but when she moved that gaze to her child's face, her look of love and longing moved him.

He fought to keep from understanding or caring about these people. His dealings with them were only part of his charade, or so he told himself. He wanted the woman and her child to leave. "For you, ma'am," he said, "a gift." He limped around behind the counter and scooped up six sweets, tying them up in paper. The woman stared at him, at the others, and at the sweets as if they might suddenly disappear, or he might be joking and jerk them back.

A lanky balding man burst in, wearing an oiled canvas coat and carrying three more. "We got to get along now and get over that creek afore it rises. We'll camp yonder, out of town."

The young mother fastened her coat around herself and the child in her arms and they all swept out without another word, taking his gift and their sad-eyed longings with them. They'd

29

already made their marks in the account book.

He stepped out, watching the wagons rattle off into the dark and breathing in the scent of rain-settled air. The village was mostly adobe and after a rain it had a particular smell, a comforting smell, like hot metal in the sun. At first he'd wondered why it soothed him, but came to understand it reminded him of the smell that lingered after battle. Cordite and the coppery scent of blood-soaked earth. How could such a smell be a comfort? Because the battle was over and he had been left alive to smell it.

He wrenched himself from recollections of war and tethered his mind to the here and now as he gathered supplies for the woman they'd saved. He latched the shutters and barred the front door before shedding his jacket, careful not to tear the seams. He pulled his shoulders back and stretched his arms high overhead. Taller than most men, he could nearly graze the ceiling with his fingers. He rolled his head around. Bones in his upper spine and neck crackled like twigs underfoot. He squatted, jumped up, then out on his hands and toes and pushed up from the floor until the muscles of his arms and shoulders burned with the strain, coiling and quivering. Strength unused would soon be no strength at all and the time would surely come when he'd need it.

He stood, stretched and shook his hair free. He wore it long these days and tied back with a rawhide strip. Before, he'd kept it shorn and brushed glossy. Now it lay lank to his shoulders, unwashed and dull with oil. He scratched at his scalp, longing to plunge into the sea and wash this whole façade away, stand tall again and ride hard, using wits and weapons to get a job done. He longed to be finished with furtive and likely useless observation.

If he had to do this much longer he feared he'd forget who

So Wild the Wind

and what he really was: a Union army officer, a patriot, a man with a burning need for atonement.

CHAPTER FOUR

This time every year—the same. The same savage wind, ferocious heaving waves. Martin Cooper pressed his forehead to the window, closing his eyes and reveling in the cooling touch of glass. He slowly opened his eyes, then scowled, all comfort forgotten at what he saw. Brown-skinned, bandy-legged little Emiliano Mirlito was stumbling up the path from the town, easily seen in the moonlight. He should be at the shoreline, not rushing to the house.

Cooper slammed out the front door and trotted down the steps in time to grasp the man's shoulder and jerk him into the shadow of an oleander bush. "How dare you come up here!"

"But all work is finished, *Señor*." The man doffed a bowler riding low over his ears, a hat useless for this climate and much too large. A ridiculous little man with seawater soaking his trousers and boots.

"Any salvage? I expected a shipment from Cuba." He shook Mirlito.

Mirlito shrugged. "Wooden crates. I know nothing more."

Cooper narrowed his eyes. "And no survivors?"

Mirlito grinned and stared at the ground.

Cooper shoved the little man away and turned to mount the steps.

"I must tell you a thing, a strange thing," Mirlito said.

Cooper paused, one foot on the bottom step. "I do not require explanations."

Mirlito sidled closer and whispered. "A little woman, *Señor.* She washes up alive, away from all others. So busy were we with the noisy ones." His teeth flashed in the moonlight, though Cooper sensed no humor in the smile. "We did not see her."

"Busy? I don't know what you mean." Desperation thinned Cooper's voice. "I don't need to know."

"No, *patrón.* Of course not. I just say, others saw this little woman. That old healing woman, *la curandera,* then also the shopkeeper. He carried her to the old woman's house." He dropped his gaze. "And the priest has come."

"Dead, then?"

Mirlito shook his head. "Not dead. I am sorry," he said, smiling at the ground.

"Sorry? Sorry for what?" Cooper spun and swung a fist, knocking Mirlito off balance, though he stayed upright. "Do you jest with me? Jest about drowning with *me*?"

Mirlito's teeth flashed white in his dark face, though angry eyes made the smile a lie.

Cooper glared. "Did the woman speak? Talk about the ship-wreck?"

"I do not know."

"Then why come to me?"

"You *must* see her. She is—" He paused, then shrugged. "You will see for yourself."

"Saddle my gray." Cooper turned back toward the house as Mirlito scurried away, shoving his hat down over his ears.

Inside, Cooper replaced his quilted smoking jacket with a more suitable black woolen coat. Then he went out again and waited for Mirlito to bring the horse, thinking about the little man's expression. Little blackbird, his name meant. Dark, like his eyes and his soul. Did an angry flame burn beneath the blanket of ice that was the clownish Mirlito's usual demeanor? Of course, in him the ice was black.

Cooper smiled. Another poetic phrase to commit to paper. He hoped to recall it when he had time. So many ideas were lost to him. He had so much on his mind. He longed for the time when a being like Mirlito knew his place and dared not stray from it. Then he, Cooper, would again have time for creative endeavors. Hunger for the old ways twisted in his belly like a blade. His longing for the past was agony sometimes.

If only all could be put right, the world would again turn as it should. He'd go back to his Charleston home, the lush gardens nudging the banks of the Ashley River. He'd return to his gracious life. His fervor had been called obsession, but since she— well, now he cared for no one's opinion.

Mirlito brought the horse and made a cradle of his hands. Cooper stepped up and swung into the saddle, then put heels to the horse and urged it into an easy lope. "Follow!" he shouted, laughing. "Stretch those stunted legs." If Mirlito answered, Cooper didn't hear over the clacking of hooves along the rocky carriage path.

When he neared the town, he held the horse to a prancing walk and drew in a deep breath. The breeze smelled as clean as it ever did in this place of exile. After the wind blew a storm inland, it wet the rocky soil far beyond the hills and freshened the air. He also liked to watch the villagers, but only from a distance through his spyglass. They scurried about like a swarm of ants, stowing things away, salvaging their pitiful goods. Years ago he'd mingled with the swarm, gone rushing to the rocks when a ship foundered. This fresh air reminded him of those days when he saw to everything himself, gathered any salvage and—he sucked in a breath. *She* had seen him and misunderstood. It was war, after all, and his way of supporting . . .

He screwed his eyes shut. He wouldn't think of her, wouldn't conjure up her hateful words and that final betrayal. He could only allow his thoughts to drift to her in the evenings, when he fixed his eyes on her portrait and allowed his heart to mourn. Sometimes he wept. Mirlito had interrupted this evening's ritual. Anger sprouted anew, blooming large. He lopped it off and smoothed the tangle inside with deep, slow breaths.

The town was empty of all but four foraging pigs, two goats and a three-legged dog. Likely everyone had flocked to the wreckage to gawk and take what they could glean, though if his men did their job there would be precious little for anyone else.

He rode past the church, the store and the tavern, all clustered around a well. The houses looked little better than the slave cabins back home. He turned down a path to the shore where villagers gathered, some with lanterns, and held his mount a little distance apart as Mirlito stumbled up from behind. The dwarf grasped Cooper's stirrup, his breath whistling. Cooper kicked the little man's grip from the tooled leather. Mirlito stumbled back but didn't fall. Again, Cooper chuckled at a surge of anger in the little man's black eyes. "All right, where is the woman?" he said.

Mirlito trotted off, then stopped and turned. "This way!" he shouted. "They have taken her up the hill."

Was Mirlito purposefully drawing attention? Cooper shot a glance toward the crowd picking through debris and murmuring sadly about bodies along the shore. Hearing Mirlito's shout, many turned like curious cats, gazing at him.

Cooper urged his horse up the hill, scattering the few people foolish enough to stand in his way. At the house where Mirlito had led him, he swung down from the saddle and stood, staring at the small but surprisingly tidy structure. A neatly built fence surrounded it, and a lantern hung from a porch encased in vines that bore sweet-smelling blossoms.

The priest strode up from behind him, his robes wet to the knees and caked with sand. "One survivor, Mr. Cooper. Thanks be to God, finally one survivor."

"Where is she?"

He nodded toward the lantern's glow. "*Señora* Rivera has offered to care for the poor young woman."

"Young, you say?"

"So sad." He leaned closer, whispering. "On the shore we found another. A woman drowned, also a young boy." The priest closed his eyes and moved his lips in what was likely prayer. "Near your son's age."

Cooper strode through the open gate, entered without knocking and pushed his way through a knot of people into a small room in the back. There he froze, gaping at a black-haired woman who lay on the bed. He could barely catch his breath.

Mirlito had followed him. He leaned close and crooked one finger, inviting Cooper to bend to his level. His lips nearly touching Cooper's ear, the little man whispered, "Now you see, *patrón*, do you not? She looks so very much like—"

Cooper shoved him away with a slap. Someone gasped, for it was the kind of blow a man might inflict on a nagging woman or an unruly child. A storm roiled behind Mirlito's eyes as Cooper jerked his chin toward the door. "Get to work. Weren't you first to get there? You work for me, so all salvage is mine." He turned his back on the dwarf, knowing he risked the thrust of a blade, but his show of fearlessness demonstrated he was not to be disobeyed.

The priest—what was his name? Father Sebastian. The priest gaped at the exchange with Mirlito and then scowled, as if he might reprimand Cooper, though he only cleared his throat. "Many are lost," the priest said. "Emotions run high."

"Yes, like the tides," Cooper said. "And the wind." He couldn't look away from the woman on the bed. Such a pale, lovely face, as if carved from marble. Would she wake if he kissed her, like in a tale of chivalry? He shook himself free of fantasy.

"God has blessed us," the priest went on. "He must have a plan for this woman."

"Yes, a plan."

The priest nodded slowly. "Many have washed up, drowned and savaged on the rocks and strong currents." He sighed. "This lady asked for a child and an infant. We have found the boy. But not the baby."

Cooper let out an impatient puff of breath. "A baby? How could she even wonder? Something so small. An easy meal for fishes."

The old woman kneeling by the bed turned a horrified stare on him. He hadn't meant to speak aloud. Appalled at his mistake, he bowed his head. "Poor little thing," he said, hoping to appear downcast, though he couldn't muster interest in the death of the woman's child, only in the woman. Struggling for control, he waved an arm at the knot of villagers crowded into the hovel, gawking at the woman like she was Christ newly risen. "Leave this poor woman in peace," he said.

One surly rascal wouldn't comply. Such disrespect! Cooper raised his fist but a hand stronger than his own checked him in mid-arc. He cursed and spun around. The shopkeeper kept a grip on Cooper's wrist with ease. He smiled, forcing Cooper's arm down.

"Be calm, Francisco," Bishop said quietly, still smiling, to the surly fellow Cooper had nearly struck. "Perhaps Mr. Cooper is right. The young lady needs privacy."

The man nodded, then spat at Cooper's feet and backed away. The old woman gibbered in Spanish, sounding angry. Cooper felt his cheeks flaming. He clenched his jaw and forced out a breath as Bishop loosened his grip.

"All right now, Mr. Cooper?" Bishop said quietly.

Cooper nodded. "Such tragedy is . . . upsetting."

"Of course." Again Bishop smiled. What could he mean by it?

Cooper brought his raging feelings under tight control again. He'd always thought the shopkeeper a weak, harmless, contemptible creature, though he'd had no direct dealings with him. Mirlito saw to any goods they might need from the store. He took William there for music lessons. Learning the violin from such a person, though inadequate, was the closest thing to culture available. When Cooper glanced up, Rafe Bishop was again the round-shouldered, gawky man he'd seen limping about the town for over a year. Could he have imagined the fellow's forcefulness?

The figure on the bed stirred. The old woman leaned forward, stroking loose black hair from the heart-shaped face. Mirlito was right. She looked so much like—why, she was *exactly* like his wife. Did no one else feel the earth shift beneath his feet? Cooper glanced from face to face, longing to ask. Everyone but Bishop gazed at the survivor. The shopkeeper still stared at *him*. No one else realized who she was, who she had to be.

He leaned closer. As his gaze roamed her face, he waited for his fantasy to pass. Not *her*. Of course not. Yet such an uncanny resemblance. The black hair, the flare of the cheekbones, the wide brow and full lips, the small-boned look of her. A beauty, even bruised and wretched as she was. Nearly as beautiful as the woman taken from him by the capricious sea. Perhaps the sea had given her back. As a reward? Or was it punishment?

"Mr. Cooper? Are you all right?"

Cooper blinked and tore his gaze away. Bishop again, with his probing eyes. He seemed truly concerned, yet who knew? After this, who knew what anything meant?

38

CHAPTER FIVE

Martin Cooper stood smiling like a schoolboy who knew every answer and wasn't above gloating. Such smugness surprised Rafe. He watched the man closely.

"Who does she claim to be?" Cooper said.

"Mrs. Alida Garrison. Should we doubt it?"

"No. Of course there's no need for doubt." Cooper stepped closer and stared boldly at the woman. He inched his hand forward and fingered the blanket's edge. Before Rafe could challenge him, Mrs. Garrison coughed, rising off the bed with the force of it. Cooper wrung his hands and knelt. "Oh, how she shivers," he said. "Like a little bird caught in the rain."

Rafe gripped Cooper's shoulder. "Move back, sir. Let *Señora* Rivera tend her."

Mrs. Garrison opened her eyes.

"My God," Cooper whispered. "I've only seen such a pairing—the eyes, the hair—once in my life."

She stared, then lifted one hand and touched Cooper's cheek. Rafe read a question in her face. "You saved me?" she whispered.

Rafe fought down an impulse to snatch the helpless woman away.

"My boy?" she said, wheezing. "Tell me the truth."

Rafe winced at the grating sound. How long had she screamed before the sea spit her out? How long, to scrape her voice so raw?

Cooper squinted up into the faces around him. "Boy? Does

she mean . . ." He shook his head. "Of course not," he whispered. "Certainly not William."

Father Sebastian shook his head as if everything was beyond him. "Mrs. Garrison, your boy has gone to God. *Lo siento mucho. Señora* Rivera will care for you and Mr. Bishop has brought medicine from his store."

"No! She must come to *my* house," Cooper said. "She will need care day and night, and perhaps a doctor. I can pay for these things."

"A kind offer," the priest said. "But we must think of the lady." He jerked his chin toward the window that framed Cooper's house on the bluff. "A woman there, alone with you. It is not seemly—not right."

"I live with a female servant and my young son," Cooper said. "She will not be 'alone' with me, as you so delicately put it. I have the room and the means. My African servant is well-trained in healing arts, herbs and the like."

"While this may be true . . ." Father Sebastian glanced around, his expression begging for help.

"And she is a woman of quality," Cooper said. "She'll be shocked when she realizes she's been spirited away to this hovel."

Señora Rivera drew in a sharp breath and sputtered a protest.

"The woman is injured and nearly unclothed," Rafe said. "How can you know anything of her?"

"Why, the cadence of her speech, if nothing else. A gentleman can always sense a lady of his own class." Cooper's own drawl intensified.

"Of course." Rafe fought a sneer.

Cooper stood and bent low over the woman. "Can you hear me? I'm Martin Cooper. I shall take care of you."

She turned her face to the wall. Tears ran from the corners of her closed eyes.

"Your name?" Cooper asked.

"I told you," Rafe said. "Alida Garrison."

Cooper straightened. "Of course. Well then, Mrs. Garrison, you'll come with me."

"My boy," she whispered. "Lost."

Cooper shook his head. "No, I saved him. He's bigger, but—" He drew a gasping breath. "No, of course you mean *your* boy. We'll sort that out. You." He pointed to a strong-looking young man. "Lift her into my arms when I'm settled on the horse."

Someone needed to step in, but Rafe hung back. He'd already been too involved, too assertive, carrying her up the hill, stopping Cooper's fist in mid-air.

Señora Rivera wrung her hands. "She must stay here! Father, Rafael. Do something. She knows her loss now. She might give up. I know of such grief." She dabbed at her eyes. "I can speak of it."

"Yes, you should care for her. She's seen you and knows you mean her no harm." Rafe did his best to be self-deprecating, bending his head, slouching. "Surely you can see that, Mr. Cooper? It wouldn't be right to move her now." He looked around the room. Some villagers nodded, some shook their heads.

"So? All are against me?" Cooper straightened to his full height, shoulders back, chin lifted. Rafe had seen such behavior from captured rebel officers. They often put on a brave face and he'd respected them for it. But in Cooper it seemed only show.

Cooper pushed through the gathered people. "My offer, of course, stands." He turned and jerked his chin toward the woman on the bed. "When she comes to her senses, she will want to come to my house." He leveled a searing glare on Father Sebastian, *Señora* Rivera and finally Rafe. "And you will send for me." He strode out.

Rafe drew a knuckle across his stubbled jaw and paced to the door, forgetting to limp, as he watched Cooper mount and ride

41

away. "This is the closest I've been to that man in the time I've lived here."

"He keeps apart," Father Sebastian said. "Drives a fine carriage. A few men work for him."

"I've seen them come and go. What do they do?"

The priest shrugged.

"He is a rich man," *Señora* Rivera added. "Drives *through* the village, but never before has someone survived a broken ship. It would interest even him."

"I wonder how he knew about this one."

She shrugged. "Someone ran to him with news?"

The priest sighed. "Mr. Cooper lost his wife to the sea. A terrible accident many years ago. So I can see why he was clearly shaken by this lady's grief."

Rafe pasted on a fawning grin, sinking into character. "Of course. The memory of his wife. This poor lady must seem like a mermaid cast ashore." He forced a wider smile while wondering how to find evidence, if it existed, of Cooper's being mixed up with the old rancher Rafe had already exposed as unrepentant rebel. He'd been suspicious of Cooper, wondering if he was a smuggler, but had found nothing. The man certainly had been a Confederate, and perhaps still was. Why was he interested in the shipwreck? Maybe if Rafe dug deeper, his months of work here would be doubly fruitful. It could go far to settle the debt he owed his nation.

"You smile, Rafael?"

"A passing thought."

Onlookers drifted away with Father Sebastian. *Señora* Rivera stood behind Rafe. "What is there to smile about on this sad night?" She crossed herself. "Lost children. The poor little lady. I fear she will lose strength to live. Yet, does she have someone else, perhaps a husband?"

"She asked only for the child. She must be a widow. So many

are these days." That she had no husband pleased Rafe in a fleeting way, but he would not think of it. He would think only of Martin Cooper. "Do you know much of Mr. Cooper's household? The little man brings William for lessons. A shy child, not too interested in music, but he likes the attention."

"The child and a servant. She is not from our village, old and African, as he said, *una misteriosa*. There is a cook, a stranger who comes to Mass and lives just outside the village. She says nothing. I do not think she can speak. For a time some months past a young woman was seen at the grand house. Beautiful, they say, but gone now. They do not bother us. So?" She shrugged. "This little woman?" She rolled up her sleeves. "She touches my heart and has a grim fight ahead. I know grief, for many times I have felt it. A heart weakens beneath grief's burden. She will need help and I will be here."

CHAPTER SIX

Alida knew she'd been saved. She lay in a warm bed—too warm. But where? Who was she with? She struggled against strong yet gentle arms. A man's voice spoke soothing words. She rolled her head and the pillow smelled of lavender.

She recalled the nubby woolen cloth of her father's coat, the smell of pipe tobacco. Some man was holding her close. She didn't want to see or know. She could barely breathe, so she surrendered. If this man was her father, it meant she was dead. He had come to claim her. How wonderful to give up grief and guilt. She sank into a soft bed that crackled, releasing the scents of sage, rosemary and again, lavender. She sighed and let go every muscle, every failing and desire.

But no. She didn't have this luxury. No rest for her. She must live and pay. She must atone. She clenched her hands, her jaw, and arched her back, struggling again to rise and remember. Rushing sea, punishing waves. She'd seen Sarah, then James in the water, but not Seth. Grinding sand scraped her skin, people crowded her, talked to her, asked her name. Her father wouldn't do that, so she wasn't dead. She pressed a fist to her chest to calm her breath. What of Seth? Ah, she remembered. Someone told her.

Quiet, worried voices wafted to her. She remembered touching a face. A man's face. She needed to see it again, someone stronger than she was.

She reached up and brushed a man's stubbled jaw. He jerked

away. She recoiled like a child grasping for a forbidden thing. But she was no child. She wanted to speak to this man but she had no breath. Her chest was aflame, a pain like knives between her ribs. She twisted away, coughing. A strong arm raised her higher. She tilted her head and it fell back like a dew-heavy flower. She opened her eyes to lamplight. The same man from the sandy beach. She remembered the scar.

"I. Can't. Breathe." She forced each word.

The man stared at her. Lines cut around his eyes, across his brow and bracketed his mouth. Limp brown hair straggled around his face.

She shook her head. Pain knifed her temple. She touched the spot and found matted hair. "Who?" she whispered.

"My name is Rafe Bishop." He scowled. "You can breathe, just don't talk."

"But I can't—can't—I'm so tired." She fell limp against his arm. Might he help her breathe? Another proof of life. Dead women have no need of breath. Yet how could she live if Seth did not?

Alida struggled to order her thoughts. The man cradled her. He was kind and didn't know that her foolish dreams of a future had led them here to death.

If he wasn't strong enough to hold her, she might slide away, tumble down into the sea. Her eyes leaked scalding tears. The bit of strength she'd mustered seeped away.

Mrs. Garrison had likely sucked in a lungful of seawater. Rafe had once seen a man plucked from water during a river crossing. Never could take a full breath after, poor bastard. He'd mustered out, but maybe lucky at that. Rafe touched his scar where her fingers had brushed him. Yes, lucky.

"You." She gasped between each word. "You washed away the sand? I remember." She plucked at the black shawl, drawing

45

it beneath her chin.

"You're safe. Be calm," he said. He had stayed to ask questions, not to care. He eased her down and slid his arm away.

"The waves," she whispered.

"What's that?" He leaned closer.

"The waves. Like mountains." She coughed hoarseness clear, then widened her eyes until the whites showed all around the blue. "Could they reach us here?"

Rafe smiled. "We're on a hill. Can't see how."

She winced. "My head throbs." Her gaze clouded.

He leaned in, searching her face.

"You're staring." Speaking stirred a fit of coughing. "Am I so odd?"

"I meant nothing by it. I apologize."

Trembling fingers pressed against his chest. Was she fending him off or bringing him close? He took her hand.

"You're sure—sure my boy is lost?"

He nodded.

She turned her face to the window. It framed the massive stone house on the bluff, lanterns burning in the windows. "Is that a prison?"

Rafe's gaze followed hers. Shadows gathered around Cooper's house, deepening at the corners. Then all but one of the lamps dimmed and disappeared. The remaining light moved from one mullioned window to another. He heard the crash of wood against stone all the way up here when the massive door slammed open, then shut. The single lamp bobbed like a firefly, welcoming Martin Cooper home. He turned again to Mrs. Garrison, thinking of Cooper. "Just some rich man's house."

She blinked. "Your eyes, so cold."

"You should rest." He didn't know what more to say. Immersed in misery, she likely remembered nothing. Questioning her now was both useless and wrong.

"Everything is wrong," she whispered.

He flinched. Good Lord, had she read his thoughts?

She closed her eyes and turned her face from him.

Seth was dead. She would tell herself over and over until she believed it. Her world had been stripped of both love and duty. She'd sometimes secretly wished for freedom, for a way to throw off duty. It wore her down, always being the one to make the decisions, to care for the others. But not this way. Never this way.

Her belly clenched. Had God misunderstood her wish and taken everything from her?

She breathed in a familiar nighttime scent. Sulfur and melting beeswax. Someone was lighting candles. She opened her eyes as a tiny flame burst to life. An old woman in a black dress, white hair braided down her back, lit one candle, then more. She lined them across a low chest and knelt for a moment before rising with difficulty. She nudged a man sitting in the corner and made him stand.

"It's cold in here, *Señora,*" he said.

"I will build the fire high in the other room, keeping this door open. She will be warm enough."

"I guess you know what you're doing."

The old woman chuckled and pushed his shoulder. "You go now. Get some sleep. I do not need you, Rafael."

Rafael. Alida had heard that name before. She kept her eyes half-closed, watching him. He cocked his head to one side and smiled at the old woman. How could people still smile? Was hers the only world to end? He strode to the door and ran his hands up and down the seams of his trousers, pausing like he had something to say, but left without another glance.

She took a deep breath, then gasped at the sudden sharp pain in her ribs. Her hand felt cool against her burning cheek.

The old woman rushed to her side and felt her forehead. "*Ai*. So, a fever now. Do not be afraid, we will get you through this, though nothing will make sense for a time."

"Was someone really here? A man?"

"Ah, yes. A good man. Sometimes strange, but is that not the way of men?"

"I don't know." A wave of self-pity warred with grief. To her shame, self-pity won. "They all left me, all of them, even Seth." She covered her mouth with one hand to hold back the whining words. She'd been misunderstood by God, by fate, by whatever oversaw the rules of life. Misunderstood and punished.

The old woman sat and pulled her into her arms. "Let it go," she said. "Let it go, *Niñita*."

And so she did, weeping with gulping sobs that sucked away what little breath she had. She curled on her side and wound her arms tightly across her breasts, shivering and clawing the blankets into a nest.

The old woman moved away, then returned to hold a spoon to her lips. "Take this. This will help you sleep."

Alida smelled it, sweet and thick, yet acrid. She knew it. She struck out and the spoon clattered to the floor. "No! Never that."

The old woman bent to retrieve the spoon, shaking her head. "That you fight me is good, I think. I will make up another kind of syrup for you, if you will not take this. I will make a poultice for your chest."

Alida could only think of breathing. She dozed and woke some time later from a dream, a dream of a list with only one name, over and over. Her husband's name. She barely remembered his face, only his pain and anger for how life had treated him. She remembered the smell of what he called his "tonic," the odor on his breath and the taste on his lips when he forced kisses on her. She remembered curses and flailing fists. He'd died angry. She no longer recalled love.

When she dropped down again into sleep, she saw Seth as a baby, rocking in a basket on the sea. He screamed for her, and when next she woke, she was being smothered. She thrust the blanket away and struggled to sit up. The door creaked open. "Help me," she panted. "Please."

A figure slid through the open doorway and melted into flickering shadows cast by three candles. The sound of her breathing was joined by a skirt swishing across the floor as the figure glided closer. "You've come to help me?" But this wasn't the same old woman. Alida raised herself up and pushed back against the wall. Who was this coming so silently in the dark? Was it a devil? "You won't have me, devil. They are dead but I am not. There must be a reason I am living. I will fight you." She flung out one arm to hold the devil off.

Candlelight flickered across the face leaning close, grinning. A woman. An old, grinning, dark-skinned woman, every tooth sharp and shining. Alida screamed and flailed with both hands. Another old woman rushed in, the one with the white braid. She bent close and reached for Alida, speaking in sweet tones. Both women dodged her blows, but the dark one grinned again and muttered something, then shrieked a warbling, high-pitched laugh.

Alida fought through a tangle of bedclothes. The devil woman grasped Alida's wrists. "Jus' ol' Cora. I got to come, for he say to come. He say, Cora. The gal need tendin'."

Alida twisted from the woman's grasp. A fit of coughing left her gasping as she calmed. She pointed a trembling finger. "Your—your teeth. My God."

The other woman pushed in. "Never mind this old thing, little one. She came with medicine, but Rafael has brought all I need. In my garden grows all else. No different from hers."

The nightmarish woman tapped her front teeth with one

long, curved fingernail. "You scared of these? Filing done in ol' Africa when Cora live by the great river." She grinned. "Little girl-child then. Had me 'nother name, don't recall it." She chuckled. "Mr. Coop, he buy me off the sugar island long time past, pick me special, 'cause these scare folks. They allus thinkin' I likely to bite 'em." She chomped down, grinning, then sobered, feeling Alida's forehead with one paper-skinned hand. "Fever." She frowned at the other old woman and pressed on Alida's chest. "Seawater a-bubbling in the breathing places."

"Buy you?" Alida whispered. "You're free—the war."

Cora chuckled. "War." She turned to the other. "We see war down here?"

"Hush, old thing. You know we did. Now, little one? You sleep. You are safe in my house. I am *Señora* Rivera, remember? I will care for you." She glared at Cora. "This one will go."

Cora's gaze roamed Alida's face. "Jus' look at you. Must be driving him crazy." She drew her fingers through Alida's hair. "This, and them eyes. Make him think what he never want to think again."

"What?" Alida asked.

"Pay no attention, *querida*." *Señora* Rivera plumped Alida's pillow and smoothed the blanket, still glaring at Cora. "You look like someone who used to live here. That is all." She stroked Alida's hair and hummed a quiet melody. After a while Alida fell into a half-sleep. She was dimly aware of both old women backing away.

Cora stared as she moved, gnawing her bottom lip with the sharpened teeth. "She a fox let loose among the chickens," she whispered. "Trouble ahead." She sighed. "Don't like it. Am partial to peaceful times."

"You hush your evil mouth."

Cora faced the last flickering candle. "Lookee there," she said. "The devil's tongue be dancing. I sees it plain." She chuckled deep in her throat. "I recall licking tongues. Sometimes soothing, I recall. Ain't never gonna be so old I forget tongues."

"No sorcery! You hush now, *Vieja.*"

"Hah! Old? Old your own self."

Alida gazed at the candle. The flame writhed and coiled like a serpent. She shifted her eyes toward Cora as the old woman moaned. "Honey-hot, poison flame." She swayed side to side.

"Stop that! Her fighting you shows me she will live, so you go. We need no talk of death." *Señora* Rivera came close again and bathed Alida's face with a cloth dipped in water from a china basin. "Go, I say, or . . ."

"She a ghost to Mr. Coop," Cora said, grinning. "Coming back, thinking she is somebody else."

"Silly old woman. The night air will do your aches and pains no good. Best you get to your own fire."

Cora chuckled. "No, I got to stay. I s'posed to tell him if she live through the night."

Alida roused herself. "What? Are you joking? Is the man so heartless?"

"He been kind to ol' Cora, more or less."

"But I do pity his boy," the *señora* said.

"A boy?" Alida whispered. "What boy? Nothing makes sense. I don't know . . ."

"By and by you will be stronger," *Señora* Rivera said.

Cora narrowed her eyes. "Huh. She likely live, but not sure that's best."

Alida shook her head, bewildered. Was she dreaming?

"Maybe you be stronger like she say, but still could be in a grave by nightfall." Cora nodded slowly. "Many a gal is dead, though plenty strong."

"You go!" *Señora* Rivera shouted. "Or I find a man to carry you away."

Cora backed out, one palm toward Alida. "Don't be staring

at ol' Cora with them ghost-blue eyes. Cora never done you no harm. Not then, not now." She stopped, thrusting her head and shoulders forward. "You sleep. See if death fit you. Try it out. Just 'cause you living now, don't mean death won't catch up again down the road. Death be a slippery fella." She smiled with lips pressed tight, squinting and drawing herself up as tall as she was able. "Gotta be watching out for him all the time. Maybe lettin' him catch you be best for us all."

CHAPTER SEVEN

Rafe limped along the strip of sand, his back in agony from his assumed deformity. It demanded relief. He eased down onto a jutting stone worn smooth by the wind and watched ruffles of white foam break in the gray of near-dawn, waiting for the sunrise to show a difference between murky sea and muted sky.

The bodies of nine men, a woman and a child had been taken to the church. Crates and barrels and even bits of wood and sail had been picked over and hauled away. He stood, stretching muscles as well as he could, and picked his way along the rocks.

Mrs. Garrison had spoken of lights. More than Cooper's blazing windows? Perhaps signal fires? A signal to smugglers, or something more sinister? Luring a ship onto rocks in a storm was nothing short of murder.

Rain and sea had washed the rocks clean of any sign of fires. Rafe ambled back up the hill, thinking. The walls of the *señora*'s house had gleamed white in the moonlight and now caught morning sun. Her garden smelled of earth made rich with goat droppings and seaweed as well as the pungent scents of growing herbs and peppers. Flowers colored every corner, a haven of peace—peace he'd been taking for granted.

The old woman's spavined horse stood patiently, its hocks as stiff as its owner's knees. *Señora* Rivera had already hitched it to the traces of a two-wheeled cart, ready should she have to drive away, for she was the only healer for miles and attended birthings, splinted broken bones and sewed gashes made by farmers' sharp hoes and fishermen's knives. Rafe patted the horse's neck as he passed.

The *señora* was grinding herbs for poultices and looked up when he entered. "So, Rafael, you return." She poured him a mug of coffee and pushed a plate of beans and one cold tortilla toward him. "You did not sleep?"

He sat at the table, staring at the food. "Likely no more than you."

"And you don't eat? The food is no good?"

"Not so hungry." He shrugged. "So many dead. It makes a man think." He waited. She was usually eager to talk and maybe the Garrison woman had said more during the night.

"*Sí.* Such a blessing to save even the one."

"Is she better?" His heart beat faster, uncommonly hopeful.

She nodded. "This village's luck has changed, perhaps. The rain was welcome, though the storm. . . ." She shook her head, clicking her tongue against her teeth.

"Well, even an ill wind blows somebody good."

She turned from stirring the blackened pot hanging over a smoldering fire, cutting off his platitude with a rap of her wooden spoon on the pot's edge. "Wind? You are saying our winds come from God and death rides them. And this means their deaths are God's will? I will not accept this." She turned back to her fire, adjusting the hook so forcefully she set the pot to swinging. "Something of man is at work—or the devil."

Startled, Rafe stammered, "I only meant, finding a survivor—saving one—some good came from it."

Her shoulders sagged. "Forgive me, Rafael. The little woman and I have fought death all night. I see in her a sign of hope."

"The village needs hope. All are so poor."

She snorted. "Not all. Not those working for *Señor* Cooper." She nodded. "I didn't like seeing him in my house, then I had to push away the old devil-woman he sent. Yes! In the night, he sent her." She slipped onto a stool across from him.

"So he thought to help, sending his servant?"

"She said he wanted news. I did not need her help. She talks too much of death and mysterious omens."

"Odd that he's so curious. Did the laudanum help Mrs. Garrison sleep?"

"She would take none and fought me like a wild thing." She grinned. "Just as she did the old devil-woman."

Rafe tore off a piece of tortilla and scooped the congealed beans into his mouth, giving himself time to think as he chewed and swallowed. "So she's a fighter?"

"She wants to live, I think, though she maybe doesn't yet know it."

He nodded. "You know, someone made short work of cleaning up the beach."

"Scavengers. *Buitres.* Like vultures, those men who work for *Señor* Cooper. They always get the biggest share of what washes ashore."

"Always? Well, I suppose if you're first at the trough, you're bound to be the fattest hog."

"Hah." She leaned forward and lowered her voice. "How do those fat hogs know when the trough is filled? And the screams we heard? Why did the scavengers not help those who screamed?" She struck the table with her palm. "They came and the screams stopped." She sat back, nodding, squinting.

"And this wreck was the fourth since I've come here?"

She closed her eyes. "Over the years, so many. More this last year. Some say *Señor* Cooper's men wreck the ships, but how? Ships are of the sea and the sea is in God's hands. Father Sebastian says anger makes us wonder, for my husband fell building that great house." As the words left her lips, she turned and frowned. "The little *señora* wakes, I think." She pushed to her feet and swept through the doorway to the room where Alida

Garrison lay.

After a few minutes she returned, poured herself a mug of coffee and slumped onto the stool.

"Is she worse?" Rafe asked.

"No. She cries out in fever dreams. I fear she will be worse, then better." She stared at him, her head to one side. "You like her?"

"You said you see her as some kind of omen."

"How do *you* see her, Rafael?" She smiled.

He felt as foolish as a boy. "Someone like me has no business looking at her. She'd not like it. A pampered lady of the South wouldn't even speak to a man like me, likely run screaming if she knew I'd touched her as I did." He fisted both hands.

"So much anger, Rafael! From where does it come?" She touched his fist and he eased it open.

He'd begun slipping back. Her touch brought him forward.

"If you could only stand straight and look a woman in her eyes, you would be a good-looking fellow. The scar only shows you suffered and survived."

He traced the raised skin on his cheek with one finger. "I forget it's there. I have little use for a mirror except to show my razor how to scrape away whiskers once every couple days."

"Your young man's body is not as it was, but you have more to give. You have music in you. The violin. You give music to our little ones."

"I'm no angel, for all your calling me Rafael." He smiled. "Teaching them fills my days, that's all. I once played well. But . . ." He flexed his fingers. "A wound here in the wrist. I believe a violin played badly is worse than no music at all."

She smiled, indulging him. "No. The children hear melodies. Some dream they too could play so well. It never hurts to dream."

"They need more than dreams." The conversation had gone

down another path. He had to swing it back around. "Mr. Cooper is rich. How does he earn his money?"

Her smile faded. "Why do you care? I should bite my tongue in half for speaking of him and his creatures. He plants nothing, keeps no cattle." She stood to stir the beans. "Building that great stone house took my husband's life, and others. A cursed house." She crossed herself and eased back down on the stool. "Some whisper of hoarded treasure."

Rafe's pulse quickened, though he chuckled as if she were joking. "So he's a pirate?"

She did not join his laughter. "Stories fly like birds from mouths to ears."

"And his men?"

"Madre de Dio. Stay away from them. They are always drinking at the old man's *cantina*."

"Isn't he called Preacher? Why is that?"

"I hear he knows every word of the Bible. He comes to Mass, but sits apart and mumbles his own words. When he painted his sign, the horse he meant to draw looked like a goat. So now some call it *El Cabrito*—he is angered by this and ill-tempered."

"I don't often venture there," Rafe said.

"Good. The man before you spent much time there. He often could not awaken in the morning to open his store."

"He was my cousin, you know."

"Ah, I forget. Forgive my speaking ill of him, poor man."

"I don't go, for men frequenting taverns often torment those they see as weak in one way or another."

She patted his hand. "My poor Rafael."

Rafe reddened at the show of sympathy, for the truth was he feared he'd forget and stand up for himself if bullied and couldn't risk it. "So, what if I wanted to learn more about getting rich, or about Mr. Cooper?"

She scowled at him.

He sensed a storm of words was about to follow. He raised one hand. "Please, good lady. Can you trust me?"

She flicked her fingers at him. "I have learned I will never understand the ways of men. If you must go to *El Cabrito*, find the little man, but I believe his heart is blacker than his eyes. The small man. How do you say—*un enano*?"

Rafe tilted his head, raising his brows.

She sucked her teeth in exasperation, holding her hand four feet from the floor. "A little man."

"A dwarf?"

"*Sí. Enano.*" She shrugged. "He bellows like a bull to make himself large."

Rafe stood. "I know who you mean. He brings William for lessons, comes in to buy tobacco. Seems a friendly sort."

The old woman snagged his sleeve and shook it. "An evil little man. You would drink and spend money recklessly like that man? Why, Rafael?"

Having to lie to her vexed him. He turned the vexation outward. "All right! I don't want to live my life in this ugly little town. I want more." He nearly convinced himself.

She paled and folded her hands on the table as if in prayer, staring at them.

He had wounded her. Remorse gnawed at him, but he had to learn more. His first suspect was traitorous, but mostly a blowhard. Rafe didn't want to leave with promises to himself unfulfilled. Martin Cooper might be only a reclusive secessionist who had somehow kept his land and fortune, dreaming of the past, but to find out, Rafe would have to stay longer. And though he hated to admit it, staying had become more attractive since yesterday.

As he limped down the hill to the store, he wondered at his own flawed character. His last dealings with a treacherous woman and her honey-dripping words had led to death and disaster for himself as well as his wounded nation. Had he learned nothing?

CHAPTER EIGHT

"Even breathing is too much," Alida said. "I must be dying."

"No." The old woman chuckled. "In you, death will be disappointed."

"You're laughing? Am I asleep or awake?"

"Fever. You fight to live and I fight at your side. This is not yet your time. I will bring another kettle."

"It's already so warm." She pushed heavy covers away, but the old woman pulled them up again.

"The steam forces the sweat to purge poison from your chest. Ah, this sheet is soaked. We need another." She peeled back the blanket. "Such bruises," she whispered, shaking her head.

Patches of blue and purple covered Alida's chest and breasts. Scrapes bloodied both arms and legs, her flesh angry, joints swollen. She wouldn't have recognized herself by sight, but the pain was clearly hers.

The old woman sat at her side and stroked her hair, then nodded sharply. "We battle. We win."

But each breath whistled from Alida, ending in a grunt. She meant to move a tendril of hair stuck to sweat on her brow but could only let her hand lie palm up beside her. She stared at it. Could she read the future in its creases?

"We wrestle the devil, *querida*. Though in your case, maybe wrestle angels to keep you from heaven?"

The old woman seemed in such high spirits, Alida felt remiss by not joining her. She wished she had more faith in survival.

She'd heard people speak of how someone had clung to life. She had scorned it, thinking it merely melodrama. Now it made sense, for she clung to life like she had gripped the splintered door in the rolling sea. Each time she surfaced from feverish sleep she remembered the swirl of murderous wind and water.

She burned. She shivered. She fought toward lucidity, a quiet island in this storm. *Señora* Rivera was always there, soothing her, smelling a bit like vinegar and plowed earth on a warm day. But she smelled of lemon, too, and roses. She moved in whispers, as if even her clothing knew secrets. She smiled with strong, even teeth. Was the fanged woman only a fever dream? Alida feared to ask.

She sometimes drifted to where she saw her husband, so wretched. His whining had once disgusted her, his bullying enraged her, but now she pitied him. An image of Seth swam near once and she cried out in sorrow. He smiled, floating past with the others. They beckoned, but when she tried to step into their soupy river, it cast her out.

Something awakened her, something different. A screech from an angry cat? Then came muted voices. A melody so pure, so sweet, drifted through the air. She opened her eyes to streaming sunlight. The door to her room was ajar, the sound coming from somewhere beyond. Yes, music after all—a violin.

When it stopped she nearly wept at its loss, but voices took the music's place. First a man's low words—encouraging, gentle. Then a boy's innocent laughter.

She pushed to one elbow. "Seth?" she whispered, rolling to her side and inching her feet down to find the floor. "You're alive." Her voice broke on the words. She stumbled forward, each step agony, but feeling oddly as if it was someone else's pain. Her boy lived. Why had they lied to her?

Each try at speaking his name ended in a whisper. She should have given him a more forceful name—something made of hard consonants, something she might bite off and spit into the air.

She reached the door and gripped the frame, but could go no further. She fell and the door swung open beneath her weight. "Seth?"

Something lifted her away as she struggled toward him. Why didn't he run to her? She blinked to clear her vision. The boy was just beyond her reach. He backed away. He feared her. But—no, not Seth. This boy was smaller, timid. He shrank from her.

"It's William, Mrs. Garrison—William Cooper. Not your boy." The voice rumbled from behind her.

Understanding sifted in through what she felt as fissures in her mind. She went limp in the strong arms holding her. "I frightened him, didn't I? Oh, God, I am so sorry."

"Just startled, ma'am. No harm done."

"Please, sir. Let me go."

"I'll help you back to bed. William? Tell the lady you're all right."

"Yes—yes, sir. I'm not so scared, ma'am." But Alida saw his tear-blotched face.

"I thought she was—Mr. Bishop? She looks like . . ."

Señora Rivera rushed in from outside, tsking and murmuring. She herded Alida back to bed and tucked her beneath the heavy blankets.

Alida closed her eyes. When she opened them again, she saw the boy in the doorway. He gazed at her in the way she must have looked at him—awestruck. She smiled. "So, William. Such a strange introduction. I hope—I hope—that . . ." Tears flooded her eyes and she turned her face to the wall. No need to frighten him more.

The man—surely she knew him—shooed him out. She heard the child go but still felt his presence. She would use it as a touchstone, a connection, but she drifted away on disappointment.

When she opened her eyes, exhausted, the light had dimmed. A man stood there frowning, rubbing his fingers and thumbs together. She must be a fearsome sight to worry him so.

He stepped closer and smiled, but warily. She struggled to recall his name. Martin Cooper? The name echoed within her. No, this man had an angel's name. "Rafael," she whispered.

"Rafe Bishop, ma'am."

"Not Martin Cooper?"

He shook his head and his smile twisted.

"Why do I recall that name? Why . . ." A sudden cough took her words. She pressed her hands to her ribs until she could speak past the pain. "No, the boy. *William* Cooper, yes?"

He nodded.

She closed her eyes. He held something to her lips. She smelled the sweet and biting elixir in the cup. "I won't take that." She rolled her head side to side, screwing her eyes shut tight.

"It will help, ma'am."

"It helps, oh, yes, it helps. But destroys."

"I suspect you've seen it happen. But we'll see it doesn't happen to you. Take it, ma'am. Please, Mrs. Garrison—Alida. Take it to ease the cough and the pain."

The warm surety in his eyes and voice broke her resolve. She swallowed what he gave her and a few sips more of cool water. Before long she felt some easing of her misery.

The little boy appeared, stepped close. Alida raised her head. The medicine had softened what she saw, and she shuddered and reached for him. "You're safe?" She let her arm fall to the bed, so heavy. "No, it's William. I remember. You're no spirit come to haunt me."

Someone pulled the boy aside. "Mr. Bishop?" he whispered. "She still thinks I'm somebody else."

"No. I remember." Alida blinked to clarity and smiled. "Don't be afraid, William."

"I thought seeing him would help, ma'am, but . . ."

"Rafael! Too soon." The old woman bustled in. "Why did you not ask me? When she is stronger, yes. But—come, William. We will make chocolate."

Alida gulped back a storm of tears. "William Cooper. And music? Did I dream that, too?"

"No. I give William lessons. I thought the music might be soothing, but it seems I'm wrong about everything. Forgive me." He shrugged. "Now I'm in trouble with the *señora.*"

She shook her head. "A surprise, is all. But to know a child exists is a comfort." The words sucked away her breath. She squinted up at him. "You're worried, sir. You think I'm dying?"

"The *señora* won't allow it, Mrs. Garrison, and I hear you're against it yourself."

"No one would care."

"Self-pity?"

She struggled against fresh tears, cursing her weakness. "Am I not to be pitied?"

"You are alive. Many are not."

She swallowed again and again to bring enough moisture to her mouth to speak. The old woman stood next to him now and Alida reached for her. "I see them in dreams. We lived along the river, but—but loved the land, you see. And now, to be forever in the sea." Speech wore her down. She let go and wept. The old woman lifted her off the bed and held her.

"They're buried. Safe on land," the man said, stepping back. "If that's any comfort."

Ashamed of her tears, she wished he would go, but when he

called to the boy and closed the door, she missed them. Both so strong and alive, the man so sure of things.

Señora Rivera sponged her neck and arms with cool water. "The fever is gone." She smiled.

"How long?"

"Days. Many days."

Alida stared at her arms, so thin, bruises fading to sickly green. "This is my body?" She closed her eyes, searching her mind. "My thinking is clearer." She smiled, but it faded when she remembered. "Too clear."

Señora Rivera fussed, sponging her limbs, changing the sweat-soaked sheet. "Five days," she said, winking. "You are back with us. The number is favorable."

"Number five has meaning?"

She shrugged. "*Quién sabe?* It sounds right." She grinned and fluffed a pillow, then helped Alida sit up. A clock ticked quietly on a nearby table.

"I recall visitors—or were they a dream?"

"Only Rafael. And the boy."

"Of course. I hope he'll come again, the boy. I hope I didn't frighten him."

"Rafael tells me the boy is eager to visit again. Rafael," she said, shaking her head as if annoyed. "He calls himself Rafe, an ugly way to say his name. He brought supplies I didn't need, for I grow the herbs I use." She winked. "It gave him reason to come."

Alida touched the side of her head and winced.

"Yes, still there is a bruise, but the cut heals. I snipped a bit of hair, but no one will notice if we comb it just so."

"I won't worry about that." Alida smiled.

"Most of the time you were feverish, but Rafael sat by you so I could rest. He listened to what you said, then said a strange thing to me. He said after truly listening to you he believes you are nothing like the other. Then he laughed, in a strange way and said he had been fooled before. He would not explain except to say maybe he is fooled again."

Alida leaned back. "I wonder what I said to prompt all that." She pointed toward the clock. "Four o'clock? But so dark. We're up very early. When does the sun rise?"

Señora Rivera chuckled. "Afternoon, *querida*. I closed the shutters, for you often said the light hurt your head."

"I would love to see outside."

When *Señora* Rivera unlatched the shutters, a breeze touched Alida's face. No longer memory's fierce wind. She drew deeply of the salt air and drank in the sight of blue sky. "Wasn't there another gentleman?"

"You mean *Señor* Cooper, William's father? He came the night of the storm. It is very strange, for when I go down the hill to church, I see him three times. Before, he only rides or drives in his carriage and never comes into the village. Now he sees me and asks of you. Such curiosity." She reached into a trunk in the corner. "This nightdress my daughter wore so long ago. Soft like a cloud, soft like . . ." She stroked the gauzy cotton and her voice dwindled to nothing before rising again. "A sweating sickness took her and her little ones. I fought for them but did not win." She smiled. "But for you? This time I am the winner."

Alida looked down at her bare arms and shoulders. She drew the sheet to her chin. "Surely no one saw me like this?"

"I kept you well covered. Rafael was the only one I trusted."

"Alone with an unrelated man? My mother would be seeking her fainting couch at the thought." She smiled.

"Well, Rafael does not think himself much of a man. He is kind. This I believe, and honorable, though sometimes impatient."

"His scar shames him?"

"More, poor man. His leg, his back . . ." She shook her head.

"So he was badly wounded?" She swallowed a sudden sour taste. "Crippled?"

"*Sí,* but strong. He carried you all the way up the hill to my house. I was very proud."

"Before he died, my wounded husband—well, he burdened me with his despair. He blamed me and—now I fear I can't bear being near someone who—I know it's wrong, but I can't be charitable as I should."

"You raved of war and after, worrying about others."

"My mother always insisted I was strong, born to take care of them." She swallowed. "Where has that strength gone?"

"It returns." *Señora* Rivera helped her slip the nightdress over her head and beneath her hips, combed and braided her hair and tied it back with a blue ribbon.

Alida closed her eyes and lay back.

"So, *muy bonita.* So very pretty." The old woman smiled.

Alida took her hand. "My own mother wouldn't have given me better care." She smiled back, her lips trembling. "Thank you."

"Ah, to see your smile is my reward."

Alida took in a deep breath and closed her eyes. "My sister, her husband, the baby and—and Seth. Did they—I mean, were they found?"

"Everyone we found, we buried in the churchyard and mourned. Our Father Sebastian said many prayers."

"It's my fault, you know."

The door opened and Alida heard a dragging footstep. Mr. Bishop. She shuddered, fearing to see his infirmity as he limped near her bed.

"Your fault?" he said. "Did they have to do your bidding? Were they children?"

"Two of them were, yes." She opened her arms and turned her palms up, looking from one empty hand to the other. "*I* had them. I was the strongest. When the ship smashed against the rocks I would trust them to no one else."

"So you blame yourself."

"Must I explain myself to you, sir?" She angled her glare up to his face, searching her mind for stronger words.

"You whipped up the wind, made the storm? Are you used to being so important? How vain."

"Vain?"

The *señora* glared at him. "Why do you torment this woman? Who knows where the hand of God will fall, who will be lifted, who crushed?" She swept her hand in an arc and ended with a gently closing fist. "Foolish to argue about this." She left the room, shaking her head.

"She's right. I apologize," Bishop said. "I spoke without thought. It's just that some people take responsibility only after something happens, when it suits them to feel sorry for themselves. This is something I know about." He formed a half-smile. "The *señora,* now. She has God as a rudder in her treacherous sea."

"And you do not?" Anger strengthened Alida's voice.

"I do not."

"Nor do I, not anymore. Responsible? I will never be responsible for another." She took a breath. "Never."

"Then you choose loneliness?"

"Better loneliness than pain."

"You are a beautiful young woman. You'll seek true love. Every woman's prize."

She narrowed her gaze. "You mock me, scorn my feelings. I say love is a trap. All kinds of love. The love of a horrific way of life brought us war." She shook her head. "My love of being right and getting my way killed my family. If ever love grows in me for anything, I will tear it away." Alida paused to calm herself.

He gave a twisted grin. "I sense passion in your voice, see it in your eyes. A man hearing you right now would fall in love with you. What would you do with the poor fellow?"

"I would not allow it."

"You take a lot on yourself, Mrs. Garrison. You fought hard to stay alive in that storm and after. Why not let it take you?"

Tears had formed, but they iced over beneath his cold words. "I prayed Seth was alive. If so, he would need me. Then, I don't know, maybe I needed to live so I could suffer and atone for what I've done."

He sneered. "Guilt. It will pass. You'll make a new life. Women like you always do."

"Like me? You know nothing of me."

"I know enough. A spoiled lady with slaves to bring her lemon water and fan her through fainting spells. I've met women like you."

"But not *me.*"

He shifted from foot to foot. "Well, I've managed to irritate you into getting color in your cheeks. *Señora* Rivera will be pleased. She's stirring up something good to eat, a fine cook." He winked, then backed out into the other room.

"Yes, I am hungry." She raised her voice so it would follow him. He had seemed to want to stand straighter, but apparently could not. She could hardly bear to look at his rounded shoulders. The way he dragged his leg, it must be shriveled or twisted.

Señora Rivera leaned into the room, smiling. "All this arguing. What good comes from it? But if you are hungry, this is good, *querida.* The body knows what it needs. Trust your body." The old woman ducked back into the kitchen and closed the door behind her.

Alida, exhausted from the confrontation with the insufferable

Mr. Bishop, turned her gaze to the window. The sky had darkened. Wind shook a tree planted close to the house. Leaves rustled, limbs creaked as they swayed, and far off on the bluff over the sea loomed a bare-walled house, forbidding and cold, as cold as she believed her heart would always be.

CHAPTER NINE

In the past five days, Rafe's visits to the ailing woman had let him learn more about her than he would have if she'd been lucid, for then propriety would have dictated restraint.

She was a fiery debater while feverish, though he never argued. She'd clutch his hand and shake it to make a point, her eyes glittering with fever and anger. Her soft drawl irritated him, reminding him of a woman's betrayal and stirring his memory of failure. Was he about to follow another Southern beauty down a path away from duty? Not likely. Yet it was like falling under a spell. He found himself wanting to lift burdens from her. Her delicate bones and ethereal beauty, her depth of sorrow, brought out an instinct to protect her. This protective urge had been his ruination before. Had he learned nothing?

He did miss living in *Señora* Rivera's cozy house. Missed her cooking and bustling ways. Already tired of burning his mess of beans over the stove at the store, he'd been eating out of tins like he had as a soldier. This evening, relieved Mrs. Garrison had recovered enough strength to spar with him, he decided to take himself to the *cantina* for a meal.

He stepped onto the road and gazed into the ragged night sky. Playful wind drove clouds across the face of a waning moon. By midnight there'd likely be a storm. He strode along at a good pace, taking stock of what he knew.

No secret that smugglers with Confederate sympathies, or maybe just greed, had operated along the coast during the war.

71

From Brownsville, far south of this tiny fishing village, cotton had made its way into Mexico and onto ships bound for European markets. The nearest town, Indianola, was taken by the North early on, yet saw its share of skirmishes. It seemed Cooper had been here all through the war. Why? What was he doing?

Tasked with stopping money and arms finding a way into the hands of men who wanted to continue fighting for their "lost cause," Rafe meant to succeed. His neglect of duty had led to tragedy greater than one good man's death and he had much to atone for. He'd do this job and be done with it all. Afterward, he hoped to be able to build a quiet life. He longed to stand beneath the oaks shading the rolling hills of his land, longed for breezes filled with the scent of sagebrush and cedar, not these stiff winds stinking of brine and fish.

He would build up his ranch, neglected through the war, and live a settled life. In daydreams, a woman shared this life, a nameless woman waving at him from the porch, welcoming him home into loving arms. Tall, long-limbed, graceful as a willow, her blue eyes sparkling, a mass of golden hair tumbling down her back, shining like the sun. Yet lately the daydream had changed. Not nearly so tall, her hair was more like the night sky, though her eyes were the same. Rafe smiled and shook his head hard. Such dreaming would not end well.

He slipped into the *cantina*. The wind took hold of the door and wrenched it from him. It slammed open with a crash and he had to lean out again, grab it and get it latched. Laughter and murmured talk ceased as every gaze turned toward him. He shrugged and grinned until folks lost interest.

Preacher Marsden stood behind a bar he'd built along the back of the room. Rumor was he'd been a ship's carpenter, once working for Martin Cooper, building the mansion on the bluff. A fall had crippled him and he stood like a wind-twisted tree. He limped worse than Rafe at his most dramatic. He'd furnished the rest of the place with six wobbling tables and a scattering of chairs.

The room stank like soured bread dough and manure. To get to a table, Rafe nudged aside two half-grown pigs rooting in a pile of potato peelings. He'd heard Marsden's pigs had once chewed the ears off a drunk who'd lain still too long. He didn't doubt it. The pigs grunted and barely moved when Rafe shoved them with the toe of one boot. They wallowed in a crater they'd dug in the floor of hard-packed earth and Preacher Marsden poured the leavings of a customer's beer over them.

In the dusky light of smoking oil lamps, Rafe made for a table closest to the stone fireplace, sat down and took off his hat. He shook out his hair, ran his hand through it and re-tied the thong holding it back, then eyed the three doors behind the bar. One, he imagined, led to Marsden's room, the other to a room for the woman, Twyla Green. He didn't know where the third door led. Some said men talked there. About what, he hadn't found out.

Twyla was leaning close and leering at a character with a scarred face and patchy red beard. She sighted Rafe and straightened. Setting both hands on ample hips, she gazed at him like a bird spying a kind of creature she'd never seen before, but maybe wanted to sample.

He smiled, hoping to appear harmless.

She simpered, making a show of looking away and winding a limp strand of straw-colored hair around one finger. Then she swung her gaze back to him and left it there.

Señora Rivera had told him Twyla was a girl off a hardscrabble homestead beyond the hills. A wild one, gone bad. Others said she'd been brought here by smugglers who left her behind. But Twyla would say nothing about her past, so either story could be true, or neither.

She sauntered to his table. He took a breath, rounded his shoulders and ducked his head, rubbing his hands nervously along his thighs, again hoping to be thought unlikely prey.

But Twyla sidled closer. "I'm likely to think your hands are cold, you rubbing them like that, shopkeeper. Maybe you ought to be warming them."

He stammered like a green kid. "Warming?"

She nodded. "By the fire is all I meant." She grinned, showing crooked front teeth. "Unless you got some other way in mind?"

"Of course—the fire." Rafe glanced at her from under his brow. She carried plenty of flesh on a large-boned frame. The fingers she fluttered around her face and twined in her hair were work-worn and grimy, nails gnawed to the quick. She could be less than twenty or pushing forty, depending on the light.

Though she worked hard at this seduction, her wide-set gray eyes were dull as a doll's. Likely she'd seen too much, too soon. She'd laced her ribs and belly into a corset over a dingy chemise and her bosom spilled over, straining worn calico. She parted her lips and thrust out her tongue to lick them, but Marsden shouted and she ducked like she was warding off a blow, though he was nowhere close enough to touch her. She snarled a reply, more surly than slavish. "Bastard," she muttered.

"Not too busy tonight?" Rafe hung his head, shrugging one shoulder.

"You're a shy one, ain't you?" She arched her back and rolled her hips, rubbing up against the table. "Busy enough. That wind makes fellas jumpy, brings out the worst in 'em. Except sometimes that ain't so bad." She leaned close and shook her breasts near his face. "If you take my meaning."

Rafe hoped it was only beans caked in the chasm between her breasts. He shifted his glance.

74

"So, Mr. Storekeeper," she sneered. "What brings you to this shit hole?"

"Should I go?"

She poked his shoulder like he'd just made a joke. "Naw. I'm just saying you ain't hardly come before."

"Others do."

"Surely do," she whispered, glancing behind her. Was that fear in her eyes?

She shook it away and dropped her gaze on him again. "I believe you are the only man in town, 'ceptin' the priest, who never once took me back of the bar." She leaned forward and tapped one finger on his forehead. "And I'm counting Mexicans. Nope, not you. Never once."

"What would people say? I have a business, and . . ."

She looked him up and down. "They'd say you was a man like anybody else. But maybe you don't like women. Maybe you're the other kind. I hear you play the fiddle."

He nodded.

"A prissy piano player come in here once, but he liked the curve of a young lad's flesh more than he did a woman's. You know what I mean?"

Rafe turned toward the fire. "So that's what you think?"

She flopped into a chair across from him. "Nah. I seen you dragging yourself here and there. You ain't a mincing kind and seem manly enough. You'd look a sight better if you'd stand up straight. You get that gimpy leg in the war?"

He shrugged.

"Don't want to talk of it?" Her voice softened. "Lots don't. Then again, some won't shut up."

"You see a lot of what goes on, don't you?"

She nodded.

Would she share gossip with him? He appraised her. Though she'd never been a beauty, her life here surely hadn't helped.

She might appreciate a friendly ear.

She spoke up before he could decide what to ask. "You got kindness in you, don't you, shopkeeper? Ain't much of that around, so it naturally stands out."

"You seek kindness, Twyla?"

"I'm getting by without it."

"My landlady is a woman of strength, though sorrowful sometimes. Women who come in my store are usually burdened with too many children and not enough coins. Some of them have a fierce pride."

Twyla sniffed. "I'm no different. I got pride too. You're talking awful pretty to me, think you can get a poke for free?"

"I haven't yet traded coins for a woman and I'm not about to start. I don't want that, Twyla. But I'd like some company. Why don't you bring me a whiskey and one for yourself?"

She shook her head. "The preacher, he don't want me idle."

"I'll pay you to sit with me."

She frowned. "You looked different just then, sittin' straight. Looked me right in the eye."

He slumped again. "Trying to rise to the occasion."

She looked vacant, then her eyes lit up and she giggled, punching him in the shoulder. "Rise to . . . ? That's a good joke for a sober man!" She stood, tugged her corset into place and slunk to the bar.

Did she know Cooper's little man? Rafe had never got much out of him when he brought William to the store for lessons. A swaggering fellow, always grinning like he knew secrets. Likely boastful to impress women. Maybe a drink or two would get Twyla talking about him.

When she returned, he stood to pull out a chair for her. Her eyes rounded and she blushed. "My, a gentleman. I've heard tell of such. Thought they was all fairytales." She set his whiskey down, holding a glass of what looked like water for herself.

"Marsden don't like me getting drunk, not so early."

Rafe smiled. "So," he began. "You heard about that woman, how she survived the shipwreck. Rarely happens. Was everyone talking about it?"

"A miracle, some say. Others grumble."

"Why grumble?"

She jerked her head toward Marsden. "*Some* say God meant her to die with the rest." She sneered. "She didn't, so she must belong to the Devil." Her sneer deepened. "Some say only dying will save her." She shook her head. "Makes no sense to me, but I heard a man boast he might see to it if paid enough, something about her looks, maybe who she looks like? Like it's gonna mess up somebody's big plans."

"Kill her? Who? Why?"

"Don't know. Some stupid drunk. Likely couldn't even go near a woman who's tough enough to come through a shipwreck. Men here can't do nothing but talk." She winked. "And who better'n me to know what they can and can't do?" She stared at him boldly before nodding toward her room, winking twice more.

He shook his head. Her face took on a sullen expression.

"Another drink, Twyla?"

She shrugged and scraped back her chair, went behind the bar and traded angry words with Marsden. She ducked a snap of his towel and came back with what looked like beer.

Rafe sighed as if he were weary. "All I ever do is argue with women trying to dicker down to rock-bottom prices. Then I listen to brats make the violin scream. Your quiet company is a pleasure, Twyla. Works just like a tonic."

She grinned, gulping her drink. "Don't you like kids?"

He shrugged. "Teaching them passes the time." He swung the conversation back around. "It seems odd someone wants that poor woman dead."

"Oh, they'll be thinking she's bad luck. Though I'd say good, wouldn't you?" Twyla leaned close and Rafe caught the yeasty scent of her breath and body. "Don't know how her looks could upset anyone. I hear she's thin as a snake. Guess she ain't gonna be taking none of my trade."

Rafe nodded and stared into the fire, seeing Alida Garrison's tangle of black hair, her full lips and sapphire eyes, the swell of small breasts beneath a ragged chemise, the curve of a calf. He remembered how she'd pressed herself tight against him, both of them shivering and drenched in seawater. Then, with a jolt, he remembered today's declaration that she would never again accept love.

Silence stretched thin. Twyla slapped the table and jerked him from reverie. She squinted at him suspiciously, yet smiled without seduction this time. "You can't understand them wanting her dead, because you're a good man," she said. "I suspect there ain't many of your sort around."

"You believe all men are evil?"

Twyla looked at him like an older sister might. "You know much about the fella you got your store from? That Mr. Lacey? The priest found him floating amongst the rocks over across from where you fished that gal out."

Rafe held his breath, then let it out slowly, staring at his drink as he moved it from hand to hand, sloshing the whiskey.

Twyla's hand flew to her mouth. "I clean forgot. He was kin, that dead man. That's why you got the store."

"Not close kin, Twyla." He sighed. "And it was an accident. I had a letter from the priest. It told of a fall. He'd been drinking."

She snorted. "Hah! Mr. Lacey? He held his whiskey fine, never so much as staggered. He'd not go wandering drunk on a pitch-black night. He had more sense." She gnawed at her lip. "I was getting right fond of him."

"Then why did the letter . . . ?"

" 'Cause the little brown man said."

Rafe's pulse gave a lurch. He licked his lips, suddenly dry.

She nodded. "Him and two others come upon poor Mr. Lacey. Guess the gulls already been at his face. Hope to God he was already dead by then." She knuckled her eyes. "Likeable, he was, talked a lot like you do. Must run in your family." She shook her head slowly. "Mirlito and his bunch dragged me there. Said somebody had to identify him. With his face gone, they showed me just his private parts, a-laughin' like it was a joke." She sniffed and swiped at her nose. "Bastards."

"Is Mirlito the one wanting the young woman dead?"

Her pallid complexion grayed. "Did I say so?" she whispered. "Please, I don't know what I was thinking, telling such a tale." Twyla grabbed her glass and scurried to Marsden's side behind the bar, cringing beneath a shouted onslaught of damning Scripture.

Rafe forgot to ask for food. He'd lost all hunger and now only craved sleep. As he stood, the door blew open. Three men stumbled in. He eased back down, his pulse pounding from a sense of something—anticipation or foreboding? For months he'd been scurrying around this unforgiving place, searching for answers to the enigmatic Mr. Cooper. *A storm blows up and a shipwreck spews out a survivor.* Was something about to rip apart here? He'd have to stand ready to catch the pieces.

Emiliano Mirlito was the first through the door. Below bowed thighs, thick muscle roped his shortened legs and he'd torn the legs of his trousers to fall just below his knees. He pushed through the doorway with one shoulder, swinging long sinewy arms. Above his stunted legs, his brawny torso was like any man's. A deep chest and thick neck held up a square-jawed, high-browed head. Pausing just inside the door, he furrowed his pock-marked face, resting an angry grimace on Rafe before grinning with white, perfectly even teeth. In such a face they looked wrong, like he'd stolen them and now only bared them to boast of the theft.

Rafe held his breath. The smell of whiskey oozed from the skin of Mirlito's two companions, as if they'd been pickled in it. They pushed past Mirlito. Rafe tensed, ready for insults or worse.

When the three sat down, it was as if the room gave a relieved sigh. Mirlito's gaze found Rafe again. He kept it there, cocking his head like a curious bird.

"Twyla, you lazy slut," Mirlito yelled. "Tequila!"

Twyla scurried past Rafe's table, the bottle already in hand.

"Please, Twyla," Rafe said, his voice low. "Another whiskey."

She planted her bulk between his and Mirlito's table, blocking the little man's view. "Go!" She kept her voice to a whisper and widened her eyes, her gaze jumping back and forth from him to the door.

Rafe smiled. "Sweet of you to worry."

"He likes to make trouble. You're the kind who . . ." She slumped. "Men," she muttered. "Fools, every damn one of you. Go on and get yourself killed."

Rafe leaned to one side to see around Twyla as she poured. Mirlito was scowling and swallowing tequila as if it were water. He pounded a fist on the table and roared at his companions in a stew of English and Spanish seasoned with obscenities. Rafe recognized a few words spiking high—something about Mirlito being treated like a dog and how he would make someone pay. He shouted for Twyla again. "The *good* tequila. This is like the piss of a sick cat."

Twyla had retreated to the bar. She edged warily to Mirlito's table with a new bottle, her gaze fixed on the little man. She set down the bottle but turned too slowly. Mirlito snaked out his long arm and closed stubby fingers around her wrist. She struggled. Mirlito's companions laughed. He yanked her closer and jerked her down, nuzzling his face between her breasts. "Why you pull away? You are happy enough last night. For a few coins, you are happy."

"I ain't never been happy," Twyla muttered. "Not in my whole life." She twisted, but Mirlito held on. "No," she whined. "I don't want to." She lunged sideways and pulled back, but the little man held tight.

"I have more coins," he said, grinning. "They weigh down my trousers, making them too tight. You want to see?"

His companions roared and slapped the table. Twyla struggled harder, but Mirlito snagged her chemise, ripping it. Both breasts spilled over the corset. Twyla froze, tears smearing her face and dropping off her chin.

How to help her without acting the hero? The man Rafe pretended to be would only look away. He stirred and then stood, but to do what, he didn't know.

Mirlito shifted his gaze to him. "You! Shopkeeper. Are you a man?"

"I am." Rafe tensed every muscle, splaying his fingers to keep from making fists. "And I have a name."

"I care nothing for your name. Look at this." Mirlito hopped down from his chair and stood close to Twyla, the top of his head only breast high. "What would you do with this, eh?" He dragged Twyla, whimpering, to Rafe's table. "What do you see?"

"I see a man acting the fool."

Mirlito froze for a heartbeat. He shoved Twyla aside with enough force to put her on the floor. "Oh, so you are like him," Mirlito said, the strong teeth bared. "Gringos talking so grand." He snapped his fingers and a man handed him a glass. He drank its contents in one gulp. When Twyla stumbled to her feet he yanked her close and groped her from behind, peeking at Rafe with an impish grin. When she tried to pull her chemise together he slapped her hands away.

"This cow is only for me and my kind, yes?" Mirlito said. "You are too good for her? Like him in the big house." He spat on the floor. "I once had a woman. A pretty woman. He took her. What do you think of that?"

"I don't know." Rafe loosened his jaw. "Nor do I care."

The little man squinted, then snapped his eyes wide. "So, you are more than a slinking weasel. You have claws." Mirlito shoved Twyla away and charged, smashing his head into Rafe's belly. He punched and kicked, swarming over Rafe and taking him to the floor. Rafe threw him off and staggered to his feet, but the little man came back growling, scrambling onto a chair and leaping from it to Rafe's back. The weight took them both down. Rafe curled up to protect his most vulnerable spots.

One of Mirlito's long, iron-muscled arms snaked around Rafe's neck. If Rafe fought back he could subdue the little man, but it would mean showing strength he'd been careful to hide. The others pulled knives. To keep from being stabbed, Rafe eased his struggling and took twice the punishment from Mirlito's fists. A blow to his head finally blackened the world.

He woke to see Mirlito and his two companions slouching in their chairs, grinning. "You take a beating well," Mirlito said.

Rafe groaned and sat up. He tasted blood and spat, then counted his teeth with his tongue. "I suspect you could have killed me."

"These two stopped me." He nodded at the others. "They say we lose shopkeepers too quickly." Mirlito laughed. "And you play music." Mirlito pretended to play the violin, then hopped from the chair and waddled near Rafe, squatting and offering his hand. "I respect a man who does not whine or beg."

Rafe blinked and clasped it.

He pressed his ribs and jaw, wincing. Pieces here and there were already swelling, but he shrugged and ducked his head, grinning like a fool. "I might have begged but had to save my breath."

Mirlito laughed and slapped him on the back.

He'd won the little man's respect. With enough drink and fawning questions, he might finally learn more about the mysterious Martin Cooper.

CHAPTER TEN

Alida watched Rafe Bishop cross the room, his footsteps muffled by a strip of carpet. "Good afternoon, Mr. Bishop," she said.

He paused in mid-stride, then edged closer. "So you have recovered."

"I'm thinking more clearly. My breath comes more easily." She smiled. "Not sure that means I've recovered. I recall being some stronger before all this happened."

He perched on the edge of a chair near the bed. "You've had good care. The *señora* is like a determined mother whenever someone ailing comes to her."

"And I came so dramatically. She said you have given up your room. Thank you."

"Yes, well. Why not? Wasn't that much of a hardship. And where else could we take you?" He scowled and gazed out the window, clearing his throat. When he brought his gaze back, his eyes seemed to probe hers.

Heat rushed to her face. She tried to think of something to say. "Mr. Bishop, my goodness. Your face is bruised."

His hand flew to his cheek. "Can't always keep both feet beneath me. Clumsy since . . ." He slapped his thigh.

"Yes, of course. I'm sorry."

"Not your fault, is it?" He stirred as if to stand. "Do you need anything from the store?"

Alida shook her head.

"Likely need some clothing when you're up and about." He

slid his gaze away. "I don't carry much in the way of ready-made garments. There's some calico."

"I'm sure Mrs. Rivera and I can come up with something."

He finally stood and clenched his hands behind his back, then parted them and ran one hand through his hair. "Your husband, ma'am, was he on the ship with you?"

"I didn't speak of him in my fevered ravings?" She managed a shaky smile. "We lost my husband just as the war ended. He was gravely wounded at Sharpsburg, a battle the northerners call Antietam, I believe? Whatever the name, that's where we truly lost him, for he was never himself after that." She sat up straighter. "I say we, but I am 'we' no longer, am I? I wonder how I will repay you all for your kindness."

"Seeing you well is payment enough, ma'am. Well, I'll go. You should sleep, now."

"Sleep? My stars, sir. That's all I've done for days."

He smiled. "Well, you've missed no parties or fancy dress balls."

She returned it. "How you do go on, sir. Such things haven't been part of my life for years."

His face went blank, like a curtain pulled over it. "Too bad that inconvenient war took so much from you. You've missed the life, no doubt."

"Why would you think so? You know nothing of my life."

"Easy enough to guess."

Silence grew between them as she cast about for harmless words. "I hope soon to be able to venture outside."

"There's an easy path to a quiet part of the sea, a secluded cove."

"Might I be able to manage it alone?"

"I'd be honored to escort you." He bowed slightly.

She glanced quickly at his leg, then just as quickly away, hoping her revulsion did not show. "I was not fishing for an invitation, sir."

"Still, the offer stands." A wry smile twisted his lips. "If you walk slowly, of course."

"Mr. Bishop?" A quavering voice uncurled from the doorway. Alida caught her breath, her heart pounding. The sweet sound was so unexpected and such a relief.

"William," Bishop said. "I asked you to wait at the gate."

Alida strained forward, one hand held out toward the boy. "Hello, William." She swallowed the lump in her throat. "I remember you. How goes the violin?"

"I'm not so good at it, ma'am." The boy edged closer, his eyes wide and questioning.

"I'm sorry if I stare, but you are like—someone else," Alida said. She would not weep.

"So are you, ma'am," he said.

"Am I?" She glanced at Mr. Bishop, but he shrugged.

Seth's hair had been a mop of brown curls, taking after his father. This boy's hair, straight and dark, fell into his eyes. But those eyes held the same innocence, the same wonder. "You must be what? Five years old?"

"I'm six, ma'am."

"Six. Such a good age to be."

He had edged closer, within reach. Yet he seemed likely to scurry off. He shot wary glances at Mr. Bishop. "Father doesn't know Mr. Bishop brings me here," he said. "He wouldn't like it. He said to stay away when I asked."

"I'm sure he meant when I was ill, but I'm better now, William. I would enjoy your company." She smiled at Mr. Bishop. "And your mother, William. Can she visit as well?"

William stared at his feet. "My mama is drowned, ma'am." He stepped closer and raised his gaze to her face. "I can read. I have read about mermaids. Maybe you are—are you a mermaid, ma'am?"

"William, that's enough." Rafe Bishop's voice was gentle, but firm. He rested his hand on William's shoulder and turned him. "Off with you now. We have a lesson yet to finish."

The boy nodded, but turned back to face her. "Goodbye, ma'am." Then he backed out, that same searching gaze fixed on her.

"He meant no harm, Mr. Bishop. I would truly like him to visit."

"He's fanciful. He might bother you with silly prattle about mermaids and such."

"It's only natural for him to wonder. He loses his mother to the sea, I presume? Then I show up, cast from it. He misses his mother. How long ago did this happen?"

"I'm told William was an infant when she died. I doubt Mr. Cooper will want him visiting."

"Couldn't you ask? Or I might send a note?"

"I haven't spoken to the man. I plan to, though."

"Well then, would you ask?"

"Not just yet."

"I see," Alida whispered. But she did not. Why would the father care? He obviously trusted Mr. Bishop with the boy. "I fear I am tired after all, Mr. Bishop. Thank you again for all you have done." She smiled and held out her hand to signal the end of their conversation, just as she had done countless times at social gatherings. He held her fingers, his thumb grazing her knuckles, almost absent-mindedly. Their gazes met and held, and Alida's smile faded. Something was wrong. What was in his eyes? He stared as if he knew her, but didn't like what he knew. "Sir, is there something . . . ?"

He released her hand and nodded curtly. "Good day," he whispered, backing three steps away before turning. He closed the door with a quiet click behind him.

Alida fell back against the pillow, one hand at her throat, calming a wildly beating heart. What was that emotion flickering in Rafe Bishop's hooded eyes? Not admiration. Something deeper, and not so pleasing. What to make of such a probing gaze?

Señora Rivera came in, balancing a tray of toast and tea and a kind of pudding. Alida leaned toward her, whispering, "I'm so glad you're back."

"What is wrong, *querida*?" She set the tray on the bed and felt Alida's forehead with the back of one hand. "The fever returns?"

Alida shook her head. "I had visitors. William, Mr. Cooper's son, is so like—well, like Seth. I wanted him to stay, but Mr. Bishop became very stern and they left."

"He must fear you would grieve anew, seeing a child so like your own."

"Perhaps, but he spoke so oddly. At first he was friendly, then he turned cold. I can't recall what I might have said." She closed her eyes and sighed. "Is there a reason he wouldn't like me, or approve of me?" She shook her head. "Oh, maybe it's just me. I don't know what I'm supposed to feel about anything." She took a breath and picked up a cup, blew the steam from the tea, and took a sip.

"Do not try just now," Señora Rivera said, plumping a pillow. "Make no decisions. You are weak yet. Maybe you fear this new life."

"New life?" Alida nodded slowly. "Yet the old one trails behind me like an anchor." She smiled. "Listen to me, how fanciful I've become. I used to be so practical. No one who knows me would recognize me." Her smile froze and she gripped the cup's handle, nearly snapping it. "But there is no one left. No one knows me."

"You spoke of your mother once. Will you return to her?"

"I don't think so. She has many friends, but they all sit and go on and on about the old days, the old ways. They were relieved to have us gone. We reminded them of how times have changed and how they could not. I must write to her, of course. Such sad news."

"Then the whole world can be yours, *querida*. Now, eat the custard. The eggs will give you strength."

Alida let out a long breath. "The whole world. You mean I can be anyone? If only I knew who that might be."

Martin Cooper glowered at Cora. "Why are you lurking about?"

She grinned. "I seen death in that candle flame. Look like she push death off for now, but it be a-waiting."

"Nonsense." Cooper's anger kindled. "Where's William? The boy's nearly useless lately."

"Poor child, slinking around staring at his mama's picture." Cora limped away, muttering. "Askin' do I know if the dead come back. Wants to know mighty bad." Her words dripped scorn. "Don't we all?"

"What? Why do you speak of death?" He took a step after her, but held back, slowing his racing heart. Cora reminded him of a snake that had just swallowed a rat, smug and too satisfied. His fingers itched for want of a pen. He must write that down. He made his way to the landing, but paused at his wife's chamber and stopped himself from knocking, as if she might be in there. No one besides himself ever entered except Cora once a week, to clean. He pushed open the door and crossed to the canopied four-poster draped in lace and silk. He fingered the blue satin coverlet, the same blue as her eyes. The furniture carved of oak and ash was from England, the paintings from France, as were the drapery and crystal lamps. No one in Texas could have an idea of their value. His wife, though from an old

Georgia family, had been like a rough jewel, polished and dropped into this exquisite setting. Polished by him.

How could she have scorned him and all he gave her?

Maybe this new woman had more sense. He closed his eyes and remembered her small, perfect breasts and waif-like limbs, recalled how she murmured to him and how she fit against him when he'd held her the night she came to them, held her against his woolen coat. He closed his eyes. She looked so much like— she *was* like—she was—no, she was not. She was Alida Garrison, a Southern gentlewoman. Like his wife in that, at least.

He'd tried once since his wife's death to fashion a lady for himself. But the woman Mirlito had found was only a creature of appetite, calling herself a *courtesan*, pretending she was a lady fallen on hard times since the war. It hadn't taken long to see her true nature. He sneered. Molly. She had purred like a cat when she spoke. Her eyes had flashed like emerald fire. Her breath came as quickly with anger as it did with passion and when she stood toe to toe with him, she was as tall as he, tall and lithe. Shining hair rippled past her shoulders like maple syrup poured from a pitcher. Molly needed no corset to show off a wasp-waisted figure and her full breasts were high, though she was past youth's first bloom.

Now the thought of her nearly undid him, a *mélange* of lust and disgust. He'd sought comfort in the canyons of her body many times, though he had never found it. Her pouting lips had too often curled with scorn when he demanded warmth, though she had the kind of lips a man wanted to feel roaming his flesh. These thoughts, unbidden, stirred the part between his legs as if it were a creature out of his control. That was what Molly did to him. She'd quickly learned to read him like *he* did clouds and sea for signs of impending storm or deadly calm. When he re-alized that, she had to go. She had once called him the devil in the shape of a man. It pleased him to know he frightened her, but he lost control too often with her and he couldn't afford such weakness. Better to be lonely. He'd tried to be kind when he sent her away, but she'd spat at him. He recalled her exact words. "Don't try that honey-dripping tone with me, Martin Cooper. You don't mean it. I'm the expert in pretending to feel something I don't."

Pretend! The thought doused him like a cold bath. He'd put her on a wagon and sent her off with nothing. That she escaped at all was testament to his self-control. He'd heard Mirlito had tracked and found her in Indianola. It was fitting the little man should have his discards, like the trousers Mirlito cut off to fit himself.

Molly could soothe his blinding headaches with massage, but Cora's potions worked better. Though neither woman could soothe his aching heart. No one ever could.

Except—maybe now. He left the chamber, glided down carpeted stairs and entered his library, locking the door behind him. He would write down the many thoughts he'd had this day. So many, so deeply felt. Yes. The woman. She could be—might be—anyone.

CHAPTER ELEVEN

Rafe took a winding path up the hill to the *señora*'s house, a longer path than usual, so he could pretend he was going somewhere else. He'd spent all morning thinking about Alida Garrison. He couldn't pretend gentlemanly concern every day, she needed no supplies from the store, and his landlady already gave him knowing smiles when he appeared. What must Alida Garrison think of a crippled, surly shopkeeper fawning over her? If only he could be himself. But why was he so drawn to her? Something moved in him the moment he'd lifted her from the sand, a kind of joy set his heart pounding when he saw she lived. It might be something so simple and shallow as feeling a hero for a change, but he suspected it was more.

The sun hung just overhead and pierced the veil of fog billowing off the sea, forcing it to swirl back over the water. He stopped halfway up the path and turned to watch the fog disappear. Cooper's house materialized from the mist. Cooper himself had come out a side door and moved about in a garden enclosed by a low stone wall. He faced inland, standing still, staring toward *Señora* Rivera's house.

Rafe turned, spurred by a sudden need to reach the little house. He jogged past an outbuilding where clucking hens scratched, and the smell of their droppings stung his nose. *Señora* Rivera was in her garden, snipping herbs and cutting flowers. He stopped and called to her. Though he'd spoken softly, the sound carried across the misty silence like a shout. She turned and grinned. "You did not visit us yesterday."

"I needed to do some thinking."

She wagged one finger at him. "You think too much."

"Does she—do you need anything? I mean, for her?"

"Come in. Find this out yourself."

He shrugged, out of breath, feeling ridiculous, for he'd hurried here as if it was imperative he protect Mrs. Garrison from Cooper's sight.

"Come," the *señora* said. "Carry this for me, yes? The little man left a basket of roses, sent from Mr. Cooper's house." She sighed. "Sick roses, I fear. Many years ago, his wife made our poor soil give life to flowers." She shrugged. "But since she died, no one tends them. Only the strongest blossoms survive."

"Cooper sent flowers?" Rafe picked up the basket, glaring at it. He followed her toward the house. Did the fellow think to come courting? That notion seemed monstrous. It pierced his already faulty armor of detachment. Who was Alida Garrison to trouble him like this? A lovely but undoubtedly spoiled Southern belle whose world had been torn away. She had suffered. Yes, she grieved, but likely lacked strength of character to move on. He'd known one of her kind. He would not succumb to another. He would take information from her about the shipwreck and be done with it.

But since she'd come among them, his thoughts had begun turning from his past and need for atonement, away from his mission here. They turned instead to her. Fantasies. Today he would put them to rest.

He set the basket of flowers on a small table by the door. The *señora* beckoned him in. Alida Garrison slept, her black hair spread across a white linen pillowcase, one hand at her breast, the other flung above her head, fingers loosely curled.

He was a boy again, blinking and gulping like a fool.

"Alida?" The *señora* leaned close to whisper. "A visitor."

Rafe shook his head. "No," he murmured, "don't wake her."

Her lashes fluttered. Her blue eyes focused. She came awake at once, no groggy murmuring. So she was accustomed to awakening swiftly and surely. Was it because she often woke to trouble? She moved only her gaze, flicking it from the old woman to Rafe. She sat up, leaning forward so *Señora* Rivera could drape a paisley shawl around her shoulders. Pinching the shawl closed beneath her chin, she tucked hair behind her ears.

Rafe nodded. "Mrs. Garrison," he said. "Forgive my interruption of your sleep."

She smiled sadly. "Ah, Mr. Bishop. Each time I wake, I remember. Everything rushes back to me. I have moments, you know, when I wonder if I should thank or curse the one who saved me."

Rafe pulled a chair to the side of the bed. "Do you know which yet?"

She leaned forward and stared into his eyes as if she knew his every thought. He checked the urge to look away. "It seems you are reading my mind," he said, uneasy but smiling to make light of the emotion swirling in the room like a storm. He couldn't quite pin down what emotion it was.

Her bright smile cut through doubts. Was she aware of the captivating picture she made, with her sparkling eyes and parted lips, showing small, straight teeth? She seemed guileless, not the scheming, drawling, vaporous belle he'd imagined her to be— needed her to be in order to keep his mind on what he truly needed from her.

"Well, I do admit, sir, I have been accused of mind-reading. Sister Sarah has always teased . . ." She stopped suddenly, as if her breath had been sucked away. Her smile wavered and disappeared. Tears pooled in her eyes.

He didn't think it through, just took her hand.

She dashed the tears away and leaned closer, letting go of her shawl and covering his hand with hers. "I remember your face," she said. "I recall your voice calling me from darkness."

"That's a lot of remembering. But, here now—please don't. Don't cry." Rafe turned to the *señora,* who bustled up, nudging him out of the way with a thrust of one hip.

"Phah! You go ahead and cry, *niñita.* Tears are saltwater too, like the sea." She sat on the bed and pulled Alida into her arms. "Saltwater nearly dragged you under. It can do so again, but from inside if you don't let them go."

Rafe had told her not to cry, meaning *be strong.* The old woman acted as if weeping itself would give her strength. He ran his hand through his hair and fled into the other room, where he snatched up an iron poker and squatted down to stir the fire, while behind him the women wept, holding on to each other.

When they quieted he stood and eased back through the open door. Alida's eyes were red-rimmed. Spots of deep rose burned on her cheeks and the tip of her nose was red. The *señora* was tidying a little table, clinking a glass into a bowl and picking up two medicine bottles.

Rafe sat again. "Better?" He still felt off balance, but managed a smile.

"Does it frighten you to see women cry? You bolted like a man possessed."

He shook his head. "Possessed by memories of other weeping women. Not exactly frightened, unless it is by my own . . ." He shrugged, searching his mind for the right word. In the past it would be disgust, but now . . . "Helplessness, I suppose. I wanted to fix what made you cry." He felt his face burn and jerked his chin toward *Señora* Rivera. "I mean, anyone so distressed. My need to fix things for people has led me into trouble in the past. Tears can be powerful weapons."

"Weapons? I can't imagine using them as such." She scowled.

"It's weeping itself that helps, Mr. Bishop. Take my case, there's nothing to be fixed. I can't help my sorrow. I can't yet stop feeling at fault."

"Well, that's just fanciful. You mustn't feel that way."

"Mustn't I? Do you presume to tell me how to feel?" She took a tremulous breath. "I fear that kind of patronizing attitude is among the worst habits of men." Her face burned as silence fell between them, broken by gulls crying along the shoreline and the whisper of *Señora* Rivera's dress as she moved about the room.

"Tell me," Alida said, at length. She sounded calmer, and gave him the glittering, false kind of smile he remembered from drawing rooms and dining tables of years gone by. "What kind of town is this? A good place? Are all the people as good to strangers as this fine lady?" She nodded toward the *señora.*

"I haven't given it much thought." The woman was clearly only making polite conversation, finding it a chore. "I came to run the store after my—my cousin died."

"Oh, I'm so sorry."

"I hardly knew him. It's nothing like your loss." Damn! He'd taken them down that path to tears again. He smiled, hoping to keep them from going too deeply. She surprised him by keeping to small talk. Good—he might turn it to his advantage.

"Mrs. Rivera told me we're not in Mexico at all, but Texas. Are you a Texan, sir?"

"Yes, ma'am. And you?"

"Vicksburg."

He sighed, again treading on shaky ground. "A terrible time there in Vicksburg, so I've heard." He took a breath and decided to tell part of his truth. "Mrs. Garrison, though I am a Texan, I did not fight for the South. Many folks still feel strongly about the conflict, but I think I should tell you. I believed in abolition. I believed in the Union. My conscience would not allow me any other course."

He waited, bracing for anger or disdain. He'd feel a great loss if she withdrew completely from him now, though he wished it didn't matter.

"You believed? In the past you believed? What about now?"

"The Union was preserved and the slaves were freed. Now I believe in peace."

She looked away, then nodded slowly as she brought her solemn gaze back to him. "I agree. Each of us must think things through, follow our conscience as you did. I fear my husband, brother, father, brother-in-law . . ." She shrugged. "All the men I knew, in fact, were caught up in the drama, the outrage of a people whose land was invaded by foreigners, ignoring the greater issues. My family held no slaves. We lived in the city and my family was in business, shipping and cotton brokering. My father owned two stores. We had servants, of course, and clerks in the stores, but always white people. We would have hired free colored, but for Mississippi's odd laws about such things. If we had been planters, I'm not sure if our convictions would have held, but I suppose we'll never know. We had many spirited debates with friends in the weeks leading up the first shots fired, I can tell you that."

"Thank you, ma'am. Here in my home state, I don't often meet with that much understanding."

They sat in silence again. Rafe couldn't think of anything to say that wasn't dull.

She cleared her throat. "So you keep a store? Is business good?"

"Business?" He had been captivated by the movement of her lips and not following the words. He needed to focus on his true purpose for coming here. "No, business is never good in a town this poor. That's why the townspeople often scavenge from shipwrecks."

The *señora* bustled up from behind him. "But he does more than run a shop. He teaches the children violin and plays for us some evenings in the square by the church."

"Yes, I recall the music. So beautiful." Alida laughed. "I believe William has far to go, though."

Rafe shrugged. "It's just something I did before the war, an amateur."

"He plays like an angel and should not say otherwise."

Alida's eyes lingered on his face. He feared to move and shatter what felt like a spell as they gazed at each other. What must she think of him? If only he could show her who he was, tell her why he was here.

She sighed and her eyes closed for a moment, her lashes shadowing her cheeks.

"You're tired," he said. "I've stayed too long." He would ask about the shipwreck, what she might have heard or seen, another time. For now, it was enough to have her trust. When he stood, she gave him her hand. He bowed over it, pre-war manners coming back to him. "I wanted to see that you were all right." He stepped back and stumbled on the edge of the carpet, feeling like his feet had grown too big. He blushed like a boy.

If Alida noticed, she was gracious enough not to show it. "Thank you for coming, Mr. Bishop. I'm pleased to speak to you without feverish ranting."

"My pleasure too, ma'am. An honor to serve you and . . ." He spun on his heel and escaped. He thought he heard the *señora* chuckle, but not Alida Garrison. She wouldn't laugh at him. Somehow he knew that much about her.

As he slipped off like a thief toward the shoreline, he remembered to hobble, slipping back into the hateful character he now had more reason to discard. He'd have to finish this business soon.

CHAPTER TWELVE

"Perhaps tomorrow? I'll try them on tomorrow. It's already getting dark." Alida bit the inside of her cheek to gain control, suddenly reluctant to leave the bed, the room. *Señora* Rivera had insisted she get up, get dressed. The woman held up a shimmering silk taffeta, clearly years out of style. Alida hadn't seen a skirt cut for a full-hooped crinoline since the war's early days.

"This is the color of your eyes," *Señora* Rivera said. "*Señor* Cooper is kind to send this trunk full of clothes. Some, like this, are not suited for this life, but beautiful. I have never before thought him kind." She pursed her lips and frowned. "Am I mistaken?"

Alida grasped her hand. "I can't. I can't yet face the world." She smiled to lessen the gravity of her words. "You've been my guardian angel."

The old woman squeezed her hand and laughed. "Angel? Sometimes you thought me the devil and cursed me when I made you drink the tea that smells like dirt and pressed the hot flannel to your chest, sticky with camphor paste."

"Never."

"*Es verdad,* though I have heard worse curses between children at play." She patted Alida's hand. "Try on this beautiful dress just for me." She tugged on Alida's fingers, making her stand, then laughed as she laced her into a corset and pulled the dress down over her head. She lifted Alida's hair and hooked up the back. "So thin, no need for this corset, really."

Alida looked down, uneasy at how her bosom swelled above the bodice. "Is there a shawl or scarf? I could tuck it . . ." She tugged at the square-cut neckline.

"Yes, we should cover those fading bruises. This dress shows off both beauty and suffering."

Alida pressed her hands to her cheeks. Heat burned in them. "It shows too much."

"God did not make flowers to turn their faces away. This I know. Flowers turn to the sun and open."

"But I'm no flower." Alida trailed her fingertips across the knobs of her collarbone where she wished a scarf might be.

"Is this not how ladies dress when candles burn brightly, dishes sparkle and silver shines? We will pretend. Step from this room, no one will see you but me. Come outside and show the horse." She chuckled.

"Many years have passed since I've worn such a dress." Alida took a notion to twirl and the skirt belled out, though when she stopped it puddled on the floor, too long without the crinoline. She embraced the old woman. "I would have died but for you."

"You are young and strong, easy to tend. Rafael's strong hands lifted you from the choking sand. He is the one who saved you." With her thumb, she traced a cross on Alida's forehead. "You owe thanks to Rafael and God. And now to *Señor* Cooper for these nice things."

Alida tsked in mock disapproval. "Oh, but so out of fashion."

The *señora* pretended to swat her, laughing. "Now I know you are well, to make a joke."

Alida glided to the window. A sickle moon shimmered on a placid sea. "How to believe that shining water could kill, and so quickly?" The memory knifed through her. She touched the spot where she had struck her head. The bruise had faded and the cut had nearly healed. She gripped the window sill, breathing deeply, calming.

"Forget that terrible night."

"Forget?" Alida crossed the room and opened the outside door. "It's not my way to forget. I take charge. I bully. I have even *threatened* to get my way." She blew out a tremulous breath. "Well, I got my way. I must find a way to atone."

"We have won back time for you. You can do what you must."

Alida lifted her chin and tamed her breathing. She turned, wanting to retreat to her safe little room, but the *señora* stood in the doorway, shaking her finger and flapping her apron like Alida was poultry flocking the wrong way. She could only step further into the garden. One lantern played its light across white blossoms of feverfew and ghostly flowers of the marsh mallow towering above the others in the garden's corner where the old woman did the wash. She had used that plant in a poultice for Alida's wounds. The intoxicating scent of wild tobacco and what the *señora* called *Dama de Noche* rushed to Alida's head. Frogs had ceased peeping when she stepped out, but a mournful owl took up where they stopped. She glided slowly, the dress whispering along the graveled path, a faint scent of another woman's perfume rising from the silk. The whalebone stays held her upright, but she felt like a candle whose flame might be snuffed out by the slightest wind.

Her thoughts turned to Rafe Bishop. Thank him, *Señora* Rivera had urged. She had done so, thanked him for fishing her from the water and lifting her from the sand. He was an unassuming man whose hands had pushed hair from her eyes and chafed her cold fingers. An enigmatic man, blowing hot and cold. Sometimes gracious, sometimes distant. Likely his wounds had made him so. He'd probably once stood straight, been true and courageous like so many others. Now crippled, rendered nearly helpless, relying on medicines and on *her*.

No! What was she thinking? Confusing Mr. Bishop with her husband?

She shuddered, throwing off recollection of her husband's bouts of impotent rage, his sour smell and the taste of laudanum on his lips when he forced her to kiss him. She couldn't even remember loving him. His death had been a mercy to them both, and especially to Seth who witnessed it all, who had tried to protect her and been thrown aside and battered.

Her eyes stung. She would not think of Seth, yet how could she help it?

She wrenched her thoughts back to Rafe Bishop. Thinking of him brought back images of the storm. The lights. Yes, the captain had shouted about lights. He said the lights would guide them, save them, but they had killed everyone instead. She would ask Mr. Bishop about the lights—why, there was one now. She turned toward the *señora's* little house.

"Do you see the lantern, Alida?" the old woman said, nodding past her. "Could this be our Rafael come again so soon?"

"You think highly of him, don't you?" Alida turned to watch a lantern sway along at the bottom of the hill. From the way it swung, she knew it must indeed be Rafe Bishop with his lurching gait, but he passed by and didn't take their path. She sighed, relieved yet disappointed. Her feelings toward him were too tangled.

"*Sí,* he is a good man, but stays too much to himself—asks no one for help or pity."

"Really? Or perhaps he is only polite for outsiders, putting on a show. Such men—you don't—you can never know . . ." Her heart pounded. She pressed one hand to her chest and was appalled to hear her voice rise with each word, knew she was sneering. "What about tending his weeping wounds, spending every hour catering to him, taking his abuse, his rage, his . . ."

Señora Rivera gripped her shoulders and shook her. "What do you say? He does none of that."

"No, of course not. Forgive me." She drew a halting breath.

"He reminds me of another. I—I lost myself in the past for a moment. How foolish. I promise it won't happen again." She calmed her racing thoughts and pulse with a deep breath. "So, where does Mr. Bishop go so late in the evening?"

"Sometimes the *cantina,* as men do. Sometimes he only walks, poor man. No special place."

"It must be painful for him, walking along the path in the dark. He risks a fall. I admire his determination, his persistence. So many men give in, give up—" Again, bitterness threatened to take hold. She throttled it. "As I said, I admire him for that."

"Perhaps you will admire him for more?" The old woman chuckled. "A strutting walk and a spine like a straight tree is not all there is to a man. He has a good soul, a kind heart."

"Of course. You would know, yet . . . well, isn't he as damaged as the rest of them?"

Señora Rivera drew herself up straight. "Some come through the fire, like the clay pot, the *olla.* They are made strong enough to hold the water to give life. Our Rafael is one of those, I think. Others come through the storm of the sea." She softened and smiled. "Perhaps, I wonder, you, *querida*?"

"No, oh, no, please. I can't think of it, not like that—I mean I must go in. I must not be out here. That moon—I thought it a smile, but it's more like a sneer—I can't . . ." Would she weep, would she fall?

"*Pobrecita.* Come in. I have pushed too far. Too soon." The *señora* slipped one arm around Alida's shoulders, helping her inside, murmuring endearments, keeping her upright, but weakening her resolve not to weep. The old woman helped her strip off the silly dress and corset and Alida curled up beneath the blanket, seeking darkness, not warmth, not on this balmy night. She fell into uneasy sleep.

★ ★ ★ ★ ★

The ship was rocking, sinking into darkness, filling with the sea. Seth was there, but smaller. Where were his tousled curls? But it *was* Seth. It had to be. He cried out for her, terrified. "No," she murmured. "Don't be afraid. I'm here. I'm here now." Yet someone was singing. Angels? Alida didn't believe in angels. Not anymore.

Light burst through. She had to open her eyes to the light, for it would not be denied. And when she let it in, she knew. The darkness, the sea, Seth—all a dream. Through the window came sunlight and *Señora* Rivera's fluting voice kept in rhythm by the chunk of a hoe into earth.

Alida breathed in and out five times, then ten more. She must remember the woman she was and be that woman again. She would get up. She would go outside to feel the sunshine on her face. She swung her legs over, sat, then stood and picked through the gift of clothing and found one dress less showy than the rest. She managed to wrestle into it. It hung from her shoulders like a dark gray sack, shapeless, the kind of garment she had worn when she was carrying Seth. Could this be William's mother's dress, worn when her baby was growing—oh, what did it matter? It would cover her.

"*Ai! Querida.*" *Señora* Rivera threw down her hoe and ran toward Alida as she eased out the door, stumbling a little and squinting into late morning sun. "What is this you wear?"

Alida shrugged. The fabric bunched across her chest. "Something William's mother likely wore when—before he was born, and I thought—"

"*Sí.* It would be so." She hurried into the house and came out with a twisted red scarf. "Here. Around your skinny waist. Pull the skirt up a bit, tuck it so. Now the skirt does not drag you down. That's it. Such a sight, you are." She fussed a bit more, then laughed.

Alida, startled, smiled and finally joined in. Dark dreams fled.

"And look who comes! But he will not care how you look."

Alida spun, her face burning. But it was William. Only William sprinting up the hill. He pushed through the gate, breathless and red-faced, looking behind him.

"So, little one," *Señora* Rivera said. "You run from *banditos*?"

"I'm s'posed to be with Mr. Rafe, Father says don't come here, but Mirlito went off somewhere before I got to Mr. Rafe's an' I sort of ran up here. I can't stay long. Maybe a little while?"

"My, William. Take a breath. We'd love a visit." Alida wiped sweat from the boy's face with the end of the red scarf. "Shall we help this good lady with her garden?"

"Oh, yes, ma'am!" Again he stared into her face and frowned as if trying to place her.

"So, you two," *Señora* Rivera said. "Here grows a patch of—"

Alida jerked William back. "Those are nettles! My goodness, they're taking over this corner. I'll help you, *Señora*. William, stay back. You will be stung."

"No, no. We must leave my patch of nettles. They sting, *sí*, but the tea can staunch the blood of new mamas when babies come."

William cocked his head. "How do babies come?"

"Never mind, young man." Alida turned him away from the nettles and toward the towering foxgloves.

"Pull all the little shoots from around those, but do not eat the flowers." *Señora* Rivera wagged her finger, scowling.

"Eat flowers? That's silly. I'm not a baby." William shook his head, as all-knowing as Seth had been.

"Be careful of the bees, William," Alida cautioned.

"Mr. Rafe says bees won't hurt us if we don't hurt them, like most people, he says."

105

"Did I not say Rafael has a good heart?" *Señora* Rivera nodded.

Just then Alida didn't care what Rafe Bishop thought or said. She only drank in the sound of the boyish words, the sight of the child's determined chin as he dug his fingers into the rich dirt around the plants. "Are you thirsty, William? I can get some—"

"Oh, no, ma'am. I'm fine."

Alida took a breath. She had to stop this. Was he Seth reborn? No. Foolish woman. She was not his mother. She was no one's mother. She'd failed, wasted that chance.

The *señora* stood and leaned on the handle of her hoe, shading her eyes with her forearm. "Now who is running up the hill?"

William jerked his head, spun and backed away into the tall flowers. "Is it Father? Is it?"

Alida stepped in front, shielding him, reaching back to take his hand. "No, it's a woman."

"Is it Cora?" William whispered.

"No, little one," *Señora* Rivera said. "Your Cora could never run so fast. Ah, I know who this is. Her daughter's time has come. I am needed and must go. Perhaps my stinging nettles are needed too? Good thing you did not pull them." She chuckled.

Alida and William stood close as the old woman rode away in her little cart. Alida slipped an arm around the boy's shoulders. He stared up at her as he'd done before. "William, why do you look at me so?"

"I think, well, you look like . . ." He hung his head.

"Your mother?"

He nodded. "She drowned in the sea. Sometimes Father says things I don't understand about it. Cora says not to listen to him. She says it wasn't my fault. But I don't understand Cora either." He shrugged and added, "I was just a little baby."

Poor child. Poor lonely child. "Well! Let's get at these weeds, shall we?"

"No, ma'am. I should go before someone really does come for me. So goodbye!"

He raced away before she could say or do anything more. She stepped back and slumped into a rickety wooden chair and let the afternoon darken into evening, thinking, dozing, dreaming.

Señora Rivera returned and they spoke of the birthing. "New life, *querida*. A hard time, the mama had, but finally all was well. A fine boy."

"Yes. Such a fine boy," Alida whispered. The old woman didn't hear her, but went on with her tale of the day's event. A light from the bottom of the hill caught Alida's attention. Like the evening before, it wobbled as the man holding it lurched along, and like before, he did not climb the hill.

CHAPTER THIRTEEN

"So," Twyla drawled. "Back again. Drinking don't seem to suit you."

"Just food, if you please, Twyla."

"Oh, it don't please me a-tall. Last time you ended on the floor, brawling like the rest."

"Maybe I *am* like the rest."

"Never thought so," she muttered as she swept away from him.

He sat and watched the fire pop and flare. He missed seeing the *señora* every day. He'd begun to care about the old woman, and now—having seen her with changed eyes—he cared for Alida Garrison. He'd even begun worrying about William up at that great house. The boy was too shy and sad. Only six, he fussed and worried like an old man.

Rafe didn't like how things were going. He needed no sentimental burdens. Twyla sauntered to his table. He was even worrying about her. Since his brawl with Mirlito, she treated him with disdain, as did some of the villagers. Less respectful now when they traded at his store, they saw him as a man who drank, fought and had been beaten by a man half his size. Father Sebastian had even taken him aside to offer words of rebuke. It rankled, but Rafe didn't dare explain.

Twyla wriggled her shoulders, scowling.

"Is that black look for me?" he said.

"Naw, this damn corset. Preacher says it ain't proper to go

without. Proper! Ain't that the limit?"

"Must be confining."

"Sure as hell is. Even if I was a less fleshy woman."

Even slender, like Alida Garrison. The thought knifed through him and cut away everything else. He closed his eyes and let the thought of her run free. She was both more and less than he'd assumed. He blew a breath over loose lips.

Twyla stood, waiting, twisting her hair.

"Sorry, Twyla. My thoughts flew off on their own. Beans, I guess. Or whatever you have cooking back there."

She snorted and turned, then paused. "You're lookin' a little peaked lately, shopkeeper."

Rafe mustered a smile.

She raised her chin. "Well, if you ask me, and I know you ain't, you best be staying away from this dung heap. Go play your fiddle, teach them kids and the like. Don't come swilling down Marsden's beer."

Rafe leaned forward. "You've been so unfriendly lately when you come in the store—I doubted you cared what happened to me."

She tucked a strand of hair behind one ear. "You got that bow-legged little bastard for a friend now." She sneered. "I can't for the life of me figure why." She spun dramatically and stalked away.

Rafe leaned back, rolling his shoulders and stretching out long legs. He stared into the fire, thinking. Too many shipwrecks, too much death. Evidence of a renewed Confederate plot dangled just out of reach. Lacey had written three letters to San Antonio. He had suspected the inland rancher and Rafe had proved him right. Lacey was finished here, coming home. He only mentioned Cooper in passing—calling him a strange, reclusive man, but no more.

Rafe slipped Lacey's last letter from his pocket now and read it once more, then fed it to the fire. It was in code, one he knew well. He sat well back on his spine, his chin on his chest, watching the letter burn. He didn't hear Mirlito come in, only noticing him when the little man rapped twice on his table.

Mirlito grinned. "Hey, *amigo*. What do you see in those flames? Tell me and I will look too, eh?"

Rafe played along. "Hmm," he said. "I believe I see the image of a naked . . ."

"Where, where do you see this?" Mirlito leaned forward, peering into the fire, nearly falling.

"There. See where I'm pointing?"

Mirlito stretched his neck like a tortoise. "I see nothing." He tapped his own temple. "You are a little crazy, my friend."

Twyla brought a plate with five tortillas wrapped around beans and pork and peppers. The spicy aroma brought tears to Rafe's eyes. Mirlito leered at Twyla as she put down the plate, but she side-stepped his grasping fingers. He blinked out of a lustful stare and watched Rafe wolf down the food. "So, you eat here. *La Señora?* Still you are not back in her house?"

Rafe shook his head, his mouth full of beans, the tortilla pinched between thumb and fingers, dripping grease.

"Twyla," Mirlito called. "Bring tequila. A bottle."

She glared at Rafe. "For you two?"

Mirlito held up four fingers. "Glasses, too. Two more come soon."

She returned with a bottle, four glasses and a glass of beer on a tray, setting the beer in front of Rafe. "Best stick with this. You ain't used to the other."

"Hah!" Mirlito laughed. "The cow thinks she is your mother."

Rafe only nodded as he swallowed. "Haven't seen you for a while."

"*Sí.* The weather is too damn good." Mirlito twisted his lips into a snarl, poured a full glass of tequila and tossed it back in one gulp. "But it will change. Always the wind blows here."

"Why so disgusted with good weather?"

Mirlito shrugged, poured another glass and sipped it.

Rafe tore off a bite-sized piece of tortilla and scooped up a smear of beans. "You work for Mr. Cooper. Does he ever speak of the woman we saved? He was set on taking her into his house at first."

Mirlito scowled. "He takes *many* fine things to his house, yet that one is pale and skinny." He grinned and slapped the table. "But if she died you'd have your room back, eh?"

It hurt to imagine it, but Rafe nodded.

"The villagers know everything." Mirlito put his hands behind his ears and pushed them forward. "Ears like donkeys. Mouths like bugles."

Rafe forced a smile. "Me coming to *El Cabrito* so often has made the good people and the priest unhappy with me."

Mirlito snorted. "To hell with them." He finished his tequila and poured another, slopping it onto his hand. He slurped down the spill and licked his fingers. "May they all rot."

"Isn't this your town?"

"Ah, you insult me. I come from a real city. People here only work, work, work, and are all cowards." He stabbed his chest with his thumb. "*I* do what is asked and fear no man."

Rafe's pulse quickened. His next mouthful of tortilla, pork and beans went down hard over a tongue gone dry. He took a gulp of beer. "So what is it you do so bravely?"

"Why do you ask?" Mirlito was beginning to slur his words.

"Just that you seem prosperous!" Rafe gulped more beer, sensing an opening in a wall around Martin Cooper.

Mirlito nodded slowly, his eyes closed. "This is a poor town for keeping a store, my friend." He opened his eyes wide, then squinted. "You did not always dream of owning a store?"

Rafe laughed. "My dreams are bigger than that."

"But shopkeepers are respected. You do not want respect?" Mirlito grinned.

Rafe picked his next words with care. Even drunk, the man was bound to be suspicious. "Respect," Rafe said. "Hah! Can a man make good times out of respect?"

"*Sí*. That takes money. But many men *want* to be rich." Mirlito leaned back in his chair, pushing the tequila bottle back and forth, slowly, gently. "Only a few can do what they must." He pulled a slim-bladed knife from his boot and carefully pared his thumbnail. "This, my friend, helps me do what is needed." He smiled grimly, replaced the knife and took another from a sheath on his belt. "And this beauty here, she is so large and lovely, who could resist, eh?" He kissed the blade. "I pity men who carry pistols. Such noisy things, smelling of smoke."

Rafe scowled at his beer. He picked up the glass, trying to look like a timid man finally grown desperate enough for adventure.

Mirlito tilted his head to one side, squinting bleary eyes.

Rafe eased back in his chair. "I've learned there are takers, and those who wait to be given scraps." He shook his head, feeling a little drunk. He hadn't had much beer, so it was likely from assuming this role. He felt excitement grow as he dove deeper into it.

"Strong talk," Mirlito said.

Rafe only smiled.

Mirlito sipped his liquor, staring into the fire. Rafe feared he'd gone too far, but Mirlito glared at him and flicked at a lump of dried beans congealed on the table. "Money comes to men who take risks," he said.

Rafe tried to appear calm and drunker than he was. "I'm not just a timid shopkeeper like you all think. I've done things." He let his words slide around as he pounded the table. "But if something's risky, the money must be worth it."

"I will remember, *amigo*," Mirlito said, smiling. "I will pass the word along."

Rafe raised his glass in a sloppy toast, slowing his breath and pulse.

Mirlito laughed. "Twyla, you luscious cow, bring something stronger for this foolhardy man. You got whiskey, Preacher? Gringos like whiskey."

The old man brought up a bottle from behind the bar, glaring at them.

Rafe grinned and nodded, unable to look at Twyla. She radiated scorn like a lantern gives off light.

Mirlito's two companions entered. With a boozy nod to Rafe, the little man got up and followed them into the private back room. The *cantina* was now empty but for himself, Marsden and Twyla.

Twyla sidled up, tugging at the ribbon where her breasts strained against her blouse.

"More beer, Twyla, if you please. Why so empty in here? The wind's picking up. I'd expect every man in town to gather around this hearth." He grinned. "Or around you."

She gave him a playful slap. "I suspect you had more'n enough." But she turned to get the beer. When she brought it back, she leaned her hip against the table. "Glad to see that little bastard has left you be. Who knows what he's up to?"

"Is he waiting in *your* room?"

She sneered and looked over her shoulder. "He ain't coming to my room again if I can help it, though I doubt I can. I suspect he's getting up to some meanness. Lately he's been nastier than usual."

Rafe sobered. "Has he hurt you, Twyla?"

She shrugged. "Not so much. It's just that he goes slipping around like a snake and you can't ever know when he'll bite. Him and those two go on and on past morning when they got plans brewing, start talking gibberish and I can't get a wink of sleep."

"They're that loud?"

"The walls are that thin." She turned away. Rafe grasped her hand. She turned back, eyes wide.

"Twyla, I've been meaning to ask you . . ."

"Ask me what, darlin'?" She plopped her bulk down on the chair nearest his and leaned forward. Her nipples, hard now, strained tight against the calico. She meant to be seductive, but all he could picture was a cow in need of milking. He felt bad to be so mean.

"I've been wanting to, you know, see your room." He nodded toward the door behind the bar. "Now, with no one here to see us go." He gave her what he hoped was a bashful grin.

Her eyebrows rose. "Well, imagine that. All right, but we gotta be quick and quiet. I don't want them back there hearing us." She took his hand and led him to her door, nodding to Marsden as they passed. Preacher Marsden took out his Bible and mumbled Scriptures he must have found fitting.

"Old coot. Got no trouble making money off what I do, but he surely gives me hell for doing it." Twyla lit a lamp, its untrimmed wick smoking, and set it on a table by the window. "That wind's howling like a moonstruck dog and this ain't much of a room." She moved the lamp a little. Wind seeping around the window glass set the flame flickering.

Rafe leaned his back against the wall between Twyla's room and the next, straining to hear Mirlito and his companions. They spoke in two languages, ending phrases with spikes of drunken laughter. The words came muffled and he could make nothing of them, though he understood how the sound would keep Twyla awake. He turned to her. How could he get out of this? He didn't want to pile more insult onto the woman.

She reclined on the narrow cot, having taken off everything

but cotton stockings rolled down below dimpled knees and a dingy white shift dipping low in the front and riding high on her white thighs. She grinned and bounced on the cot. The frame squeaked. She covered her mouth and giggled. "Maybe I can keep *them* awake for once."

Rafe sat and bent to pull off his boots, hoping to appear too shy to move any faster. She ran her fingers down his spine. "Twyla," he said. "It's been a long time. My wounds and all, you know? And, well . . ."

"Come on, darlin'. Come here to Twyla. I ain't never had a fella in my bed who played the fiddle."

"I suspect we're all built pretty much the same." He tried to laugh, but Twyla's hand had worked itself around his chest and found the shirt's opening. Her fingers plowed through his chest hair, then inched lower. She murmured and muttered and gave out little gasps and whimpers. Then her hand slipped out again, tugging his shirt from his trousers. She let her fingers follow the trail below his navel. She paused at his trousers, reached in and grabbed hold, squeezing hard.

He gasped, surprised, and jerked away. His head struck the wall and his foot kicked a coat stand into her mirror. It crashed down. Before he could disentangle himself from Twyla's grasping legs and arms, the door flew open and Mirlito's companions stumbled through. "What the hell?" one yelled. "You trying to kill that harlot?"

Mirlito pushed through the doorway, saw Rafe and laughed, bending over and pounding his knees. "See, *compañeros,* I told you the shopkeeper was more of a man than you thought." He turned and pushed the others out the door, throwing words back over his shoulder. "Go ahead, my friend. Have your fun."

Rafe heard them take their places by the fire, their business presumably done. The lamp's chimney was shattered and the guttering flame had blown out. He was alone again with Twyla in near darkness. He stretched out his hand and touched warm flesh.

"I'm sorry, Twyla. Those men rushing in like that, well, I fear I've disgraced myself. You know—too soon. Your hand on me like that, I couldn't wait. It's been so long and . . ." He made a show of adjusting his trousers, tucking in his shirt and looking forlorn.

She grabbed a short broom and swept the shards of broken chimney aside, picked up the lamp, found a match and lit the wick. "Marsden's gonna make me pay for this lamp," she said.

"I'll pay, Twyla. For the lamp and, you know, the other."

"All right, honey," she said, sounding weary. Her voice quavered, whether from fear or anger or hurt feelings, he couldn't tell. "Don't hardly think I earned it. Them busting in like that has dampened my fire as well."

Rafe heard the rustle of her clothing as she dressed. "Twyla," he whispered. "Sit here a while."

She sat on the bed again. In the glow of the lamp's smoking wick, tears made snail's tracks down her face.

So here was another woman whose tears were not simply part of a game. Her despair went deep and twisted something in him. She suddenly seemed to stand for every hopeless thing he'd seen in the last few years. He slipped one arm around her shoulders and tugged her close, holding her while she tucked her face under his chin and wept.

Finally he kissed the top of her head, tipped her face to his and kissed her lightly on the mouth, as if she were precious, as if she were fragile. Then he stood and took her hand. "Let's go out there, girl, and look 'em in the eyes. No one need know about my shame and your sadness."

She wiped her eyes. "You can't tell me you've not been with women, Rafe Bishop. You surely do know your way around a woman's heart."

"Well, I can honestly say no one has ever said that to me. A woman's heart?" He shook his head. "Up to today's lesson I would've said most of you have no heart. So for me, it's unknown territory."

CHAPTER FOURTEEN

Alida woke to a swirl of clouds and paintbox colors. She stretched her arms high, rejoicing. So much of the strength she feared lost had returned. She slipped out of bed and padded to the window. A cool morning breeze had already chased the fog back to blanket the sea. Far down the hill was a strip of white sand. Three days had passed since her night-time foray into the garden. Three days helping *Señora* Rivera weed and water. Today she felt ready for more.

The old woman had been called to a birthing, hitched her horse to the cart, and left. Today Alida would be alone. She watched the distant waves. She feared the sea, thinking it a monstrous, heaving mass. She must conquer this fear if she was to go on.

She dressed quickly in a gown she had altered, one from Mr. Cooper's trunk. Its bodice was now shorn of gold lace and the skirt cleared the floor by nearly two inches. She took a knitted shawl from a hook by the door and laced up a pair of short boots, also a donation from Mr. Cooper. Every item was a perfect fit.

She slipped from the house and down the hill, taking in deep, full breaths. The sky and sea shimmered as the sun rose, changing from pearl gray to ever darker shades of blue.

She meant to plant her feet and stare down the waves, but this morning the water lapped so gently at the sand it seemed impossible it had ever stirred into murderous storms. Alida was not so easily fooled. She had felt its violence. She inched closer to the water, gazing south toward the rocky shoal where the ship had smashed, then glared out at the waves. "What did you want with them?" she whispered.

Where the sea and sky met, where the fog still lingered, they were nearly one color. She lifted her face and glared at gulls wheeling overhead—squawking, demanding birds, screeching like she longed to do.

"Why them and not me?" She bowed her head. Should she try to pray rather than demand? She squeezed her eyes closed and clasped her hands at her waist, but anger fueled every thought and kept her from prayer. She could not believe as *Señora* Rivera believed. God had a plan? She couldn't believe in anything that could play with lives so capriciously, so heartlessly. She opened her eyes. Her feet had settled into wet sand and each froth-capped wave inched closer. "I dare you to take me now," she shouted, holding her ground. "I'm strong again."

As the waves splashed closer, she felt foolish. The sea, like the wind, was mindless in choosing victims. It took rich, young, old and poor. It took happy and sorrowing people. Yet she fancied the sea remembered her and now played with her. She hated its arrogance. Mesmerized by the rhythm of the oncoming waves, she wondered why she didn't give in. Why not let it take her? She wouldn't have to grieve anymore, wouldn't have to question. The weight of guilt would no longer steal her sleep and dull her appetite. She could simply stand here, let the tide roll in and take her to where the others waited.

But when the first impudent wave tugged at her hem, the cold splash on her ankles jarred her. She jerked her skirts high and stumbled back. "No," she whispered, then shouted. "No!" She whirled and ran through a screeching flurry of feathers, her shouts startling the gulls so they rose in a cloud. She waved her arms and fought them off, but stumbled in the wrong direction, across the sand toward the rocks. The tide had turned. Waves rushed toward her with more energy. Of course the sea feared nothing, least of all her.

"Stop! Not that way." A shout came from behind her, sharp with command. She stopped and turned, pushing against her whaleboned bodice to catch a breath. Wet sand sucked at her boots. She staggered off balance.

She had to keep running. The way ahead was the only way she saw. She wrenched her boots free and stumbled forward, slowing as someone slogged through the waves behind her. A strong hand grasped her arm and swung her around. She twisted away, taking another step, panting now, turning to see who had tried to hold her.

Rafe Bishop stood straight and tall. She teetered just beyond his reach. He stretched out his hand just as a wave, bolder than the others, knocked her to her knees. "Here!" he said, pushing closer. "Grab hold."

When she raised her hands he gripped her fingers, then her wrists, pulling her toward him. "Stand, then run," he said. "The tide won't wait." He tugged harder. "Get up!"

She shook her head and slumped where she was, half-crouched in swirling water. "Let it take me," she said. "It was always meant to have me."

He grasped her wrists tight enough to hurt. "Stand," he shouted. "Stand up so I can help you. Are you such a coward?"

Alida lifted her chin. He looked so cross. A little wave sneaked in and tugged at them both and she remembered he was wounded, a crippled man. If he stayed with her and drowned, she'd have yet another death on her account.

"Quit pulling me," she shouted, wrenching from his grasp. She lifted her skirts and struggled upright from her crouch. The water swept sand from beneath her feet. "I can get up."

"Not likely." He snaked one arm around her waist and lifted

her high and tight against his chest, carrying her onto firmer footing.

"Mr. Bishop! Let me down. You can't lift me. Mr. Bishop, please."

He gave her a bleak, tight-lipped smile and heaved her over one shoulder. Not until they reached a place far beyond the sand did he let her down. She fell to her knees.

"What in God's name were you trying to do?" He leaned over, hands on his thighs, breathing hard.

She scrambled up but tripped on her skirt. He reached for her. "Don't touch me," she said, relieved to be alive, yet angry— and unsure why.

He pointed behind them. "Look there."

She turned. Waves crashed against the rocks near where she'd just been. The sea had nearly swallowed the sand. "It roars like an animal," she said, covering her mouth with one hand.

He rested steadying hands on her shoulders and pulled her against him, turning them both. His body shielded her back from the wind. "Now you'll fall apart? Now, when you're safe?" He turned her to face him and held her at arms' length, his hands still on her shoulders, firm but not unkind. He bent low enough at the knees to look into her eyes. "Is this what women do? Be brave during danger and fall apart after?" He offered her a sudden disarming smile. Creases fanned out from his eyes and around his mouth, nearly hiding the scar. His eyes were lively and warm.

The smile stunned her. "Likely men as well," she said. "And I am not falling apart."

He pulled his hands away. Without them she stumbled, but quickly righted herself, stepping to one side to peer around him at the sea before moving back to face him. "Thank you," she said. "I assure you I wasn't trying to drown, if that's what you think." A sudden dizziness came over her. "At least I don't think I was." She touched her temple. The bruised place still throbbed at times. "It was as if the sea called to me, wanted me." She barked a laugh. "Seems ridiculous now."

He shook his head. "Well, the tides are under the pull of the moon and it's on the wane." He leaned forward a little and smiled again. "Nearly gone, the moon. Maybe it was the moon calling to you." When he straightened, he was taller than she recalled. She couldn't see over his shoulder, standing so close. She stepped back.

"What brings you here, Mr. Bishop, so early in the morning?"

"Perhaps my morning patrol for mermaids." He turned and gazed out at the sea. "I found one on a stormy night, you know. Did I find another this morning, or did I find the first one again?"

She felt her face go hot. "If I were a mermaid, I would not have needed help."

"Ah, logic. I wonder how the sea could seduce such a logical woman." He glanced at her. "I was watching the sun rise and burn away the fog. It's a good place to ponder the ways of the world. And why were you frisking about? I heard shouting, but couldn't pick out the words."

"Indeed. Why *was* I shouting at the sea like a fool? Some nonsense about standing up to it." She spread out her soggy, sand-caked skirt and smiled. "And now look. I've only made more work for myself. I'll have to wash this dress, hang it to dry. I'm not sure Mrs. Rivera has an iron to heat, and . . ."

"Yes, I see she found you some clothes."

"Mr. Cooper donated this. He sent a trunk full. Many things too fine for daily wear, but such generosity!"

"That *was* generous. Likely William's mother's things?"

"That's what I thought. I must find a way to thank him."

Mr. Bishop's smile had slipped away. When their eyes met,

the smile returned and Alida was again struck by the change in him. She glanced up the hill. "I should be getting back or Mrs. Rivera will set the dogs to find me." She shrugged. "Except she has no dogs."

Mr. Bishop bowed slightly and offered his arm. "We're closer to Mr. Cooper's house than the *señora's*. I could escort you there. Do you want to thank him now?"

"Oh, I can't let him see how badly I've treated his gift." She laughed, feeling foolish indeed.

"Likely better to approach him another time, then. He seems a solitary man. Some people hereabouts fear that house. Workers suffered all kinds of accidents in the building of it. Some died." He leaned down, whispering, "They say it's cursed."

She took his offered arm. "Surely you don't believe so."

He shrugged. "It makes an interesting story in a place where little happens."

"You say little happens? Mrs. Rivera mentioned how many ships have broken on these rocks."

"Well, yes, I believe three that I know of, and more, I've heard. I wonder . . ."

She shuddered. "Please. I'm sorry I mentioned it. Can't we speak of something else? Must it always be of tragedy or war, or . . ."

He nodded, but kept silent as they walked up the path. "William is quite taken with you," he said. "Usually a quiet boy. He's nearly mute sometimes. I worry about him."

"I felt drawn to him from that first meeting. I don't believe it's only that he's the same age as my own boy. I'd like to spend more time with him."

"He talks about you all through our lessons."

"He's lonely, I imagine."

"I think he needs more lively company. He rarely speaks of his father."

Only the wind and screeching gulls broke another silence. She looked up into his face. "Do you come to the sea often to think? Is there no better place?"

"It's solitary." He covered her hand with his. "Usually."

His palm felt warm against her fingers. She glanced down at his hand. A crescent-shaped scar curved around his left wrist. "Did that wound hinder your playing the violin?"

"Doesn't look like much, does it?" He wiggled his fingers. "But it keeps the last two fingers from bending as they should. I should be grateful I have the hand." As he spoke, he slumped gradually and slowed his pace. He'd likely been trying to put on a brave front and hide his infirmities. So unlike her husband, who had boasted of his wounds even as he raged against them.

She spoke before thinking it through. "I think you are a very brave man."

"Oh?" he said quietly, gazing out to sea. He cleared his throat. "You sound surprised. Because I'm a Yankee? Are you surprised I even have wounds? Seems you all believe only your gallant boys in gray have suffered."

Alida stopped walking. He turned to her, his head tilted to one side, a cold smile on his face.

"All?" she said. "All of us?"

The chilly smile faded. "Well, some."

"I've seen suffering on both sides. Heavens, sir, I have suffered myself. It just happens that I have never before *met* a Yankee to speak to. How would I know what one might suffer?"

They glared at each other. Then his expression softened. "I'm sorry," he said.

She sighed. "As am I. Must we fight the war all over again?"

"I hope not."

She suddenly remembered the lights. "Mr. Bishop, I—"

"Please. Call me Rafe. I have saved you from the sea twice. You've put me in my place at least as often, so it's only right to

124

use first names, and I intend to call you Alida."

"Then I have no choice, Rafe." That smile of his again. It drove all other thoughts away.

"What were you about to say?"

She shook her head, not wanting to recall it. "I've forgotten it already."

"We're nearing the house. Stop for a moment. Let me get a good look at you." He stepped away, moving his gaze from her tangled hair to the soaking, sand-encrusted hem of her dress. "Just to make sure you're all right."

Her discomfort grew under his scrutiny, but she held steady, lifting her chin and pulling back her shoulders.

"Madam, somehow you've managed to become more beautiful."

"Please," she said. "Considering how you have seen me up to now, that wouldn't be difficult." Her face burned with embarrassment. "I'm unaccustomed to gallantry, sir."

He raised his eyebrows. "Really? Were all the men in Vicksburg blind?"

"I meant you should not be so free with compliments."

"Me in particular?"

"No—well, yes. . . ."

"Do you mean," this time, his smile didn't reach his eyes "a cripple has no business gazing at beauty?"

"Of course not. How—I only mean—Lord, we are as cross as two sittin' hens, as my granny would've said." She strode forward. "And here we are at the gate."

"Had I known we were so close, I would have slowed our pace even more." He smirked. "I should have traded on my infirmity."

"Rafe, stop that. I doubt you do anything slowly, sir." Her face flushed again. Was she flirting? She had never flirted in her life.

125

"Why, Mrs. Garrison," he drawled in a parody of her speech. "You are minus a fan, madam, yet I'd swear we were sparring at a cotillion in the bygone days of the old South."

She chose not to be offended and laughed instead, dipping into a deep curtsy. Her sand-encrusted skirt fanned out across the ground.

"I meant no offense with my comment about your appearance," Rafe said. "I have little contact with young ladies, or even old ladies unless they're trying to talk me into giving them a bargain. I have never honed a skill in drawing-room flirtation."

"By the look in your eyes just now, sir, I cannot altogether believe you. I never thought very highly of such banter and never learned the knack myself. Instead, I took lessons with my brother." She leaned closer and whispered, "Sometimes I took them *for* him."

"Did your brother suffer from his lack of education?"

Alida's smile dimmed. "We'll never know. He didn't survive Sharpsburg. Seth's father lost an arm and a leg there, and was burned on one side of his face."

"I'm so sorry. Please, you don't have to speak of it. I have an inquisitive way, I fear, and am too blunt."

"My heart beats." She put a fist to her breast. "But grief keeps it captive and cold. Grief and guilt."

"Again you speak of guilt?" He ran his hand through his hair and gave her a look as if he'd like to say more.

"You think my sister had a choice in coming, that I should take no responsibility. But you don't know what I did to her. I threatened to go alone and take Seth." She sucked in breath, remembering the arguments, the tears and recriminations. "They loved him as their own. During the war I struggled to keep us fed and my sister cared for Seth. Her husband returned whole in body, but was wounded in his mind. Mine returned also, but neither could help me feed us. Seth knew his aunt and uncle as his true parents."

"Surely . . ."

She stopped him with a glare. "My sister was warm and sweet. My brother-in-law, though distant with others, adored Seth. Seth's father was no father, he was barely a man." She swallowed the bile that rose to choke her.

"But you blame only yourself for every ill?"

"I should blame circumstances?" She took a breath. "Should I blame you, or every Union soldier, or every freed slave? I threatened Sarah and James with the loss of a child they loved. I 'shouldered the burden,' as everyone said, basking in their gratitude. I only learned to be a mother to Seth on board that ship. I saw him as the person he was, the person he would become." She let go a tremulous breath. "But he's gone. Sometimes I wake up whispering, 'I'm sorry,' and look about me. No one is left to accept my apology, but also, no one is hungry, hurt or angry. Here is the worst thing. Sometimes I am thankful to be left so alone. Sometimes I am even—even glad they're gone."

"No, how can you—"

"Maybe that's the guilt I wallow in. Guilt for not feeling guilty." She took a breath, feeling lightheaded. Had she lost her mind, telling him such a thing?

He opened his mouth to speak, but closed it again.

"Yes, now you know I'm horrible. A cold, unnatural woman."

He stared at the ground for a few seconds, shaking his head slowly. "You've looked deep to dig out that truth. Let me tell *you* a story." He swallowed and looked her in the face. "I once had a simple job. To protect an important person. I lied, saying I was ill and couldn't take another man's place that evening as I had promised. I wasn't ill, I wanted to be with—to be . . ." Rafe sighed. "The man we protected was too talkative for the state I was in, my wounds and the war still fresh. The person I wanted to be with had just returned to me." He took a breath. "She wept and begged forgiveness. I had to take her back, take her in and make things right for her, for that was my way."

"You don't have to tell me."

"I think I do. My story for yours. Over and over, I keep thinking I could have stopped the killer if I had been there. I could have prevented everything that followed. But, like you, often my relief at *not* being there lies heavier than the other. So like you, I am guilty of, what, relief? And for that I seek redemption."

He drew something small from his pocket, tied with a black ribbon. He held it out to her. She stepped closer. A tintype in a tiny, ornate frame with a mourning ribbon lay in his palm. Though the enamel had begun to wear off, showing spots of rust, she recognized it and gasped. Who in the North *or* the South did not know it? "Lincoln? You were his—you were there?"

"That's just it. I *wasn't* there. Maybe it wouldn't have changed anything, but we won't know, will we?" Rafe stared at the tintype, then replaced it in his pocket.

Finally she spoke, for it was clear he would not. "It seems neither of us is so delicate we've shattered in the face of our shame, sir."

His eyes had gone hard, his gaze distant. She looked quickly away, wondering if he carried more secrets. Just now she didn't want to know them. She wished she could recapture the ease they'd achieved. "My story was mostly foolish, melodramatic. As, I suspect, was yours. Aren't we the pair, though?"

"I'm honored just the same to have heard it, Alida." He searched her eyes, tilted his head and smiled gently. "You're upright and strong, no longer a mermaid cast from the sea or a grieving, feverish woman who once accused me of bullying her. Today you are real. Your story made you real."

The intensity of his gaze frightened her. She looked at her hand where it lay on his arm. He lifted her hand to his lips. As they brushed her fingers, she trembled and drew in a sudden breath. She let it go in a sigh and slowly pulled her hand from his.

"Until next time," he said.

"Yes, until then," she said as she passed through the garden gate.

CHAPTER FIFTEEN

Rafe glanced both ways, sneezing as his broom stirred the grit and dust from the porch into a rising cloud. Satisfied no one was about to visit, he stepped inside, returned the broom to its corner and tugged the rolling ladder into place. Without an audience, he could scurry up the rungs like a man with two good legs to stash goods on the high shelves. He had to at least appear to run a store, but had let chores pile up.

A week had passed since his talk with Alida. Alida—he liked her name, liked how his mouth felt saying it, especially when he spoke it slowly under his breath.

Able to reach far to one side, he could quickly rotate his stock. Tins of baking powder and something new he'd brought back from Indianola two days past. VanCamp's beans. Beans in a tomato sauce right from the can. He wished he'd had such a thing when on the march. He'd borrowed *Señora* Rivera's cart and horse on the pretext of stocking up on goods in town, and managed to send a telegram to San Antonio, telling them of his growing suspicion of Martin Cooper, though as yet he had no proof of treason. Sometimes he doubted anyone still cared. The nation was moving on. Even Indianola thrived, rebuilding after a recent fire, though he heard talk of some kind of sickness sweeping the town and was relieved nothing held him there. More anxious than he used to be to return to the little windswept village.

Now, as he climbed down to gather more goods, he noticed

the diminished supply in the pickle barrel. The locals were likely to rise up and throw him out if he didn't start doing a better job. He smiled, imagining women storming his porch in their dark dresses and shawls. Like *Señora* Rivera, they would be formidable.

He scrambled back up the ladder just as the bell over the door clanged. He turned sharply and the ladder wobbled. He grabbed a shelf. Two tins of beans hit the floor.

"Mr. Bishop! Rafe! Be careful. What on earth are you doing up there?"

"Why, Alida. Hello. Uh, well, work must be done."

"You shouldn't be climbing ladders. Have you no one to help you?"

He muttered a curse, stiffened his leg and did his best to climb down, hopping on his "good" leg and almost falling. "I apologize. I imagine I don't cut a very heroic figure."

"Oh, who cares about such a thing. Didn't heroic figures on both sides turn this country on its head? I believe you heroic for what you just did, climbing a ladder, risking a fall." Her eyes shone with conviction and admiration.

He longed to kiss her.

"Believe me," she said. "Many men do nothing but glory in their infirmities, expecting those of us without visible wounds to cater to them while bearing their abuse."

"Well, I appreciate your fiery defense."

"Forgive me. I can't always put the past so completely behind me. Sometimes I . . ."

He waited, but she said no more for the time it took him to roll the ladder into its usual place and turn to face her.

"Would you let *me* help you?" she said.

"I can't have *you* climbing ladders."

"I suspect I can climb as well as you." Her face flamed as she spoke.

"So, is that a defense of your own abilities, or a comment on my lack thereof?" Again, he quelled his desire to take her in his arms, to confess all. He grinned, imagining it.

"Silly man. It's good you can joke about it. Can you straighten your back at all? It looks very painful."

He sobered. "I can truly say it is."

"Don't be offended, I'm only trying to help. Since we've shared our deepest, darkest secrets." She laughed. "We're certainly friends now. I helped nurse the wounded before Vicksburg fell. I cared for my husband's wounds." She paused and shook herself. "So, if you will, turn around and let me see." She moved close to him. "Would some kind of brace help?"

He feared what she might do next. "I'm really fine, Alida."

"Fine? I don't think so. I've heard that braces and prostheses of all kinds are being designed these days." She touched his back just below his neck, running her hands down the muscles along his spine.

"Alida, really. You shouldn't . . ."

"I'm sorry. Does that hurt?"

He closed his eyes. "Not really hurt, but please don't. Don't concern yourself. I've learned to live with, well, how I am, how I must be at least for a while more."

"A while? If you don't do something now to stretch those muscles—why, I can feel how knotted they are even through your coat—you'll be like this forever."

"I sincerely hope not." He smiled, glad she could not see his face.

"Can't you remove your coat? Please, just for a moment."

He shook his head, biting his lip.

"Why so reluctant to be helped? Aren't we friends?"

He nodded, his face bright red, his eyes tearful. Alida sighed. Men and their pride.

"I just don't think that would be such a grand idea, Alida."

She had thought him about to weep, but he sounded like he was on the verge of laughter. "Well, I don't understand," she said, insulted he would make light of her suggestions.

"Of course you don't." He sidestepped. "Uh, I need to fetch something from my room." He gestured. "In the back. I'll be right out."

As he limped away, pity flooded her and made her warm toward him. Such a good, brave man. He didn't want to be a bother. She'd have to go more slowly. How different he was from her husband. "I'll take up this apron and your broom, all right? I hate to stand idle. I may as well sweep the porch."

"I suppose, if you want to."

He sounded so sad. She should probably leave the poor man alone. He clearly did not relish thinking about his infirmities. She was actually surprised she'd had any notion to help, for she'd vowed never to be in the position of nurse again, never have to take the kind of abuse a suffering man might give. She supposed it was a testimony to their growing friendship. Perhaps he might agree to let her help in the store. They would be partners, not mates, of course, but partners in business. It would be of mutual benefit, for she had to find something to do, at least while she stayed here. She thought it through as she swept.

Martin Cooper returned from a punishing, early morning ride. Both he and the horse were lathered. He threw the reins to Mirlito, who looked half-asleep, and strode to the house to pace in his study. How might he see the woman again? He'd sent the clothes and she'd sent a note of thanks. A note! Surely his generosity merited a visit. He'd begun watching her with a spyglass, watched her move about the old woman's garden for the past week, and today watched her at the store. She seemed to be working there in some capacity.

133

He closed his eyes. She was, of course, a stranger. And might she not disappoint him as before? His head felt heavy. Pain slashed behind his eyes. Before? There was no *before*. The woman was Alida Garrison, not his wife reborn. He dug his fingers into his temples, kneading his skull just there. He needed Cora. He rang the bell on his desk. Where was she? She and her potions. He waited, trying to read. He forced himself to think of the woman. She might fill his mind and push away the pain. Her hair, her eyes, the slender body lying so briefly in his arms the night she was cast ashore . . . so like the other, but different in how she had clung to him, not pushing him away. He saw no revulsion or reproach in *her* eyes.

He squeezed his head between his hands, trying to crush the throbbing and slashing lights. Where was Cora? He rang the bell again, louder. Her remedies were the best, but she didn't come. There was nothing for it but to surrender. He took a small bottle from his desk—tincture of opium. He poured out a carefully measured dose and swallowed it down. He hadn't had to use it for some time, for Cora had managed his headaches perfectly until the night of the shipwreck. Since then he'd turned to the opium's restorative powers five times, maybe six. It was the woman. She'd weakened him.

The pain eased enough that he could think. He stared at the portrait of his wife, desperate to find—what? A sign? The artist had captured her sweet serenity. Cooper longed to have her again before him, but as she was on canvas, not as he'd last seen her, angry and screaming, her hair whipping wildly in the wind.

The door creaked open.

"Go away," he said.

"Father?"

Cooper turned. "William, I said go away."

"Yes, Father." But the boy edged in one step. "I only came to look at Mama's picture."

"Are you disobeying?" Though astounded and displeased, he felt a stir of admiration for the child's pluck. He had little to do with William beyond making sure he wasn't a dolt. The boy had picked up reading quickly enough, though often Cooper had to drill the lesson into him. "You have no business in here, William." Cooper growled the words, but didn't really care. He closed his eyes. The pain in his head was receding. Relief overpowered everything.

"I won't stay, Father." William crossed the room and leaned against the arm of his chair. "Is the new lady—is she Mama come back to us?"

Cooper scowled. "Nonsense."

"She looks just like Mama's picture, but her face is pale. Cora says that's because she's sick and Mama wasn't."

"Who told you this about her pale face?"

"I saw her. I went for a lesson and Mr. Bishop said we could go there. He played music for her. At first she called me another name. But then she knew I was William."

"Bishop dared take you there?"

He must have spoken louder than he knew. William blinked and started to cry.

"It was right she wouldn't know me, 'cause I was a baby before." He snuffled and wiped his nose on his sleeve.

"Don't be silly, William." But could it be? If the boy saw it, too—she would have had many years to forgive him, and she had once said she loved him more than life. Ah, but maybe not more than death. He squeezed his eyes tight shut. This was only the laudanum. It put pictures in his head. It was why Cora said he should use her potions instead. But they took so long, and—he sighed. "People don't come back from the dead, William."

"I *wish* it was Mama. I miss her."

135

"Don't be ridiculous. You can't remember her."

"Cora says a baby always knows its mama."

"Just more of Cora's nonsense." Cooper sprawled back into his cushioned chair. "Go! Just—just get out of here, get away from me!"

William spun and ran, slamming the door behind him.

Cooper jumped to his feet and began pacing. After three rounds of the room, stopping to finger the spines of his books, he paused at the globe in one corner. It squatted, as big as the armchair next to it. He gave it a spin as he would have spun the world if he were God.

He had to write. Words were pushing their way out. Likely the cause of his headaches. He would be the savior of the South, and as such, his every word would be of importance. He gazed out the window at the gray-blue, heaving water. It looked more petulant than angry now. The night before, a quarter moon had lurked behind wisps of gauzy clouds that trailed across the sky like shrouds. He had tried to write about it, but the morbid turn of mind had led him into restless sleep.

The door clicked open. He startled and spun on one heel. "Cora, about time. Didn't you hear the bell? Where have you been skulking around?"

"I bringing coffee just now, Mr. Coop. Didn't hear no bell."

"I got on well enough without your potions. Maybe you're no use to me after all."

"Now, you don't want to be takin' that other so much. What I make up for you is better."

"I will concede that point. You have proven more valuable than I would have imagined when I first saw you gnashing those teeth." He smiled, remembering.

"Always know what you thinkin', that's the truth of it. Been knowin' that since the day you buy me and not the others. You didn't care about no wailing and carryin' on, nossir."

136

"One must be strong at such times, Cora. I saw immediately you were that kind of strong."

"Oh, yessir. Time make Cora mighty strong. From that time is when I can see what is in your mind."

"Really? Then it shouldn't take you so long to come when I call." He took the cup from the tray and sipped the rich, black coffee, sugared just right. "I was speculating about what might have become of that shipwrecked woman."

"I jus' *bet.*"

"What's that? I didn't quite hear what you said." He sneered, amused by her little tries at independence. "I went to town the other day, thinking to ask, and those people gawped at me like sheep in a meadow. Don't they know who I am?"

"Oh, they know. You never go among 'em. This land ain't like no farm or plantation I ever seen. No crops, no cattle. Them brown folks hatin' you for how you hold your land."

"And how do you know all this?"

"Emiliano tells me. I gets to talkin' with him sometimes."

"I care nothing for the opinions of others."

"Not nobody?"

Cooper was ambushed by a sudden vision of his wife standing on the rocks, her hair windblown, the infant William shrieking in her arms. Pain scissored through his head. Just like on that horrible day, he was speechless. He dug his fingers into his temples, as if he could pry out the pain.

"Yessir. You cared 'bout *her.* That good lady showed you what she think of you that last day. Sure did."

Cooper shook his head, squinting at her. "Do you see the future in your candle flames? Tell me, Cora. Has she seen the error in what she did? Has she come for . . ."

"Never say nothin' about no future. Who you mean?"

He shook his head. The pain shrieked in his skull. "You know who! You see it, too. I know you do, I'm not insane."

Cora only smiled.

"You old crow. Quit grinning, showing me those hideous teeth. I have never seen something so old still walking upright."

"I is spry as the day you take me off that block in Barbados."

"You were a bargain, a leathery old crocodile. My wife believed I took you out of kindness, you clutching that child. He's the one I wanted to buy. What was it you said? He was a grandchild?" He managed a half-smile. "Probably a lie to play on my wife's sympathy. Your kind have no idea of family." He managed a half-smile even with the pain. "Whatever happened to that child?"

She glared at him. "He stay behind when we come down here."

"Ah, that's right. You put on quite a show that day."

"I speak up, yessir. I got grit, though it do me no good. You like grit. That Molly gal, she had it." Cora took the empty cup from him and backed toward the door, grinning now.

The change of topic seemed to ease his headache. "Yes, she did have a certain spirit about her." His pulse quickened, thinking of the fall of Molly Bank's shining hair, her glowing green eyes. She'd been obsessed with parasols and hats, boasting a creamy white complexion. She'd never let her skin turn to saddle leather.

Cora narrowed her eyes. "Hope wherever she be now, she ain't sunning herself."

Cora's ability to read his thoughts rattled him, as always. It was one reason he let her stay when all the others fled. She was a reflection of his thoughts, a sounding board, and she had found a way to soothe him with her tonics. He called them potions, of course, joking, and . . .

"That Miss Molly, she was a lusty gal." Cora showed her crocodile smile. "That little man still plenty mad you take her from him."

138

"Too bad she couldn't see—couldn't understand . . ."

Cora squinted, tilting her head. What was she looking at him for? Did he say something odd? "She was wild," he said. "Nothing like the other." He stared at the ceiling. He'd had it painted blue like a summer sky. It soothed him. "So serene. Small and gentle. Her cloud of soft black hair, her eyes like sapphires."

Cora scowled. "What gal you meaning? Get hold of what's real, Mr. Coop."

He shifted his gaze back down to the wizened black face, suddenly appalled at how she was speaking to him. "You! How has such a creature as you become my only confidant? What kind of world has this become?"

"The only world we got. I know you. I knowed *her*. Who else gonna let you talk about her? So, now. Who you mean?"

"I don't mean my wife, if that's what you think. I mean Alida Garrison. My thoughts occasionally slip their leash and go running to the past," he murmured.

"William doing the running today," Cora said. "Slammed outa here, ran off toward town. Probably to that shopkeeper. You got to go get him. I can't be chasin' after no running child."

"Where did you say?" He started for the door.

Cora scuttled in front of him, crossed the hallway and bounded to the front door, agile for one so ancient. "Likely where he get lessons."

"I saw *her* there. Just this morning with the spyglass. I saw her."

"Then you better get after William before he say what he's bound to. She'll think he's crazy." She grinned again. "He bound to tell her about his mama, for he been running off ever' morning for a week. Running to that ol' woman's house."

"Why didn't you stop him?" He raised a fist, but she didn't even blink.

"He a slippery little fella. Ol' Cora can't be watching him.

Got too much to do."

"Get out of my way. I swear, Cora I will sell you yet."

"Huh. You think I ain't knowed freedom has come." A sly smile grew wider and she narrowed her eyes. "Freedom." She spat the word at him. "Where this ol' carcass gonna go to find freedom? Need to stay right here, but you ain't sellin' nobody no more. You promise me. You say, bide here and raise that boy and peace will be my reward. I hold you to that." She crossed her arms, glaring at him. "There be powerful fussin' if you take up with that woman. I see trouble down that road. Ol' Cora likes peace and might leave yet. Then what you do when the pain comes a-blindin' you?"

"Stand aside. I must go and see—I mean—I must see William doesn't bother her."

She grinned, every spiky tooth wet and shiny. "I know what you thinkin', and that ain't exactly it."

Cooper turned and stalked away from her, every limb stiff with anger. "Why do I put up with you? As meddlesome as my own grandmother. Is it a common trait of crones, no matter what color?" Something more to write down. Stories of his time with his aristocratic grandmother would enliven his memoir. The thought lightened his mood, though the pain remained. "The potion, Cora. I need it now."

"I see you do, yessir." She reached in her pocket, brought out a flask, and poured a good amount in his empty coffee cup.

He gulped it down. So bitter. After some minutes, relief came like a fresh wind. All in all, it had been an interesting morning. His fingers itched to grip a pen and put his latest thoughts to paper. Did he have enough ink? Lately he'd been partial to blue, but . . .

No. First he had to bring William back.

CHAPTER SIXTEEN

Rafe left the door open, taking advantage of breezes from the sea. He had spent the early morning rearranging goods in bins and on shelves, then Alida came to set up a method of keeping books. She wore a grim expression, maybe just determination, for his records were a mess.

Having her near—he liked it in a way he'd never thought of before, a woman as congenial companion, a friend. He wanted more, though he doubted he could expect any deeper emotion to grow, not when he had so many lies spinning. He felt like a circus clown twirling plates on sticks. He didn't yet dare tell her what he was really doing here, but he couldn't deny she was always in his thoughts. He grabbed a broom to sweep sand off the porch and nearly knocked over the small person running up the steps.

"William, here again so soon? We just had a lesson, what, two days ago? Are you alone?" He glanced beyond William, toward the big house, scanning for the hired man or the boy's father. How to learn more about that man? He'd need entry to that looming gray house. Maybe through William? No. He had to draw a line somewhere. He wouldn't use a child, and possibly Cooper was merely a lonely man living in the past. Rafe turned back to William. "So, Master William, what brings you here?"

Panting, the boy answered, "I—I ran away, Mr. Bishop."

"All the way down from the house?"

William nodded. "I been going to see Miss Alida in the morn-

141

ings early, but today I couldn't 'cause Cora was watching." He swiped one hand across his runny nose. "I know Miss Alida comes here in the day and—and Father shouted. He told me to go away and—and I *did.*"

"Your father likely didn't mean go away quite so far, William." Rafe squatted by the boy, using the corner of his apron to wipe his face.

"I was only looking at my mama's picture, sir. Father doesn't like me in his—his liberry—lib*ra*ry." He hiccoughed twice. "But I had to see. Had to see Mama's picture."

Rafe stood, smiled and rested one hand on William's tousled hair. "It's not wrong to think of your mother."

"No, sir. But she's—she's . . ." The boy turned his head and took a sharp breath, staring with wide eyes.

Rafe turned around. Alida stood framed in the doorway, her smile changing to a concerned frown.

"William?" she breathed. "I thought I heard you. You didn't come this morning. I missed you." She stretched one hand past Rafe. William grasped it and she tugged him close. He pressed his face tightly to her waist. "There now, William. Why are you crying? Everything's fine." She sighed. "I'm happy to see you."

"William comes every day?" Rafe asked.

Alida drew the boy along with her into the store. "He does. Comes running up the hill just as dawn breaks." She tousled William's hair. "I think of him as bringing the sunshine."

He sniffled and wiped his eyes. "But, Miss. Sometimes it's foggy."

"Yes, William. But I always know the sun's there somewhere, ready to shine."

The boy nearly melted in the warmth of her words. Rafe felt a spike of jealousy, then grinned at his own foolishness. Jealous of a six-year-old boy? His infatuation with Mrs. Garrison ran deeper than he thought. "Your father doesn't mind, William?" he said.

William hung his head. "He's always sleeping then."

Alida held William away from her. "I didn't know that, child. I assumed you had permission." She gave Rafe a rueful smile. "Now I really must meet Mr. Cooper and make my apologies. He'll think I'm stealing his son."

"Oh, he doesn't care, Miss. I'm very bothersome to him."

"I doubt that," Rafe said. "You're the quietest boy I've ever met."

"I shall certainly want to speak to your father. You'll have to introduce us, William."

"But you've met, Alida. Don't you recall?" Rafe said. "The night of the shipwreck. He came, offered you his house and servant?"

She frowned, touching the place on her temple as she often did when having to think of that time. He'd seen it more than once. "Such a vague memory." She shook her head, chuckling. "I'm sure I can make a better impression now."

"I recall you made impression enough then."

She looked quizzically at him, half-smile, half-scowl.

He laughed, trying for a lighter mood.

"Have you had breakfast, William?" Alida asked.

"Oh, yes, Miss. Cora makes me eat breakfast no matter when I get up." He leaned close to Alida. "I don't think Cora ever sleeps, Miss."

Alida laughed. "Oh, I'm sure she does. Everyone must sleep."

He shrugged. "Some people think Cora is scary, but I don't. She's always been here. She's very, very old."

"Why do people think she's scary, William?" She shot a quick smile toward Rafe.

William tapped his teeth and nodded.

Rafe nodded at Alida's puzzled look. "She's been in the store a time or two. An old African woman. Her teeth are filed sharp. *Señora* Rivera knows her. I think those two are rivals for who's the best healing woman in the village. Sort of a good versus evil struggle. Each has her factions."

"Then I *do* recall her. She came to Mrs. Rivera's house that first night. I thought it a dream."

"No, Miss. Cora's real. She helps Father with his headaches. She even teases him sometimes. She's the only one who can, I think."

"So he counts on her for many reasons?" Rafe said. "And the little man?"

"I don't think he likes me. His friend, Molly, came to stay for a while, but Emiliano didn't like her to be visiting Father."

"Well, a lot's going on at your house." Alida smiled at Rafe, opening her eyes wide, clearly trying to change the subject. "Let's look through the readers Mr. Bishop has here, William. We've finished the one I took home. William reads very well, Rafe."

"Father taught me."

"How good of him to take the time. Many fathers wouldn't," Alida said.

"He says he won't have me be a—a dolt. But I don't know what that is."

"Well, you're not one, William. You're a smart boy, a good boy."

Alida and the child gazed at each other like each thought the other hung the moon. Again, Rafe felt that foolish pinch of jealousy.

Cooper couldn't find Mirlito and cursed the man. He saddled the horse himself, and it didn't take long before he reined in by a sagging pine porch tacked onto a squat adobe structure. The shopkeeper, Rafe Bishop, lurched toward him. There, just behind him, stood a woman holding William's hand.

What a picture they made! Cooper had experienced visions before, usually after one of his headaches, especially when he took the opium instead of waiting for Cora's cures. Had he taken two doses today? He couldn't recall. His head still throbbed. He needed Cora, but it would have to wait. While he stared, the woman stayed visible, so this was no vision.

"Mr. Cooper? Have you come to collect William? We'd be happy to have him here a bit longer," Bishop said. "I can bring him home later."

We? The man seemed terribly eager to escort William. Probably wanted a gander at the inside of Cooper's house, which was most likely grander than anything he'd ever seen. It took great effort to ignore Bishop's impudent offer. "Yes, I am here to take William home."

"Please don't be angry with William, sir." The woman inclined her head. "And though Mr. Bishop has failed to introduce us, I am pleased to meet you. I'm told we met before, though I wasn't in my right mind at the time."

The woman from the shipwreck. Cooper felt a sharp stab of disappointment.

"We all need to be in our right minds, of course." Bishop gave a sideways smile. What was the man playing at? "Please, Mr. Cooper, come in. I don't recall ever seeing you in town."

"No. I send my man and my servant. I'm otherwise occupied." He dismounted, tied the horse to a sagging fence and followed Bishop in.

The woman and William had gone ahead. As he stooped to pass beneath the lintel, he noticed the storekeeper's stoop-shouldered posture was a help in this regard. No danger of him hitting his head. Cooper had the urge to take hold of Bishop and shake him. He had never tolerated slovenly posture on any of his crew, not when he captained a ship. But that was a long

145

time ago. He took a breath, scattering the memories.

How had men like Bishop, grubbing for a dollar, put down the South's fight for independence? Such a sorry lot of shopkeepers, factory workers and sons of bankers. The thought stirred his always-smoldering rage, but as he glanced around the room, he was surprised at how orderly and well-stocked the shelves were.

"Mrs. Garrison put coffee on the boil," Bishop said, limping toward the pot-bellied stove in one corner. "I surely do appreciate having coffee again. Why, I believe there was a time we'd have traded our powder and shot for a pot of real coffee."

"*You* fought in the rebellion?" Cooper blurted out the question.

. The man fingered his scar and let his hand drop to his gimpy leg. "I did indeed."

"I can't imagine—surely not an officer."

"A lieutenant, sir." He rousted three cups from a cupboard. "And what you see is how many a soldier can end up." He grimaced. "Even officers."

"Of course. I was trapped here all during the conflict. Once a ship's captain," Cooper said quickly, before the man might use his wounds as bragging rights. "I was building the house. Indianola was bound to be an important port, and I had dealings in the West Indies. I was kept away by blockades, but I did what I could. I've heard stories that Confederate soldiers lacked many things we think of as staples." He shook his head. "They fought on bravely nonetheless."

"As did *we*." Bishop let his gaze fall away. "I fought for the Union, Mr. Cooper." He poured the coffee.

"Aren't you a Texan?" Cooper's contempt for the man doubled.

"I knew the Union was bound to win." He shrugged. "Just expedience, sir."

"Rafe," Mrs. Garrison said. "That's not what you told me. Don't make light of your sacrifice."

Bishop only sipped his coffee, nodding in a self-satisfied manner.

"Well," Cooper began. "I was here when they fired on Fort Sumter. Though I tried, I couldn't get back. And you, Mrs. Garrison?"

"I have come from Vicksburg, sir."

"Such a gallant defense, I hear."

"Gallant? I saw it as futile. Appalling waste."

"Perhaps. My wife and I made a life here out of necessity. She—she died before it all went so badly for the Confederacy, but no doubt she, as sensitive as yourself, madam, would have felt the same." He shrugged. "Ladies have no head for war." His headache was inching its way back, probing fingers of pain, but he managed to smile. "After the surrender, I saw no reason to return to the Carolinas where I once had a thriving plantation. Nothing was the same—nothing." His head suddenly pounded along with his pulse. Cora. He needed Cora.

Bishop gestured for Mrs. Garrison to sit in one of the chairs just inside the door and for Cooper to take the other. "I've been meaning to compliment you, Mr. Cooper," Bishop said.

Cooper sighed, weary of obsequious men. He waved his hand, deflecting praise.

Bishop tilted his head and smiled. "I mean your son. William here is perhaps the most talented boy taking lessons from me, if not always the most enthusiastic."

William ducked his head and beamed up at Mrs. Garrison, who gazed fondly at him. William leaned against her shoulder as if he'd done so many times.

"I'd forgotten about the lessons," Cooper said.

"Yes, your man brings him down twice a week. He's doing very well."

"I see." He turned to the woman. "I understand William has been visiting you, Mrs. Garrison. I hope he's been no bother."

"Oh, no, sir. I cherish our visits. I'm getting on well now, helping at the store, for Mr. Bishop's records are in a horrible tangle." She smiled at the shopkeeper.

Cooper's pulse raced. His breath caught in his throat. He knew that smile, the affectionate one, playful. A thread of silence stretched near to breaking. He managed a deep breath. He blurted his next words without thought. "And you, Mr. Bishop, so eager to accept this lady's help. Are your motives pure, sir? Or might they be other than they appear? Are you something other than you seem?"

"Mr. Cooper!" Color burned in Mrs. Garrison's face. "What *do* you mean?"

"A jest, madam." He did his best to smile, to get hold of himself. "Only a poor jest."

"Indeed," Bishop said. "And you, sir?"

"How do you mean?"

"You have no ship now? No interests beyond this rocky shore?"

"No. All in the past. I live in isolation, but am not ignorant of the world, of course."

"So *you* could be more than you seem." Bishop smiled. "Or less."

Did Bishop really say that? Was his smile less than friendly? Cooper rubbed his temples. "So, madam. What are your plans?" It was hard to speak more than three words together.

"Sir," she said, her voice so gentle it nearly brought him to tears. "Are you unwell?"

"A slight pain. Not new to me."

"I understand. I seem to be afflicted similarly since—but you asked for my plans. Just now I'm helping Mr. Bishop. But I imagine I should have something in mind for the future." Her warm concern washed over him like sunshine. "Maybe I'll make my way to a city, perhaps into Mexico where I first meant to go. I could teach English, perhaps, or work as a lady's companion or governess." Her soft voice was tentative. "I'm not fit for much else."

Yes, the uncertain quaver gave her away. She was thinking even as she spoke. "Were you a teacher before this?" He waved vaguely toward the sea.

"I was a gentleman's daughter, a gentleman's wife, a little gentleman's mother." She chuckled, but her voice cracked on the last words.

"And where were you bound when the ship met with that storm?"

"As I said, Mexico. The captain, my father's old friend, said the emperor, although beset by troubles of his own, has been welcoming to Southern settlers."

"Oh, but we mustn't leave our country like whipped dogs. No, madam! We must stay strong and rebuild."

She patted William's hand. The boy beamed at her. "I fear that kind of strength is beyond me," she said.

"You might stay here." He thought quickly. "You could teach William! I've often thought it time he is taught by someone with more patience than I have. He cries too often with me. I can be, well—he needs the guidance of a cultured lady. I had planned to send him away to school, far away. But he cries if I speak of it, don't you, son?"

William looked startled but nodded, always eager to please.

"Alida?" Bishop said, scowling. "Is that what you want?"

How dare he use her Christian name so familiarly? Yet she didn't seem to mind. She caught her lower lip between her teeth. "Why, I hadn't thought of it, but William is very young to be sent away."

"William has visited you more than once, I understand, and

has clearly become quite fond of you, madam. It would seem an ideal situation for all of us." Cooper reached toward William, but the boy shrank back against her. Cooper shrugged. "See how he clings to you? I can pay you what a governess makes. No, I'll pay you more."

Alida shook her head.

"Why can't you accept?" Desperation strained his voice. "You were never so stubborn," he murmured.

She raised an eyebrow. "You don't know me, Mr. Cooper. I can be mulish." She tilted her head to one side. "I only meant I must think about it. I'm not a teacher, sir. Can I meet William's needs?" Her gaze softened. "I'd not want to fail another child," she whispered.

His head was pounding now. He ground a fist against his temple. Bishop's gaze was on the woman, hers on William. Neither appeared to notice his frailty, thank Heaven.

"Well, William." She leaned close to the boy, brushing his hair from his eyes. "Aren't you lonely? If you went to a fine school somewhere you could make friends."

He shook his head. "No, ma'am. I don't want to go away."

She smiled and looked up. "Let me consider your offer, Mr. Cooper."

"Can't you answer me now?"

They all looked at him oddly. Was he pushing too hard? Did he sound sullen? He must stay calm. She stared at him with such wide eyes. What had he said? The pain built behind his eyes, rolling in like waves. He had to get home.

She'd had a boy and lost him, he remembered. William was the key. William was actually useful to him. Thank God for William.

She turned a curious gaze on him. He tried to beam at her, though his eyes watered with the effort.

"One month," she said. "That's all I can promise. And I must keep my independence. I'm only employed to teach William. I am not a housekeeper or . . ."

A fiery blush tinged her alabaster complexion. Could it be she was thinking the same as he? Was it possible she knew they could be so much more?

He nodded. "Of course not. Independence, yes. Good! Good enough for now."

CHAPTER SEVENTEEN

"You want me to come right away?" Alida asked. "All of us on the horse?" She, William and Rafe had followed Cooper outside, and stood on the porch in front of the store. Cooper stood next to his mount, one hand on the horse's bridle, the other stretched back toward Alida.

"Yes, yes. Now," Cooper said. "You and William ride, I'll walk along."

Such urgency in his voice, such need. It stirred Alida's alarm, as well as pity.

"Please come, Miss Alida." William tugged her hand.

"But, William, it's getting late in the day to begin lessons. I must prepare and . . ."

"You can settle in," Cooper said. "Have a good night's rest and start fresh in the morning."

"You want me to *live* at the house?"

"Well, of course. My governess came from England and took over from Mammy when I was William's age. You will be much more than a teacher. Your constant presence will mold William's character, as hers did mine."

"But I must gather my things. I can't leave without telling *Señora* Rivera goodbye." Alida smiled at William, then glanced back at Rafe. How had this gone so far, so quickly?

Rafe stared at Cooper, his face like stone. "You haven't been given a chance to think this through, Alida."

"Only for a month, Rafe. Isn't that right, Mr. Cooper?"

"Yes, yes. A month. Come, madam. I must get out of this blinding sun. My eyes—the pain."

"You do look unwell, Mr. Cooper. Could *Señora* Rivera help?" Pity softened her. "She knows many remedies."

"No, Cora has what I need, or I have other medicine. But I must get home." He stepped closer to his horse.

"Go on ahead, Mr. Cooper," Rafe said. "I'll bring her later."

"I see no horse or buggy. Will you carry her on your back?"

Rafe stared without speaking. Such a challenging glare. Finally Mr. Cooper looked away.

"Gentlemen, please." Alida tried to laugh, to ease the sudden tension. "I'll gather my things and come later today."

"There's more clothing at the house." Cooper flapped his hand toward the manor. "Plenty of womanly frippery."

"And of course, I thank you for your thoughtfulness." A touch of defiance blossomed. "I've already made your first donation mine—alterations and such."

"Oh, yes. All right. Come, William. No whining. Come now."

Alida hugged the boy. "I'll be along soon, William. Don't worry."

Mr. Cooper mounted and pulled William up into the saddle by one arm. William looked back as they rode away, crying. His father spoke sharply to him. Alida's heart ached for the boy. She turned to Rafe. "He's so unhappy," she whispered.

"Cooper?"

"William, but maybe Mr. Cooper too."

"I wouldn't worry much about Mr. Cooper, Alida." His scowl eased a bit. "But William? Yes, he is unhappy, poor child. But is it your job to fix that?"

"I've agreed to teach him, so yes."

"He's not yours, Alida."

She sucked in a breath. Her throat swelled as she fought to quell tears. "How cruel!" she hissed. "How can you say such a thing?" She spun away, her back to him.

"Because it's true. Pretending he's yours may hurt you."

"I'm not pretending anything. He is William Cooper, an unhappy boy with an unhappy father, hungering for love. I know he is not Seth. I know what's true and what's fantasy. What right do you have to say otherwise?"

He touched her arm and she realized she'd tensed every muscle. She slumped a little as he gripped her shoulders gently and turned her to face him.

"I care about you," he said. "I'm not sorry you're staying in this town, but up there?" He jerked his chin toward the big house.

"I don't want such cruel criticism from a friend, Rafe. I'll be fine."

He took her hand, touched her chin and lifted her face to search her eyes with a heated gaze. "A friend. Yes, well. I wish I had the right to say more. But you *should* leave this place. Many things here are more *and* less than they seem."

She shook her head. "Not William. He is exactly as he seems. He needs me. Maybe he's, I don't know, my chance at redemption for failing Seth." Her voice trailed to a whisper. "I can't help feeling so." She tried to laugh, to make light of her words, wishing for less gravity.

He let his hand drop, his expression unreadable, and swallowed like he had something stuck in his throat. "Redemption, is it? I guess we're both looking for some of that." He turned and went back inside the store. She followed. He smiled at her, but with worry behind it. "You'll still be living on a hill, but looking on us from a castle. Is the king of that castle merely miserable, or might he be evil?"

"I'm no princess in need of rescue. Why so suspicious?"

He took a deep breath, grasped her shoulders again and tugged her close. He stood so much taller than usual. The effort to stand so straight must cost him. The change in him was confusing, but the warmth in his eyes was familiar. "Please, Alida. Keep an open mind about, well, everything. If only I could make you see me as I really am."

"I see you," she said. "I see a kind and sorrowful man. I see who you are."

He shook his head and seemed about to say more. She feared he was only going to belittle himself. She placed a fingertip to his lips and stood on her toes to kiss his cheek. He turned his head. Their lips met. Startled, she tried to speak, but as her lips formed words, his moved as well. The kiss was fleeting, barely a kiss at all. She should push away, but found it difficult to do. She pressed her cheek to his for a moment more and then stepped back, suddenly aware of the silence in the store and the starch and sunshine smell of cloth, the sweet scents of soap and washing powder, the dusty burlap sacks of oats and flour.

She and Rafe stood barely a pace apart. She reached up slowly and cradled his face between her hands. "You are kind and good and brave," she said. "Never complaining, always worrying about the rest of us."

He shook his head. "I've forgotten everything," he said. "The mission, the disguise."

"What do you mean, disguise?"

"I can't keep on with this, not with you. Please, listen now, I . . ."

The bell over the shop's door clanged. Poised to listen to Rafe's words, the interruption startled and irritated her. She felt she was missing something important.

"Alida? Rafael?" a familiar voice said. *Señora* Rivera. Alida reached up to make sure her hair was in place. Rafe looked at her, and they both smiled like guilty conspirators.

"*Señora,*" she said, stepping past Rafe. "I must tell you my news."

"And later," Rafe said, sighing as if the news was not to his liking. "I'll need to borrow your horse and cart, for we have an errand."

CHAPTER EIGHTEEN

Rafe tucked the pencil behind his ear and grinned. He hadn't seen William for two weeks and was happy for the interruption, desperate for news. He also truly disliked keeping accounts, though the sight of Alida's writing on the pages pleased him. "Here for a violin lesson, William? I feared you'd forgotten me."

"Oh, no, sir. But I brought a note." He held it out.

Rafe read the terse note written in Cooper's cramped hand and lost his smile. "No more lessons?"

"I shall stay home. Miss Alida will teach me."

"She plays the violin?"

William laughed. "The piano. We have a piano, you know, Mr. Bishop."

"I didn't know, but I am not surprised."

William wrinkled his nose and raised his gaze to the sky. "Father said she is to teach me everything, for she is my—my . . . what, sir?"

Rafe smiled gently. "Governess, William."

"That's it, sir. Governess." William spoke the word slowly, carefully, as if it were as precious to him as the lady it described.

Rafe's smile disappeared again. Alida hadn't left Cooper's house in all this time. He'd gone twice to visit, but was told she was busy with William and wouldn't like being disturbed. He'd doubted it, but short of shoving his way in, couldn't think of how to see her. He'd have to find a clever reason to speak with Cooper. He had come very near confessing to her everything about himself and now fervently wished he had. Would it have kept her from going? Likely not. She'd be worried about William nonetheless. He scanned the boy's face. "Is anything wrong up at the house?"

"No, sir."

The little bell over the door jingled. The new arrival swept Rafe out of a fog of worry. Alida glided up to stand just behind William, one hand on his shoulder. Rafe slipped off the stool he'd been perched on and nodded to her. "So, here you are," he said. His voice had gone scratchy and foolishly gruff. He cleared his throat.

She nodded and smiled. "So I am."

"Miss Alida," William said. "I didn't know you were coming too."

"I—I decided on a walk at the last minute."

"Miss Alida says she's going to practice the piano right along with me." William grinned.

She touched his hair with a lace-gloved hand. "Going to make sure you learn more than I did when I was your age."

"I see." But all Rafe saw was her smile and her eyes. Did they seem wary, worried?

He offered William a manly handshake, then squatted by him. "Maybe you'll take to the piano with more enthusiasm than you did the violin. You'll definitely have a prettier teacher." He gave William's shoulder a squeeze as he stood. "Watch over her, now, you hear?" He turned his gaze to her just as she paled and glanced toward the door, as if expecting, or even fearing someone.

"Isn't she supposed to take care of me?" William laughed. "Isn't that the way of it?"

"But you know your way around that big house. You know all the people in it." He couldn't read Alida's expression, but kept his gaze on her as he talked to William. "I'm hoping you'll look after her." He knelt by William again. "If something's ever wrong up at the house, you'd come running, wouldn't you, William?"

The boy nodded, frowning up at Alida, then back at Rafe. "But what could be wrong, sir?" Then he gave a knowing smile. "You like Miss Alida, don't you, Mr. Bishop?"

"William!" Alida blushed and shot another glance at the door, edging two steps toward it.

"No reason not to like her, is there?"

"Oh no, sir." William gazed after her. "I love her," he whispered. "She looks just like my mother." He dropped his voice even more. "I think Father sometimes forgets. He looks like he thinks that's who she is. I *wish* she was and sometimes I pretend." He blinked fast, as if holding back tears. "Is that wrong, Mr. Bishop?"

Sometimes Father forgets.

Rafe managed to give William a smile in spite of a stab of fear. "No, William, it's not wrong. But it's only pretend. I hope your father keeps it in mind, too. Miss Alida is likeable just the way she is. She doesn't need to be anyone else."

Alida had moved away. She was stroking a bolt of calico as if it was satin. Did she hear his last words? Did she hear the sentiment behind them? She smiled uneasily, then glanced again toward the door.

"Are you expecting someone, William?" Rafe said, watching Alida.

"No, sir, but Father might be waiting for us up the road. He doesn't like to come in, but he says he will watch over us."

"I bet he will."

"Father likes Miss Alida very, very much. He doesn't shout at me when I'm with her."

"Is that right? Then stay with her as much as you can. Promise me."

"Well, yes, sir. I—I guess so," William stuttered, clearly confused.

"William, come along now. We should go," Alida called.

"Wait," Rafe said. "Maybe we can have some coffee, some . . ."

"No, it's best we return before I'm missed." She strode out the door.

William tugged twice on Rafe's sleeve. "Miss Alida is sad, I think," he whispered. "She looks sad when she doesn't know I'm seeing her. I don't understand why."

"I don't either, William. But stay by her. Maybe you can cheer her." He watched them go. If only he hadn't left her there these past two weeks. He should have rushed the house, taken William and swept them both far away, everything else be damned.

He closed the store and limped his way home. He was relieved to be part of the *señora*'s household again. He turned and stared over at the forbidding gray house on the bluff. Off to one side loomed a high stone wall with a solid door in the middle. He'd never paid it much heed before, nor how confining it looked. But now he noticed everything, and everything was suspect.

He'd asked around about Cooper. No one knew the man, or no one cared to carry tales. He fisted his hands, tamping down frustration. He had to show his true self to Alida Garrison, though surprisingly and to her credit, she seemed to like him well enough as she thought he was. He touched his bottom lip, remembering the glancing kiss. Did it come from pity? She was a compassionate woman. Cooper had used that to breach her defenses. He took Alida's pity for him and William, used his loneliness, his headaches, to make her do what he wanted.

Rafe's belly churned and bile rose in his throat. He swallowed, disgusted at the thought of Alida pitying him, that she might think he was like Cooper. He spat, then turned and strode into the *señora*'s garden, forgetting to limp and not caring. His fingers splayed, then clenched again. His enchantment with Alida had blossomed alongside his growing suspicion of Martin Cooper. Which drove the other? He calmed his racing heart, using logic. Was he suspicious of Cooper only *because* of Alida? Simple jealousy? Was he hoping Cooper was involved in something treasonous so he could rid himself of a rival? He slowed his breathing. Surely she was in no real danger. If she was, she wouldn't have returned to the house with William today.

A rich man with a child, grieving for a dead wife who evidently, according to the besotted William, resembled Alida. William was shy, but Rafe had never seen fear when he spoke of his father. Sadness, but not fear. He was letting this get out of hand.

"Get hold of yourself, Bishop," he muttered. He was a man with a blossoming passion for a woman of the type he had vowed to shun forever, and he felt seven kinds of fool.

He came up on *Señora* Rivera, kneeling in her vegetable patch and scratching at rocky soil with a small wooden rake. He hunkered down beside her. "You should have a metal tool for that, good lady," he said. "That thing is too flimsy."

She jerked when he spoke, startled, then shaded her eyes against the setting sun and peered at him. "Many should-haves in my life, Rafael." She smiled. "Do you have such a metal tool?"

"The blacksmith could make one." He spoke vaguely, still thinking of Alida and himself and of how trapped he felt.

"You have money for the blacksmith so he will make me this tool?"

He shook himself free of the reverie. "No, I have no money. Maybe I should find out how to get some."

Her smile faded. She pressed trembling lips together. "I joke, Rafael. I need no such tools. My garden is happy and I am content." He stood and held out one hand. She clasped it, taking it to her lips, then against her cheek. "Stay away from the men who spend money like it is nothing to them. You are no match for them. We have a saying, '*Pobre con puro es ladrón, seguro.*'"

"And that means?"

"A poor man with a cigar is a thief for sure." She gave a firm nod to make the point.

He smiled. "But I don't smoke."

"Ah!" She punched his shoulder.

"And if I told you I am more than I seem? That I could handle those men and more besides?"

She shook her head. "Ah, Rafael. We all wish for life to be different."

"I'm serious."

She cupped his chin with gnarled fingers. "You need be no other kind of man. You have a good and honest heart."

Rafe winced. "Honest? *Señora,* I must—"

"You must do nothing. Stay far from those men."

"You worry too much." Rafe kissed her cheek, tasting tears but pretending not to notice.

"Chocolate is what you need, Rafael."

"Your answer to every ill, good lady. I could stand warming up, that's true enough."

She warmed the milk and melted the chocolate, then set a mug before him. "I saw the little *señora* go into the store today. You spoke to her?" She shook her head. "Also, from behind the last house at the edge of town, I saw *Señor* Cooper come, riding his horse. As she and the boy walked up the hill to that cursed house, he kept the horse walking slowly behind them, like a man herding the cows, you know? Strange, I thought."

Rafe's heart quickened. He busied himself stirring the chocolate. "Did she seem frightened?"

"No, I don't think so. She held the boy's hand and they sang, I think. They both sang."

"She wouldn't want William to be afraid."

"Afraid of what, Rafael? *Señor* Cooper has given her a place in his grand house. Perhaps he is a kind man after all."

"Have you seen him so generous with anyone else?"

She froze in her walk from table to stove. "What do you say?"

Rafe shrugged. "She's more than just passing pretty."

"She is an angel." The old woman eased into a chair, her spine rigidly upright. "You cannot mean she would—*estúpido,*" she said, sputtering. "You can think such a thing about her?"

Rafe lifted his cup. "Not her. I just don't think Cooper is quite what he seems."

"Hah! Because you are the same."

Rafe jerked his mug. Chocolate slopped over. "Now wait. What?"

"You want money, you want to be rich like him." She nodded and leaned back, arms folded. "I know I am right."

Rafe calmed, staring into the steaming chocolate. "I think I'll go to the *cantina* for a while."

"I curse the day I told you about Mirlito, curse the day you made him your friend."

"Friend?" He glanced into her tear-filled eyes and touched her clenched hand with one finger. "I'm not trying to be like him or Martin Cooper. I am only trying to be myself."

"Do you know what that is? Sometimes I do not know, but I feel you are not bad to your soul."

Rafe squeezed her hand. "Well, thank you for that."

"I fear to see you hurt, maybe drowned like—" She broke off and looked away.

"Like who?"

163

"Your cousin, too, was a stranger."

"Did he seek out Mirlito?"

"I do not know."

"I've heard how he was found—gossip at the store. You know how folks talk. But what's the truth of it? I'd believe what *you* say."

She sighed. "I only know Mirlito and his men found him on the rocks, in the water. He had fallen, they said, and drowned." She leaned closer. "But many heard him argue with Mirlito."

"You think he was killed?"

"I cannot know, but I fear it." She shook her head and sat back, gripping his hand. "You are as a son to me," she whispered. "I would die myself if you were killed in such a way."

Rafe pushed his chair back and knelt by hers. "I don't plan to be killed in any kind of way, not for a long time."

She pulled a handkerchief from her sleeve and dabbed at her tears. "You plan? Our plans mean nothing to God. He laughs at them."

"Well, to please you and your God, I'll make no devil's pact with Mirlito. That I promise."

She clasped her hands on the table, eyes closed, nodding.

Rafe stood and touched her bowed head. "Everything will come right." He tugged her shawl a little higher.

"You have words enough to confuse angels."

He managed a low chuckle, though he didn't feel especially mirthful.

"But, my son, words will not help if Mirlito wants you dead."

He shrugged. "Didn't you say he and I are friends?"

"Your cousin asked many questions and looked around this village with big, searching eyes."

"I ask nothing. Mirlito just tells me things, for he's a boastful little man." Rafe made himself laugh. "A generous man, loose-fisted with money at the *cantina*."

"He buys your friendship."

Rafe kissed the top of her head. "As I said before. All will come right. You'll see."

She rested her hand over her heart and stood, turning toward him with a sad-eyed look. "I am weary. Go on. Do what you must. It is the way of every man. All of you thinking that to tread with caution makes you less a man."

"You think that harshly of me?"

She sighed. "Even good men are like babies piling blocks one upon the other without care. Then, so surprised and frightened when they tumble down." She sighed again and seemed about to say more, but only pressed her lips tightly closed and shook her head as she walked away.

Chapter Nineteen

William needed stories about heroes, fables to teach him right and wrong. Seth had needed them too, but Alida had not been there for him. If she'd had the time for stories, what could she have told him? Their world had been blown apart, set afire. Life's sweetness had mingled with blood and tears and leached away into the Mississippi, torn from the soil by shot and shell.

Gunboats had battered Vicksburg, but she had kept her family alive, convinced them there was a future. Then, through what she'd come to see as arrogance, she'd lost them all. Each time the thought slammed into her, she could hardly breathe.

But she'd been given a chance to do some good, cast up on William's shore. She meant to give him all her time and affection, for he seemed desperate in his desire for what she could offer. Their bond would be a life-saver for them both.

On the first morning in the house she'd gone to the library and examined Mr. Cooper's books. The library, like every room she'd seen, was richly furnished but nearly ghostly in its stillness. She found one volume of poetry by Byron and two novels by Scott—perhaps Mrs. Cooper had been a romantic. The rest were philosophical texts or scientific works, most supporting the basis of slavery throughout history. She had hoped to find a novel by Dickens, maybe *Oliver Twist* or *David Copperfield,* stories of boys in dire circumstances and how they overcame them. Mr. Cooper had taught William to read, though he hadn't given the boy the love of reading. She wanted to awaken it.

A piano, slightly out of tune, took up one corner of the library. Alida had only a beginner's mastery of the piano, but William had learned basic music instruction from Mr. Bishop, so they'd get by.

Alida's thoughts often flew to Rafe Bishop. She'd become used to talking with him as they worked in the store together. An unlikely friendship, yet it had blossomed. She thought of the way he had gripped her hands, saving her from the greedy sea the day she'd been so foolish as to challenge it. He'd been strong and sure that day, lifting her, carrying her. How it must have cost him in pain. She touched her fingertips to her lips, reliving the gentle, awkwardly glancing kiss the day she left to join William and his strangely aloof father, a handsome yet brooding man.

Rafe was handsome too, in his unassuming way. The scar on his face was a badge of honor these days, as were his bent back and dragging leg. Did the wounds make him so timid, or was it his memories of war? Perhaps his heartbreaking story of failure. He seemed always on guard, hiding his pain. Still, her recollection of his easy smile and warm brown eyes comforted her in this increasingly odd household.

Today she chose books on history, thinking she and William might read them aloud together and discuss them. She thought herself a poor teacher, but vowed to make up her lack of knowledge with affection and her undivided attention.

Mr. Cooper had insisted she teach in the library, so she readied the books on his desk. While she waited for William to come in from breakfast, she browsed the rest of the collected books and then wandered idly into a corner nook. A portrait hung between two bookcases. She gasped and drew back.

For a moment she thought it was a mirror, but the woman staring out from the portrait wore her hair in gathered ringlets, a style from pre-war days. Still, the hair was as black as Alida's own, the eyes as blue, the face shaped the same as the one Alida saw every day in her own mirror.

Martin Cooper's wife, William's mother. No wonder the man stared at her so oddly at times. He couldn't help imagining his wife walked these halls again. He'd never mentioned the resemblance, though many of his strange statements now made more sense. She understood his sadness, his brooding ways and protective nature, though it often bordered on possessive. This picture certainly explained why William had taken to her so quickly.

Oh, but could the boy's affection for her be an unhealthy attachment? When the time came for her to leave, as surely it must, mightn't he feel doubly abandoned?

Martin Cooper's resonant voice reached her from the doorway. "She was never fond of that portrait. She felt it flattered her, that she was not so beautiful. But of course, she was mistaken. It was a perfect likeness."

Alida spun, her skirt nearly toppling a small table. She grabbed at it. "Mr. Cooper," she stammered. "I—I'm waiting for William."

He smiled. "I'd begun to feel the onset of a headache, but it has receded. You must be the cure for my ills." He spoke as if completely sincere.

Alida chose to treat it as a jest and curtsied. "Why, thank you, kind sir."

"I wish to show you another room," he said.

"Could we make it into a school-room?" She joined him at the threshold.

"Certainly not." He drew back, turned and led the way upstairs, where he unlocked and ushered her into a richly furnished bedroom. The ticking of a mantel clock cut through the silence. As she scanned the room, she sensed he was watching her closely. Too closely. When she looked at him, he smiled so suddenly, so openly, it completely changed his face. She realized she'd never seen him smile. A smirk, a sardonic lift of one corner of his mouth, yes, but this was dazzling, incandescent.

She searched for something innocuous to say. "That scent, Mr. Cooper, so very soothing. Is it lavender?"

"Yes. I've changed nothing. This room is exactly as it was. I keep it locked. Each of the bedchambers has its own lock and a key made specifically," he said. "Remember?"

Remember what? "Have you mentioned this before? I'm sorry, I don't recall, but there's so much to take in. Your house is quite—quite overwhelming." She smiled, hoping he wouldn't take her choice of words as criticism.

"But I told you. I must have told you about the locks. Yes, I'm sure I did." His smile flickered and died as pain blossomed behind his eyes.

"Well, perhaps. But why would you have so many keys, Mr. Cooper? In my family's home one key opened every door." She leaned a fraction closer, offering him a smile of secret understanding. "It made things easier, for someone was always losing a key."

"Losing a key? That could not happen here, Mrs. Garrison, for I keep every key carefully labeled in my library."

"I see," she said.

"Do you? My wife thought it a foible of mine, and often gently teased me. But a man has to be in control of his home."

"And such an impressive home. So unlike what I'm used to. Many of the houses along the Mississippi were built like Grecian temples. This one, the gray, fitted stones, its pointed arches—like a gothic cathedral, or even a castle."

"I wanted it different. It had to be different, to be sure it would never be my *real* home. The one taken from me . . ." He bowed his head and shut his eyes.

"Your headache has returned?"

169

"If my mind were a stage, pain would always be lurking in the wings," he said, his smile gone now. What might have been a joke seemed serious.

Reluctant to witness his pain and perhaps embarrass him, she moved to the window. The arresting view of the sea captured and held her attention.

A shadow in the corner shifted. Cora stepped out, grinning. Alida gasped and drew back, nudging Mr. Cooper, who had followed her with such a soft-footed tread she hadn't noticed his nearness.

"Cora," he said. "I am not amused." He stepped around Alida, standing between them. "She often bares those filed teeth unnecessarily, but is not nearly as fierce as she looks."

Alida peered around him, smiling at Cora. "Of course not. We've been getting along just fine, I think. A lovely pot of tea arrives in my room each evening, as well as coffee in the morning. I've meant to thank you, Cora."

The old woman clamped her lips, scowled and limped toward the door, one hand pressed to her lower back.

"Cora has many duties," Mr. Cooper said. "She won't bother you."

"But I'm not at all bothered, I . . ."

"Death be a-waitin' here," Cora said, pausing at the door. "Air is stinkin' of it."

"Ignore her, madam. She has a certain way about her." Mr. Cooper chuckled, a sound like crumpling paper. "I can't imagine what you think of her. For me, she serves as a reminder of old ways, better days. Surely your family had their own old people who grew garrulous as they aged."

"My family did not own slaves, Mr. Cooper. We've spoken of this before."

He blinked and shook his head a little. "But your father . . ." He paused and took a deep breath. "Well, I see. Quite unusual

170

for . . ." He rubbed his hands together. "So, have you had breakfast?"

"Yes. I was waiting for William to finish his. He's likely wondering where I am." She nodded once and swept past him, heading out of the bedroom and down the stairs. Again, she felt confused. What did he mean about her father? She had spoken of her father's businesses and mentioned the family's unpopular stand on slavery. Had Mr. Cooper not been listening? She looked in the dining room, but William wasn't there. She poured a cup of coffee and eased into a chair as Mr. Cooper entered.

The cook slipped in, ghostly quiet, and left an egg cup in front of Mr. Cooper. He cracked the egg with the side of a gleaming silver spoon, lifted off the top and took a bite, closing his eyes, seeming to savor the taste of the yolk. "Perfect for a change, almost bitter," he said.

"Such a deep orange color." Alida could think of nothing less banal to say.

"Of course. My hens are fed on greens and grit. And this morning, just the right amount of solid white and fluid yolk. The preparation is not always so correct." He reached for a crystal bowl of coarse sea-salt and sprinkled a pinch over the egg, again taking up his spoon.

The door burst open and Mr. Cooper flinched. His spoon cracked against the edge of the eggshell's crater. "Now the symmetry is ruined," he muttered, his teeth clenched.

Cora shuffled in with a tray of biscuits and honey. Mr. Cooper stared at his egg as the yolk seeped out and down the cup. He took a deep breath and reached for his coffee. "Where's William, Cora? His governess is waiting."

"That boy spill porridge all down his shirt. I make him go up and change. Sure a clumsy boy, William."

Alida smiled to soften criticism. "Please, Cora, can I ask you not to speak so about William? He's no clumsier than any boy his age, is he?"

"Huh. So you say."

"Cora!" Cooper raised his voice. "Your age does not excuse your manners. You are too hard on poor William. How many times have I said so myself?"

"Never, is what I recall," the old woman muttered, sidling out into the hall.

Alida smiled at Mr. Cooper. "It's admirable that you keep her on, give her a home. I understand many former slave-holders have not been so generous." She stood, as did he. "Shall I wait in the library for William?"

He was at her side in an instant. "No, please. Take your coffee here in peace." His gaze drilled into hers. What could he be searching for? Such intensity brought heat to her cheeks. She fought the impulse to break away.

"Such uncommonly light blue eyes, and your hair like darkest night," he said. "I always thought, who but she could have such eyes, such hair?" He lifted one hand, reaching toward her. She dipped to the side. He lowered his hand.

"You mean William's mother. I admit, the resemblance to the portrait is remarkable, but I assure you, sir . . ." She smiled, again trying to soften her words. Living here was like walking a tightrope. "My coloring is quite common. Why, in my family alone, my mother, four cousins and my—my sister." She took a breath. "Blue eyes, sir. All of us. Blue eyes and dark hair like me and like the portrait."

"I have upset you by stirring sad recollections of your lost family. I apologize." He gave a half-bow, grim-faced, and backed away two steps before turning toward the door.

"Please," she called. "Please wait, Mr. Cooper. You suffer with your own grief. I cannot wallow in self-pity forever."

"Yes, grief can flay the flesh from us." He stood with his back to her. "Best if we don't speak of the past, mine or yours. It does us no good." He turned and gestured toward the table, returning to his chair. "Coffee awaits us." His smile was unexpectedly open and sweet.

Grateful for his change in mood, Alida said, "I'd forgotten how pleasing a lovely table setting can be. My mother kept her china gleaming and used snowy damask cloths like these. And the fresh flowers are lovely." Her eyes burned with foolish tears she blinked away.

"Are you again upset, madam?"

"Forgive me, Mr. Cooper. Wistfulness for times gone. A woman's failing, no doubt, sentimentality, and just when we'd agreed not to dwell on the past."

"I'd say it was a woman's charm. Sentiment and gentleness are things we men evidently have too little of." His smile curled into a sneer. "Someone once made a point of telling me just that."

Alida frowned, tilting her head. Before she could speak, William dashed in. "There you are," she said, hugging him to her side.

"I see a bond has grown between you two already," Mr. Cooper said.

"We'd become fast friends over the days before I came here," she said. "Now I hope to be more." She glanced down at William. "Up and ready to learn, are you?"

Mr. Cooper gave her a wistful smile. "Yes, you will be much more, I'm sure." He glowered at his son. "And you, young man, have squandered much of the morning. Don't waste Mrs. Garrison's time."

Alida made for the door, where she turned and held out her hand. The boy actually scowled at his father before clasping her palm. The action seemed unlike the shy child she'd first met. She hoped being with her had given him courage to stand up for himself, but she'd have to be sure this independence didn't slip into rudeness.

Fearing Mr. Cooper would find it offensive, she managed to hide her amusement. William and his father were alike down to the scowls on both their faces. "You are so quiet, William," she said as they moved to the library. "After our lessons, I rarely hear you about the house. My boy was always running, laughing and knocking things over." She pushed away thoughts of the past, yet she recalled that even when they hid in burrows from Yankee cannons, Seth found something to amuse himself. She had been frightened enough for them both and did not appreciate his courage.

"Father likes the quiet," William said. "When his head hurts I go around like this." He tip-toed around her with one finger to his lips, but his eyes were open wide, full of mischief.

The cold fingers that squeezed her heart whenever she thought of her own boy released their grip. William's smile let her think of life ongoing, not irretrievably lost. She had feared the wind and sea had stripped her barren of everything but guilt and grief, but William's innocent happiness stirred hope.

He prattled to her, tugging her hand. She nodded, half-listening while thoughts of his stern-voiced father's fault-finding scratched at her mind. Cooper's words were so often cold and most of the time he seemed to be looking not *at* her, but *through* her. Would this change with time?

Cora walked by the open door, carrying a tray laden with dishes from the dining room. She strained to keep it level. Alida longed to help, but recalled times past when she'd tried to help slaves on a distant cousin's plantation, women too old or children too young to be hauling heavy things but punished when they failed. She'd been accused of abolitionist leanings, the cousin's worst insult, so she'd learned to hide any compassionate impulse at an early age. Well, no longer.

"Cora, let me help you." She stepped into the hall and

reached for the tray.

"Let me be. You got your job, I got mine." The old woman lurched away down the hall.

Alida shrugged and turned to William, who stood behind her. "Cora is grumpy and likes to do things herself," he said. "Miss Alida? I know what my name means. Father told me. It means protector, though Father says it was a poor choice. I don't know why he says that, do you?"

"I don't, William. I suspect you would be fierce in protection of anyone you love."

"Oh, yes, Miss!"

"Now, my name? I was named after a distant relative. An aunt from Holland, a country far away across the ocean. We'll find it on the globe later. The name has something to do with being noble." Alida smiled. "Evidently they had high hopes for me."

They sat close together on a settee and she took up the history book she'd chosen. "We can read about a king named William," she said. "He was a conqueror."

The boy stared into her face like she was a puzzle he wanted to put together. "The lady you were named after, was she beautiful like you?"

"Why, thank you for the compliment, William. So gallant. I never knew my aunt. My father often said she was like a fairy queen."

William stared, wide-eyed.

"I was never quite sure what that meant," she joked.

"Oh, I know. It means she knew magic." William nodded. "Did she teach you spells?"

"I doubt she knew spells, but if she did, she couldn't have taught me, for she died before I was born." The boy's excitement captivated Alida. Seth had loved stories of magic and quests too, though Sarah usually read them to him.

William's voice dropped low, almost to a whisper. "I bet she did know magic. Since you're named for her, can't you use magic to be anybody you want?"

Alida blinked, surprised. "Well, no, William, I can only be myself. Don't you want me to be myself?"

"Oh, yes, Miss. But couldn't you . . . ?" He slumped back against the settee.

"William, those are all good questions. It's been a while since I've had someone new to talk to. Thank you." She gave him a hug and coaxed a smile from him.

"Mr. Bishop saved you, didn't he?"

"Yes, William. He found me and lifted me from the sand."

"I'll miss lessons with Mr. Bishop. I like him very much, don't you?"

"Of course. I do like him. And I will miss working with him at the little store. He seemed to need the help."

"But you're helping *me*, aren't you, Miss? Will I be enough for you to help?" The child had paled and a deep furrow formed between his brows. He bit his lip.

"Of course! William, of course. And you will be helping me."

"I will? How, Miss?" Color blossomed in his cheeks again. His features cleared, an eager boy, no longer a worried old man. Curious again, as children should be.

"Just by being yourself, William. I can't explain it any better than that."

"I never knew I could be help to anyone. Sometimes I try to help Cora and sometimes she lets me, but all at once she'll get crabby and say something like, 'I don't need no child clingin' to me, lookin' fer help.' Then she'll tell me to go away."

His impersonation of Cora's scratchy voice was nearly perfect. Alida smiled and took his hand. "As you said, Cora likes to do things her own way."

William nodded, thoughtful. "Are you here because you had

a little boy and lost him, Miss?"

Alida blinked away threatened tears. "In a way. But I don't want you to think of it like that. You are William and just fine the way you are."

"Like somebody said. Was it Mr. Rafe?"

"What, child?"

"Like you're Miss Alida. Not my mother. Just fine the way *you* are." He smiled, his blue eyes sparkling. He sobered again. "But is it right for us to be happy if Mr. Rafe is sad without you?"

Alida felt heat rise in her face. How red she must be. She turned from William. "You are a kind and thoughtful boy to care. But we don't know if he is sad about that, do we?"

Ah, but was he? Could he be? Did it matter?

"Oh, I think he must be, Miss. I would be if you went away." He beamed at her with such longing, such hope.

"The little store was quiet," she said. "I do miss it. But your house is quiet, too."

"Oh, but a different quiet, Miss. The store smells good, of pickles and sometimes of bread. My house doesn't smell of anything, does it? Maybe of Cora's medicines sometimes."

"I suppose so. Your father is often ill?"

The boy shrugged. "His head hurts very much. He hits it like this." William thrust one fist against his temple, again and again."

"William! Stop. You'll hurt yourself."

"Not really. Father does it much harder." He shrugged again, as if it didn't matter. "Cora gives him medicine and he has another kind, too. He takes it sometimes and then he doesn't talk for a long time. Days and days. But that's really not so bad." He brightened. "Now you're here it will be better."

"You think my company will help your father?"

His face fell. "I mean for *me*. Better for me than when Father is angry. I guess that's selfish?"

"No, William. Whatever is better for you is good for me as well." She drew him close. He threw his arms around her waist and she knew her words were not simply to console a sad child. They were true.

Yet she remembered the soft light in the store, the satisfying sounds of someone moving about without expecting anything of her but company, where moods didn't rush in and out like tides. She missed the simple satisfaction of adding columns of numbers so that they ended up just right. Would she find such satisfaction in this quiet, yet uneasy house?

CHAPTER TWENTY

The old woman whose mouth bristled with daggers instead of teeth said Alida was always busy, couldn't see him. And what had William said? "Sometimes Miss Alida looks sad."

Rafe swept the front porch with more vigor than necessary, his broom fighting the wind for possession of the dirt. He wished he had a broom to sweep away fear and doubt. But just as the wind did the dirt, his mind carried his thoughts swirling back to him. Why should Alida be sad, especially if she was in truth so busy? She had William, a boy to mother, someone to love. Someone else to love, not him, not Rafe Bishop. No, he wasn't the one.

Good God, was he truly jealous of a child? A needy child? If that was true, besides making him a selfish fool, it was just possible such jealousy had taken him down the path of suspecting a peculiar man with puzzling habits of treasonous acts, even murderous acts. Such suspicions could only be proven with cold, hard evidence. He'd have to find some or give over to the possibility that Martin Cooper was merely a rival. Who would Alida feel sorrier for, a madman or a cripple? Which pitiful man might dupe her into loving him more?

Rafe was so disgusted with himself he actually felt dirty. He craved a bath, but a swim would have to do. He put up the broom and closed the door, tipping a ladder-backed chair across the front of it. He used the chair to show people whenever he was unexpectedly away and the store was closed, having quickly

179

understood few villagers could read signs in any language.

The sea was fairly calm, but brisk. A quick dunking was enough and the sun warmed him through the shirt and trousers he'd pulled on over wet skin. Too risky to sit naked till he dried. Someone might see his back was unscarred, his leg not withered. As he limped along toward the store he put a plan in place. He'd go to the *cantina* and do his best to glean information from whoever was there, though it was early in the day for most. Twyla would be there, though. He'd been staring at the ground, thinking, but when close to his rickety porch, he looked up.

"Well," he said, startled. "I was just thinking about you, Miss Twyla, and here you are."

The woman was hunched over on the bottom step, drawing a vague design in the dirt with a stick. "Seems you should be open, it being full daylight and all," she muttered.

"You sound out of sorts. I take it you've come for an important purchase."

"Might say that." She tossed away the stick and stood, throwing back her shoulders.

"Follow me inside, then, won't you? There's untold delights behind this door."

"Huh. I never can make out if you're just being friendly or making fun of me. I can't see that I've earned such disrespect."

Rafe paused in lifting the chair out of the way. "I'm sorry, Twyla. No insult intended. Just feeling frisky from my cold dunking in the sea."

She shivered. "I ain't never gone in there and never will. I hear there's fish that can swallow a full-growed man."

"Not close to shore. If ever you want to give it a try, I'd be pleased to escort you."

"I just bet." She stepped around him and up to the counter.

"So, what can I get you?"

"I believe I need some vinegar."

He nodded and took down a jug and an eight ounce bottle, then reached for the funnel.

"I'll need more'n that."

He grinned. "Planning on doing some pickling, are you?"

Twyla glared at him. "I got another use for it. But I imagine it's my own business." Her face burned red. "And give me some a' them Dovers Powders."

"For pain, Twyla? Or—are you poorly?" He lost his teasing smile. "Maybe *Señora* Rivera can help. She has all sorts of medicaments and—"

"She don't like me."

"She doesn't know you, does she?"

"She don't want to. Seems gals don't get on well here 'less they're wives. Even then, not all of 'em."

"Who do you mean?"

"Mirlito was in last night going on and on, laughing about that poor woman who drowned years back. The rich lady from the big house. I don't know what set him off, but he said Mr. Cooper got what he deserved back then, losing her like that. Mirlito said he hadn't known she was so fierce. Then he laughed and laughed like he does." Twyla shrugged. "I got no idea what he was carrying on about, I just felt lucky he got so drunk he passed out and left me alone."

"What do you think he meant?"

"How should I know? Said the wife was powerful mad at Mr. Cooper for things he'd been doing. So, will you sell me what I come for?"

"Of course. I still wish you'd let me take you to see the *señora*, introduce you."

"Introduce? Now I know you're making fun of me. You put that vinegar and the rest on Marsden's account, too. He don't know it, but he owes me. All part of him doing business, leastways that's what he says to me all the time." She sniffed and wiped her nose, took her parcel and flounced out as if truly insulted by the world in general.

His concern about what might be wrong with her paled as he thought of what Mirlito had said. Cooper's wife, angry at her husband for doing—what? Gambling, women—or smuggling and worse?

Rafe closed up shop again, planning to follow up with Twyla. Maybe she'd be less prickly on her home ground. As he passed the church he was hailed by the priest, not someone he had much to do with, though the man seemed a decent sort.

"Ah, Mr. Bishop. When will I see you inside my doors, eh?"

"Can't say. Not much for your ways."

"But the *señora* is, as are those who come to your store. Do you want to always be an outsider?" Father Sebastian wagged his finger like he was chastising a child.

Rafe didn't like it much. "How about Mr. Cooper?"

The priest's face saddened. "No. Poor man. Poor lonely, lost man. Alone since his wife drowned. Such a tragedy, yet people here tell stories that she did not die at all. She abandoned him, they say, for her body was never found. This gives rise to silly rumors about our castaway woman, Mrs. Garrison. She does look so much like Mrs. Cooper."

This was a tale Rafe hadn't heard. "But William. He'd have been an infant then. Surely she wouldn't have left him."

"Unlikely, but people still talk. You know how gullible superstitious people can be."

"I do, indeed." Rafe swallowed a smile. "When Mr. Cooper's men come to you, do they speak of it, or of the cursed rocks that claim so many ships and lives?"

"They do not come in, sir. Even if they did, I could not share the words of the confessional. You must know that."

"Of course," Rafe muttered. *So everyone's glad to share gossip, but never truth?* He had to swallow the words, not wanting to of-fend the man.

"Your cousin, poor Mr. Lacey, came often to church. He said he was Irish. As are you, sir?"

Rafe shrugged.

"Well, he was a believer, though far from family and fallen away from faith."

Rafe felt a stab of disquiet. What would Lacey have said in that dark little confessional? "So you must have known all about him. I fear we weren't close. Distant relatives, actually. I often wondered what led him to settle here." He scrambled to distance himself from what truths Lacey might have told about their work here. "He wasn't fearful of anyone or anything hereabouts, was he?"

"I would not know. I fear your cousin did more asking than telling. Never once did he come to confession. He visited me privately, but only asked about the town and people. I think he wanted to make a success of his business. I had hope, but, alas, he died. I cautioned him many times to stay away from some others in town. I once had to come between him and some men. All had been drinking too much, I fear."

"You mean the men who work for Mr. Cooper? You suspect they had something to do with—?"

"Oh, no. I fear only they are lost creatures, lost to God, those men." Father Sebastian shook his head and turned from Rafe. "Lost men doing the devil's work."

Rafe lurched forward. "What? What do you mean?"

"Only that they profit from the tragedy of others." The priest frowned over his shoulder, perhaps confused at Rafe's pressured question. "The salvage. Of course, someone must take it from the shore, but I feel profiting from such tragedy leads to an unbalanced scale in life. You see?"

"I do." Rafe's heart pounded. He was on the trail of something. "I'm beginning to see things much more clearly."

Father Sebastian entered his church and Rafe went back to the store. No need to bother Twyla any more today. Yes, he could put jealousy aside as motive for suspicion, though jealousy was still there. He'd think of it as concern for Alida. If that was a delusion, so be it. There was indeed something here. Something real and very wrong.

CHAPTER TWENTY-ONE

Wind moaned outside Alida's window. Inside her room, the mantel clock's ticking grew louder with each passing second. Which was more irritating? She put aside the book of poetry she'd found. Keats was an unlikely choice for this household. So romantic a collection had surely belonged to William's late mother. Alida found it tucked beneath some lace-edged linen in a dusty corner cupboard.

One line in a poem, "the jumbled heap of murky buildings," made her think of Vicksburg. She consoled herself, thinking at least she was free of that horror though she had yet to climb any "flowery slopes," as the poem described. She sighed at the thought. No flowery slopes here, just sea and sand, cliffs and wind. She knew she was too agitated for sleep just yet. Maybe another book would help. Something dense, the history of . . . lace-making, perhaps.

She smiled at the idea and glided out onto the landing, then tiptoed down the stairs. Though none of them creaked, she stayed mid-center on the carpet runner anyway, reluctant to break the silence. She paused, as she did so often in this house, listening, scanning the air and wondering if she felt a breath, or smelled a scent, all the while trying to seem as unassuming and flawless as milk and as smooth as the glass that would hold it.

A lamp burned brightly from the half-open door of the library. She rapped gently, but no answer came. She pushed open the door, found the room empty, and let her breath go. He was not here. No need for stilted words or her having to disentangle his confusing references to the past. Those times came more often these days and worried her more and more.

The lamplight showed her a shelf with just the kind of book she sought—a treatise on the cultivation of rice in the Orient. She chuckled as she took it down. Such a heavy book. Who would have thought the subject could warrant so many words?

As she turned, a muffled sound carried in from just outside the French doors. Not quite a shout, more of a growl, animal-like. She sucked in breath and stepped back, her hand to her throat, peering past distorting glass into the dusk.

The faint spill of light from the room showed two bodies, one huddled on the pavers, the other leaning over the first with an arm raised. Alida knew William had been tucked in bed for an hour. The huddled form must be someone else. And the other was clearly Mr. Cooper.

Alida tossed the heavy book aside and threw open the doors. The wind snatched one and slammed it against the wall. "Mr. Cooper!" she cried. "What on earth?"

Cora lay on the ground, her stick-thin arms curved over her head, her face hidden against drawn-up knees, voluminous skirts and a shawl barely cushioning the open-handed blows her employer rained on her bent and bony back.

The man did not appear to hear Alida over the wind and his harsh breath and guttural curses. Alida rushed forward and pushed between the two, falling across Cora and glaring up at Mr. Cooper. "Sir!" she shouted.

His hand came whistling down. Alida closed her eyes, waiting for the blow, but the hand stopped inches from her face. She blinked her eyes open. Mr. Cooper staggered back and Alida rose to help Cora to her feet. "Are you hurt, Cora?"

"When you think I never *not* been hurt?" The old woman adjusted a head-scarf and tugged at her shawl. "This ain't nothing new. Like a lid on teapot, that man. Jus' have to pop off when something is on the boil. Gotta hunker down and take it. Don't make much difference to ol' Cora, no ma'am." She sneered at Alida and gave Mr. Cooper a disgusted, yet pitying glance, then hobbled away into deeper shadows.

Alida watched her go, confused, feeling somehow in the wrong herself. She turned the confusion on Mr. Cooper, and quickly shifted to outrage. She fisted one hand at her breast to calm her breath, then pointed toward Cora's retreating back. "How cruel. I would not have believed you capable of it, sir."

"But why did you come out here in the dark?" he stammered, pushing hair from his eyes. "It's late. You should be in your room."

Alida sucked in breath, her nostrils flaring with the effort. "That, sir, is not the issue."

"Your eyes glitter like an iced-over stream," he whispered, straining toward her. Then he abruptly held back with what seemed great effort. He bent at the waist, pressing his head between trembling hands, fingers digging into the temples. "Ah, I can't—visions run rampant sometimes. I confuse you with—I . . . Mrs. Garrison. Madam, please." He straightened slowly. "We must talk."

Her outrage cooled to bewildered indignation in light of his misery. "On that," she said softly, "I can agree."

He approached, but warily, as if he feared she'd bolt. "In the library, we'll talk there." His face had gone ashen. He stumbled toward her and past, leading the way through the open doors.

He was clearly unwell and her concern for Cora shifted to him. Using the time to calm herself and think of what to do and say, she gazed at the paintings and the rich furnishings adorning the library in the glow of the lamp.

"It *is* a fine room, isn't it?" he began.

She nodded and sucked in a deep breath, appreciating the

scent of leather, books, lingering smoke from good tobacco and even the undercurrent of a fine brandy's tang. It was a masculine scent, reminding her of better times.

"My wife loved this room. I brought someone else here once, but she hadn't the wit to appreciate it so I banned her from entering, then banned her from my life. But you, Mrs. Garrison, can understand how it symbolizes our gracious Southern culture."

"Oh, can I?" She touched the globe and set it spinning, walked the perimeter and trailed her fingertips across the spines of the books. "Did slaves build this house?"

"Of course, a few I brought here with me. But villagers, too." He scowled. "Why does that matter?"

She gaze at him and raised an eyebrow. "Are you so oblivious to the pain of others?"

His scowl deepened. "Please. We must resolve—please, sit down."

"I prefer to stand."

"Do what is most comfortable, of course."

She waited.

He stared at her, appearing calm, but then his features contorted and he slammed the heel of one hand to his temple.

Alida started toward him. "Mr. Cooper. You're ill. Please sit. A chair is just there, behind you. Perhaps a brandy, some water . . ."

He waved her away and managed a charming smile, though pain roiled in his eyes. "You are so different. Not angry anymore. Not like when—back then." He frowned again as if working out a thorny problem. "What has changed you so? The sea?" He stepped to a shelf above his desk where a cut-glass bottle full of amber liquid sat among a set of stemmed glassware. "Brandy, a good idea. And you?"

"No, thank you."

"Of course. You never liked it," he muttered. "Not a lady's drink." He turned. "But you are, Mrs. Garrison, you are so gracious to speak with me. I regret offending you with the offer of strong spirits."

"It is your cruelty to Cora that I find offensive."

He blinked, pushing fingers through his hair. "What? Isn't that best forgotten?" He stumbled back a step. "I hope you don't mind if I sit, though you choose to stand. I haven't been well for days." He sank into a leather chair that seemed to swallow him with a sigh. He closed his eyes.

"I must wonder, sir, if you can treat an elderly woman with such violence, what might you do to William if he displeases you. Or to me?"

He sat forward, gripping the arms of the chair. "I did as I must. Cora doesn't listen to me most of the time. I rarely raise a hand to her. Usually a small willow switch is sufficient."

Alida backed away, one hand out toward him, appalled. "A switch? You feel you have the right to command and instruct her in this violent way; do you feel the same about me?"

He smiled, wriggling his shoulders as if uncomfortable in his coat. "Oh, now, madam. How silly."

"I'm sorry you think I am silly. The difference in how we think will be of great difficulty if I am to stay here."

"If?" He stood and crossed to the window, where he gripped the low sill, leaning on his arms. "You *must* stay. For William. Yes, you must stay. But now I fear my pain is such that I must ask you to leave me for a while. And again, if I offended you, I am sorry."

"I believe you owe the apology to Cora."

He spun to face her. "Cora?" His voice lost its studied calm as he paced from the window and back again. "She was telling tales! Ridiculous, vile lies about you and that shopkeeper. I will not tolerate it." He took a breath. "That man tries to look harmless, but I see something there. In his eyes. I don't trust him. When I said this, Cora laughed! I had no choice but to chastise her."

Alida shook her head. Pity had overcome all other feelings. "Mr. Cooper, many men have been displaced by the war. Mr. Bishop is one, and you as well, both of you haunted by what you've seen and done, by what has been done to you and by what you've lost. I believe that's what you see in his eyes." She smiled. "I see kindness, and gentleness. I have seen it in you as well, sir, which is why I was so stunned by—"

"What? Then you see him often? You meet with him." He sputtered the words. "The scoundrel has been following you, hasn't he? Has he been watching the house?"

She raised her chin. "I doubt he has any interest in this house. He told me he walks along the shore in the early mornings."

"Not at night? Does he come during storms?"

"I don't understand you, sir. He seeks solitude." She sighed, impatient. "Is it our business to know what he does or where he goes? He saved my life on the shore and—"

"What? You recall that. I thought you'd forgotten the shipwreck, forgotten the horror. What else do you remember? Lights? Do remember the rocks?" He reached toward her with grasping fingers, then let his hand drop.

She backed away. "Not the shipwreck, though it's something I'll never forget. I meant another time. If he hadn't been there I'd have been swept out to sea."

"Oh," he whispered. He took a breath and crossed the distance between them in four long strides, gripping her arms above the elbows. "Don't be misled. He's underhanded and will do anything to get what he wants."

She eased from his grasp. "Who do you describe, Mr. Cooper? I don't believe it's Rafe Bishop."

"Don't be taken in!"

"So you order me? Should I cut you a switch, or will your open hand be sufficient?"

"Now, madam. You jest. I think only of your welfare. I am responsible for you and—"

"You are responsible for your own actions, as I am responsible for mine, and for William's education and behavior, unless you mean to dismiss me."

"Never! I will never let—I mean, you must not think of going. Your return, I mean your coming has been a miracle for us—for William."

Alida could only shake her head in dismay. She left him standing rigid in the center of the room. Rather than clear up misunderstandings, the conversation had stirred deep feelings and made it all so much murkier. Leaving would be best, but not for William. How could she ever leave him now?

CHAPTER TWENTY-TWO

Alida readied herself for bed, but couldn't sleep. She crept to the window. Earlier, clouds had veiled the moon and stars, but a howling wind scattered them. She felt flushed. Was she ill? She pressed the back of one hand to her forehead. Her skin was dry and cool. She had an uncommonly powerful thirst, but her bedside carafe was empty. Cora usually filled it. The old woman had such trouble this evening, though . . . no wonder she'd forgotten. Alida pulled on a robe, tied it firmly at her waist and high beneath her chin, and ventured out in search of water.

A lamp flickered on a table hugging the wall. Otherwise, the house was dark. She crept toward the stairs, the carpet soft beneath bare feet. Every door along the landing was closed, but a voice carried from behind the door to Mr. Cooper's room. One voice, his, raging.

Alida reached for the knob, meaning to defend whoever he berated so angrily, Cora again? Or maybe even William. But the voice fell away into harsh and heavy breathing. Had he been raving in his sleep? She stepped back and took hold of the banister, then eased down the stairs.

The massive clock in the foyer chimed three as she passed it, startling her. It seemed both alive and sinister. She hurried through to the kitchen where one door led outside. Another, slightly ajar, showed faint, flickering light. Alida edged closer.

"You there." Cora's voice unreeled from the murky darkness. "You got a powerful itch to come in. Need to get it scratched, seem to me."

Alida pushed at the door with her fingertips. It swung wide enough for her to step through. She closed it behind her. Cora sat in a rocking chair a few feet from a fireplace. "So this is your room?"

"You never think I got me a room?" Cora chuckled. "Think I go wanderin' off to pasture at the end of the day?"

"Of course not." Alida raised her chin, her face burning. "I just haven't thought about where you slept."

"Huh. No surprise there."

As the old woman's scorn washed over her, Alida flushed but let it go unanswered. She had deeper questions, and without thinking, let them burst from her. "What's going on here, Cora? I don't understand Mr. Cooper much of the time. Is he ill? Or am I?" She touched the side of her head, the place that had once been so tender.

"Ol' Cora tell you true, for something got to bring peace to this house." She straightened in her chair, her back rigid for a moment. Then she slumped against the cushion. She frowned and stretched bare, twisted toes toward the fire. "I figured you be coming sooner," she said.

Firelight flickered. Alida edged closer, seeking light and warmth. "I wouldn't have thought you'd want company tonight, Cora, after the episode upstairs."

The old woman smiled. "No, I mean *days* sooner. Took your time."

Alida glanced warily around the room. A neatly made cot with a bright red blanket, a covered bucket half-hidden next to the bed, likely a night-time commode. A low stool by the fireplace. Nothing else was clearly visible in the dim light.

Cora leaned down and rubbed her bony feet, sighed, sat back and set her chair rocking. "Why you lookin' around? Lookin' for magic to help you? Think ol' Cora got power over fate?

Look all you want."

"I don't believe in magic." But Alida *did* look. A tidy little room, nothing sinister. A faded calico curtain stirred in a breeze from one half open window, and on the wall was . . . Alida moved a little closer to the fire. "Over your bed—a cross."

Cora lifted her gaze, searching Alida's face. "Ah, yes, ma'am. The pitiful, dyin' Jesus."

"So you're a believer?"

"Believe in lots of things, Missy. All kinds of paths go twisting up to a better world. Every one of 'em climbing to a clearing in the woods."

Alida sank onto the stool by the fire.

Cora shifted. The musky scent of dried herbs and dead flowers rose around her. She scratched the tip of her nose with a ragged fingernail. "So what ails you?"

"It's Mr. Cooper. Usually he's a gentleman, of course, but often he speaks confusing words, and he can be insensitive, even cruel. As he was with you this evening."

Cora rocked gently in her creaking chair, the only sound beyond the crackle of the fire. "Not cruel as some I knowed. Why you be worrying so? He won't be hurting you. He crazed with lusting for the past and you fit in with his thinkin', looking like you do."

"Surely he can't believe I'm his wife. Is he joking, and only pretends to be serious? What should I do?"

"Never knowed the man to joke in all the years I been around him. Don't do nothing. Your power is in being." The old woman chuckled. "Little William see the goodness in you and love you for motherly ways. He always sneaking peeks at you." Cora nodded. "But Mr. Coop? He don't care if you scared of him. He don't care nothin' about a woman's fear. He maybe likes it. Had him a woman a year past. He used her up and throwed her away. But you be like a flower with scent he think he smelling

before. You keepin' that scent from him, makin' him crazy."
Cora leaned closer to the flickering fire. Shadows danced in her
face. Her eyes glittered amid them. "You be so like young Miss."
She cocked her head and appraised Alida. "You seen that
picture?"

"Yes, the portrait. William said his mother drowned. That's
all I know."

"Her hair, black like night. Eyes like summer sky and skin
like cream been poured and smoothed, over little bones like a
bird's. You the same. He yearnin' for her and seein' you." Cora
nodded again. "Middlin' age for a man, feelin' his power passing and wantin' it back. You come out of the same water what
took her away." Cora leaned closer and stirred the fire. "That
Molly gal he had, she love him, but he don't care."

Alida stirred on the low stool, watching the flames.

"He tryin' to make you love him."

"But I'm not her."

"Which? Young Miss or Molly?"

"Neither, Cora. I'm not his wife. And I'm not this Molly
person."

"That's so. You finer than Molly." Cora smiled and licked her
teeth, making them shine in the firelight. "Molly set on taming
him, but found too late she couldn't." She arranged herself
more comfortably in her chair. "I heard you raving about the
cold, deep water, how you feared it. Heard you up at that ol'
woman's house. It still scare you?"

"Why does it matter?"

"You lose everything you love to it." Cora nodded once. "All
you got left is shame for being the one left alive. It's eating a
hole through you."

Alida closed her eyes.

"Fetch me that pipe, won't you, Missy?" Cora pointed to the
mantel.

Alida stood and plucked up a round-bowled pipe with a long, curving stem. She handed it to Cora, then slumped down again. While Cora filled the pipe from the pouch in her apron pocket and tamped it down with her broad thumb, she hummed a three-note tune. "I believe you stronger than you look," Cora said. "You fightin' off death and winnin'—so far." Cora ran her tongue across her teeth again. When she grinned, they glistened like river stones.

Shivering, Alida folded her arms across her chest. "It's cold in here," she said. "Is there no more wood?"

"Not so cold as the sea or the grave." Cora's grin faded. "I don't much like big fires near me. I once seen death in that candle flame in the old woman's house. I don't want to see it no bigger."

"You saw my death?" Alida inched closer to the puny warmth of the smoldering fire.

Cora made a show of glancing around her room. Then she slapped her knee and laughed, setting down her unlit pipe. "My Lord! Look at you, so scared!"

Alida pushed to her feet. "He hurt you and I defended you. Why do you dislike me so?"

"Don't dislike nobody and don't need no defending. I just need peace to come back to this house." Cora sighed and closed her eyes. "I am tiring of this talk. You go on, now. Leave me be."

Alida's shoulders ached with tension. She stretched, rolling her head around, her bones crackling like the fire.

"You believin' in spells?" Cora kept her eyes closed.

"I told you. I don't believe in magic."

"Likely wise. Neither spells nor old magic workin' no more, world's gettin' too smart, or I am gettin' too old. There ain't nothing in this world I want no more but peace. If too much is going on, it wears ol' Cora out." She waved toward the door. "You go on, now." She rocked her chair with more vigor. "He got a couple men watchin' this house. You know that? He means to keep you here, so you best find a way out."

"What? How?" Alida felt chilled from more than the cold room. "Can you help me?"

"This all the helping I got in me. I give warnin'. If you want him, I figure that'll bring us peace. But if you don't? You got to get away from us. Got to go alone, can't be taking the boy, and you got to walk away in the full daylight."

Alida managed a smile. "Now, *that* sounds like a spell."

Cora opened one eye. "Close as I can come these sorry days."

Alida stepped out and left the door ajar, just as she'd found it. A lamp flickered on a long work table in the kitchen. A ewer of water stood there and Alida filled her carafe. As she stepped away, her foot nudged something beneath the table. The object toppled. She leaned down to set it right and saw lanterns. More than twenty, lined up in soldierly rows beneath the table. She stared at them for several seconds, then returned to Cora's room.

"Cora, are you awake?"

The old woman kept her eyes closed. "Could be I am."

"The lanterns, Cora. Beneath the table. So many. What are they for?"

"What lanterns usually for? Light, Missy. The little man and the others, they take care o' them lights. Don't have nothing to do with ol' Cora, no ma'am."

"Lights along the rocks," Alida whispered.

"One more thing a-tellin' you to go and leave us as we was before."

CHAPTER TWENTY-THREE

The wind caught Alida's skirts and whipped her hair into her eyes. She'd only managed a loose knot at her nape this morning, eager to get out of the bewildering house as the sun began fingering its way through the clouds. They seemed to float on the light gray sea, yet would soon be no match for the wind. She gathered her sleeved cloak more tightly and managed to confine her skirt.

The unrelenting slap of waves against the sand and rocks and the cry of gulls overhead comforted her. She needed sound. Too much silence in Martin Cooper's house. She inhaled the dark smell of salt-crusted stone and the open-drain stench from a pool left behind by last night's receding tide. How she longed for the sweeter scent of *Señora* Rivera's flowers and herbs.

A gull swooped near her head. She ducked, then shaded her eyes with one hand and watched it soar away. If only she could be that free.

Something moved atop the rocky spit of land ahead. An animal? No, something human. Could it be Rafe? Of course not. He'd not be able to climb such an outcropping, but the forlorn hope had set her pulse pounding. She missed his steadiness. Perhaps he'd be able to make sense of the confusion in the Cooper household. But who was it standing up there?

Cora. It was Cora. Somehow the old woman had climbed to the top. Alida stared at her, waiting, though for what she couldn't have said. Cora appeared to be staring out into the sky, or the sea. She slowly raised her arms and spoke. Too far away to hear the words, Alida was fascinated by the display until Cora spun to face her. The old woman clutched her hands together, shaking them.

Alida moved closer to the base of the rocks. "Cora?" she called. "Are you all right? Do you need help climbing down?"

Cora turned and abruptly disappeared. Had she fallen? Alida hitched up her skirts and scrambled up the rocks, slipping on surfaces made slimy by sea-spray and bird droppings. "Cora? Can you hear me? Are you there?" Panting, she reached the top, her fingers scraped bloody, her skirt and two nails torn.

Cora sat on a flat stone two feet down from the top. She puffed on her clay pipe and exhaled smoke that smelled like burning rope. Languid, she squinted through it. "It's a wonderment how you made that climb. I am surprised, an' that's the truth."

"I thought you had fallen, Cora. I feared . . ." Alida worked to catch her breath.

"Guess you got goodness in you. Being good, being kind? That won't matter none to him, no ma'am. So best you go and leave us be. Leave us peaceful."

Alida found a rock of her own and sat down. She took Cora's long-fingered hand, the skin so thin she feared it would tear. "I can't leave William. Not now. Something is so wrong at the house. The lanterns, the storms, Mr. Cooper himself." She gave Cora's hand a gentle shake. "What's wrong with him, Cora?"

"Lots wrong with Mr. Coop, but nothin' you nor me gonna do to help. I see now how you is kind and brave both, but I say it won't do you no good." She slowly withdrew her hand from Alida's. "And don't you never say we been up here on these rocks. He don't let nobody come here. I fear he'd kill me, knowing I ever come here."

Alida sighed and gazed far out to sea, then focused on the

jagged rocks just below. "Is this where she—his wife—fell?"

Cora nodded. "Right here is where she left him. Most days since, I is comin' out here just when the sun is risin'. I call out to her and tell her what's going on with us. She always kind to me. She try to help best she can. She got the kindness you got, but not so much strength. Course, she never answer me. I ain't crazy enough to think she will, but I tell her anyways. I know I got to keep going on my own, lookin' for peace as best I can."

"Cora? I'll take William away and you come too. We'll slip away and—"

"No, ma'am. Where you think we be going? Us an' the boy? He find us. You think that ol' lady gonna help us, or that crippled-up shopkeepin' man? Mr. Coop'd find us. He'd kill 'em, probably me too, maybe even the boy, but not you. Oh, no, Missy. Never you. You jus' wish you was dead."

Alida felt as if she'd been punched with each word. She could think of nothing sensible to say. Cora knocked the ashes from her pipe and pocketed it. She grasped a heavy stick that lay beside her and used it to push to her feet and balance as she picked her way down to firmer footing. Alida watched her go, watched the clouds scud away, and drew the cloak tighter around her.

"You're not eating this evening, Mrs. Garrison. Are you poorly?"

Alida caught Mr. Cooper's worried scowl. Before she could answer, Cora, ladling the soup, spoke. "Miss Alida had a little scare this mornin', is all."

"It was nothing," she murmured, remembering Cora's warning not to say anything. She gave the old woman a puzzled look and a furtive shake of her head.

"Now, Missy. Nothin' to be shamed of." Cora set down the soup tureen with a show of effort. "Good thing ol' Cora come by, is all."

Mr. Cooper choked on his wine. He scowled at Cora. "What are you talking about?"

Alida smiled, trying to inject some light-heartedness into the void left by his cold question. "Cora, that wasn't how it was. You were—I was . . ."

"Why you makin' light of it?"

Mr. Cooper set down his wine glass with precision, stared at it, then sat up very straight. "By God," he said quietly. "Someone had better tell me."

Alida glanced at William who sat very still, open-mouthed and pale.

Cora nodded slowly, her eyes glittering like a mischievous child's. "Them rocks. Ain't I ask before? I ask an' ask. Fence off that piece so nobody—" She nodded toward Alida. "Be climbin' there."

"Miss Alida?" William's voice was high and thin. "Did you fall?" His face crumpled. "Oh, Miss, don't go there. Not like Mama." He hid his face in his hands.

Alida jumped up and took a step around the table to touch William's shoulder. "Don't cry, sweetheart. I was never close to falling." She glared at Cora.

"You climbed the rocks?" Mr. Cooper's voice rose in volume with each word. "Why?" He pushed upright, his fists on the table. "Were you looking for something? Did you see something?"

"No. I took a walk down the beach and—and—"

"No one is to go near those rocks. Cora, you know that."

Cora thrust out her lower lip. "If you builds a fence . . ."

"You are not sheep, are you? Must you be fenced away from what is obviously dangerous? You are not cows."

Cora smiled, her lips closed, hiding her teeth. She slowly raised her gaze to meet his. "Nossir. No, Massa Cooper, *suh!*" She gave the words a mocking twist. "Though you think it so, I ain't no kinda animal."

Mr. Cooper merely glared at her, then turned to Alida. "And you?"

Alida stared from him to Cora, who squinted up at the ceiling. "Cora was—I mean, she was there." How to speak up without getting Cora into deeper trouble? She swallowed with revulsion, recalling the violence done to the old woman the night before.

Cora locked her gaze with Alida's. "I begs Missy's pardon. Seems I is gettin' old. Shoulda' said we can't be climbin' them rocks. Forgettin' more and more as time passes."

Alida's thoughts whirled. She felt dizzy and touched her temple. It often throbbed when she was overtired. "I'm just a bit wobbly." She tried to laugh. "I haven't eaten all day, and . . ." She moved back to her chair but stumbled, missed the chair and clutched at the table, snagging the cloth. Dishes clattered and she fell to her knees.

"William!" Mr. Cooper roared. "Bring the brandy. No, wait. Bring that vial. My medicine. There on the sideboard."

"Oh, best you not give her that. She don't need that, Mr. Coop. Up at that ol' woman's house that time, I hear how she don't like it none."

"Shut up, you old hag."

"Just sayin'."

Their words drifted in and out like waves. Mr. Cooper's arm slipped around her shoulders and he thrust something to her lips, forcing them open. "Swallow," he commanded.

Alida smelled it. She knew it and would not swallow, not that. But he shouted and she startled, sucking a mouthful in with a breath.

He began to lift her, but she pressed her fist to his chest. "I can stand, sir." She gagged at the taste of what he'd forced on her. "The sun was hot. Then climbing . . ."

"That subject is closed."

"Of course."

Cora's face appeared over Mr. Cooper's shoulder. "That's right, Missy," she said. "Don't be sayin' more. Some places ain't good for you to be going. Some not good to be stayin,' neither."

Alida closed her eyes. Yes. She should not be staying. The room spun. "Cora," she whispered. "Does the sea still mean to have me?"

The old woman shrugged. "Seems something does."

Alida stood, Mr. Cooper helping her. She backed away from all of them, turned and walked slowly out of the dining room to the bottom of the stairs. Their gazes seemed to burn into her back. She turned slightly and glanced through the doorway to give poor William a smile. He returned it and gave her a little wave. She held her head high, to be strong for William. But she clung to the banister as she climbed the stairs, and stumbled into her room, then leaned against the closed door. After a moment she slipped the buttons of her dress from their loops and unhooked the corset, easing down across the bed.

Some minutes later Cora entered with a tray. "Ain't nobody eat civilized no more," she muttered. "Be climbing here, climbing there, bringin' trays. Bad enough I got to bring you coffee in the morning."

"You don't have to do that, Cora. I can come down." Alida could hardly focus on the woman. She was so tired . . .

"Nope. He say bring her coffee like you did young Miss. So I do. But you need to eat. And drink what's there." She stirred up a fire and shuffled out again, her hand pressing her lower back.

Alida drank a glass of nearly purple wine, hoping it might fortify her. She nibbled at some roast chicken and sipped some strong tea, an unusual brew, but sweetened and not bad. Soon she lay back and dozed. Half-awake, she imagined the rocks and Cora standing on them like a giant with raised arms. The rocks were a sea dragon's head, eyes burning. Lights. Lanterns. Lights seen from ships, from *their* ship. Murderous lights. The thought rattled her to wakefulness. She shivered and gathered a comforter up to her chin, then slept again.

A deep-throated rumble woke her. The fire had died to glowing coals. Her room was dark as a cave. Thunder crashed, lightning flashed. She sat up, confused. She still wore her clothes, her shoes. She could recall nothing after that bewildering supper. Her mouth felt bone-dry and she reached for the teacup, but only an inch of liquid remained. It smelled, not like tea at all. A bitter, acrid smell. She'd smelled it before, years ago. A friend had grown a tomato plant in her hothouse as a curiosity. No one they knew dared to eat one, but did people make tea from such plants? She set down the cup, trying to think sensibly. Was she still addled by the opium Mr. Cooper had forced her to swallow? Or was it the tea, something concocted by Cora?

Lightning flashed and thunder rumbled again, rattling the window. She perched on the edge of the bed, shivering, and pulled the comforter around her shoulders. She didn't want to leave the bed to build up the fire. She felt safe where she was. She could think.

Cora had known the rocks were forbidden. Did the old woman lure her there? Cora wanted her to go, could have pushed her. Alida would have been swept out to sea and the old crocodile would have the peace she craved. But Mr. Cooper's obsession would grow if she drowned like William's mother. Cora wouldn't like that, would she? Oh, and poor William.

Alida fought to think more clearly. All right. Cora wanted her gone. Alida would oblige. She'd run to *Señora* Rivera. She'd run to Rafe. They'd help her come back and take William. Yes. That would be the way. She padded across the room, gripping the comforter beneath her chin, and cracked open the door, peering both ways. The grandfather clock loomed at the end of the landing. Another lightning flash showed the hands pointing straight up. Midnight in the house of a grieving child, an obsessive man who wanted her, and a conniving old woman who wanted her gone. She was torn between them all.

Still dizzy, she crept forward onto the landing and eased down the stairs, leaning nearly her whole weight on the banister. She staggered across the tiled entryway to the front door and tried the handle. It wouldn't open. She tugged harder. The door frame seemed to swirl. Alida shook her head, but it didn't steady what she saw. She slipped to her knees, pulling and shaking the handle of the door that barred her only way to freedom.

CHAPTER TWENTY-FOUR

Rafe slapped rain from his hat and slipped into the *cantina*.

"Sad doings today." Twyla Green stepped from a shadowed corner to his side. "Did you know that little fella that died? I hear you played your fiddle." She rubbed at an imaginary spot on Rafe's table, lingering like a dog waiting to be petted. "Seems babies die all the time around here. Lots of bigger kids, too," she said.

"Some kind of fever, poor child. *Señora* Rivera couldn't do much, though she tried. Father Sebastian asked me to play at the funeral, said it might comfort the parents." He shrugged. "Not sure anything could. Nearly everybody in the village was there, but I don't recall seeing you."

"Oh, I don't never linger at the church, or the graveyard neither," she said, her voice low and rough. "Not me."

Rafe smiled. "Afraid of ghosts?"

"Huh. Ain't a ghost alive worse than most men I seen."

"I don't believe ghosts are likely to be alive, Twyla."

"Oh, go on and laugh at me. You know what I mean." She eased into the chair opposite him and leaned forward. "It's that priest. He looks like he's wanting to slap the sin right out of me. Has that godly look."

"Appropriate for a priest, I'd say. Yet what good is a church if it won't take a sinner? Remember Mary Magdalene?"

"Don't recall nobody by that name. She never worked around here or I would've run her off."

Rafe hid a smile and leaned back, stretching his legs beneath the table. "Do you have a good memory, Twyla?"

"Not for names. Fellas don't use their right ones, so I don't bother with 'em. But I remember faces and got a real good memory for hands. Some are rough and a few are awful sweet." She chuckled. "You'd think I'd likely recall other manly parts, wouldn't you?" She shook her head and sobered. "No, them parts are pretty much alike, though men are mighty proud of 'em. I, for one, can't see why."

Rafe sat up and leaned forward, wanting to keep her talking. Never know what she might have heard. A fist slammed on the bar, making them both jump. Twyla heaved wearily to her feet. "It's clear to Marsden that me settin' here talking to you ain't gonna bring money to his hand," she whispered. She backed away, simpering and lifting her skirts past her knees. "That is, unless you . . ." She jerked her head toward the back rooms.

"Sorry, Twyla. Funerals pretty much put me off."

"You know?" She stepped forward again, resting her hands on the table, her face creased in thought, breasts nearly in his face. "That is something. Funerals put starch in some men's peckers." She nodded. "Even the burial of their own kin. Ain't that strange? A thing to ponder."

"Twyla," Rafe said, shaking his head, "you should write a book."

She threw back her shoulders, shooting Rafe an injured pout. "Oh, go on. Make fun of me. I know some things."

"I'm sure you do. I meant no insult. I like to talk to you."

But she stalked away, lifting her chin high.

Rafe sighed and cradled his head in his hands, his elbows on the table. While he waited for Twyla to get over hurt feelings and come back, his thoughts drifted to Alida Garrison, as they did most days and nights. He imagined her as a woman he'd want as a partner in life. His ranch was still rough and raw, but she'd probably roll up her sleeves and get to work alongside him like she'd done at the store. She wouldn't play womanish games.

Thinking of her brought Martin Cooper to mind. Now Alida was part of that household, maybe he'd find a way to get in. Nothing unusual about a friend visiting. He could bring the *señora* and . . .

He stood. It was past midnight. He'd get some sleep and visit in the morning. While he'd been daydreaming, the storm had sent gusts of wind inland like an army does its scouts. Wind howled at the door before Rafe got to it. The door slammed open and the wind spit Mirlito through, so hard the little man sprawled on the floor. As Rafe reached him, thinking he was hurt, Mirlito laughed, climbed to his feet and turned to lean his back against the door, shutting it against the gale outside.

"Ah, *amigo.* Help me celebrate." He gave a grand sweep of his arm. "You, Twyla. Bring us drink."

Rafe looked up. Twyla sneered at them both before bringing the bottle. He poured two glasses, one to the brim for Mirlito, less for himself. "What could be worth celebrating? Didn't we bury a child today?" he said. "A sad day and now a stormy night."

"Ah, yes. The child." Mirlito turned his mouth down and closed his eyes for a moment, then clapped his hands once and grinned. "You see? Not even children are safe from death, so best to get on with living, eh? And stormy nights? They are good for many reasons." Mirlito leaned forward and winked as he picked up his glass. He drank it fast, gasped, coughed and held up the glass for more.

Rafe obliged him.

"Many ships, my friend." Mirlito brought his shoulders up high and then let them drop. "Many ships are lost in such storms. These terrible rocks always find them." He made a show of shuddering. "Perhaps even tonight." He nodded slowly and pursed his lips, as if deep in thought.

"Like Mrs. Garrison's ship?"

"*Sí*. That poor little woman." He knuckled his eyes, pretending to cry. He eyed Rafe as if a thought had just hit him. "So, you are liking that skinny woman?"

Rafe nodded toward Twyla. "You've seen the kind of woman I like."

Mirlito giggled and threw back another drink. "A good thing. If you fancied the other, my friend, how could I do what I have promised her?"

"Promised Mrs. Garrison?" Rafe felt confused. What connection could Mirlito have with Alida?

"Not *that* one. Another. Ah, you don't know her and never will. She is again for me, and I celebrate. She is in town, in Indianola. Five nights ago she asked me—*me*—she knows I am a true man." He winked and swayed side to side in the chair. "I will not betray her."

"You need to get home."

Mirlito nodded. "*Sí*. My little house. She will come to me there. We will look across at the great house where once she lived. We will laugh at him. I showed her off to him, for I was proud." He struck his forehead with a fist. "*Estúpido!* He took her and dressed her in silk and velvet, clothes I could never give her. Then he took it all away. Now my house, my bed, will again be hers." He sagged slowly forward until his face hit the table.

Rafe laid down coins, hauled Mirlito up and across one shoulder, and shoved out the door into the storm. Thunder and lightning had ceased and rain held off. Only a fearsome, wild wind screamed off the sea, scouring the land. Rafe climbed the bluff where Mirlito's shack shuddered in every gust. Its door stood ajar. Rafe kicked it completely open and eased Mirlito down into a nest of tangled blankets. The little man came awake kissing the air, cooing to his pillow.

Rafe found matches and lit a lamp.

Mirlito patted his bed. "Right here," he said. "Here is where she will lay herself down for me." He smirked. "The great lady from the great house. I told her . . ."

Rafe raised the lamp. The little man winced, raising his hand against the light. "Hey, *amigo!* Why do you blind me?"

"Great lady?"

Mirlito sat up, held the pose of an insulted man for a second and then collapsed, laughing and falling back. He rolled side to side, kicking his feet. "That's what she wanted to be, my Molly. Cooper threw her away, but she did not go far. Today I saw her in town. Did I not say this?" He sighed. "So silly, that Molly. She wanted to be his wife. He *did* have a wife, a kind lady. She gave him a son, but would give him nothing more after she saw him working that morning."

"You mean his wife left him and the child? I thought she died."

Mirlito sat up. "Always I have thought she meant to take the child." He beckoned Rafe closer with a crook of one finger. "A storm comes. A ship comes along, as often they do. In early morning she hears talk. Many more servants in those days," he whispered. "She takes the tiny one." Mirlito held his hands apart about twenty inches. "Alive for only a few weeks. He cries into the wind as his mother climbs the rocks, wanting to see." He nodded. "Cooper laughed as we claimed the salvage. He picked up a flag, laughing. A Union flag and all around him lay dead men." Mirlito winked. "He never liked to think of what must be done with survivors, never saw it done." He nodded. "But she sees the dead and the flag and hears his laughter and knows the gossip is true."

"She thought he had something to do with killing?"

Mirlito shrugged. "Maybe." He pursed his lips, smirking. "He sees her, climbs to her, but she runs screaming, calling him names. Just as she throws herself down he grabs for her, but snags only the little one." Mirlito shook his head. "A pitiful sight, *amigo*. Before he could get down, the sea lifts and carries her away." He moved his hand in a gentle wave.

"My God."

Mirlito nodded. "Cooper said the same. Over and over he said it and screamed her name. He could not fight the sea." He let his face droop and closed his eyes. Suddenly, like a child who had only pretended sadness, he laughed and fell back again, rolling side to side. "So." He wiped his eyes. "When the little black-haired woman washes up on the beach, Cooper thought the sea had spit his wife back."

"Are they so much alike?"

"*Amigo,* she is the same. She and the dead wife like twins." Mirlito struggled to sit up again. "I think maybe this one is smaller." He slapped his thigh. "Maybe the sea took his wife and shrank her. What a fine joke."

"So Cooper's not just having you take salvage, he's luring ships to the rocks. Has he lost his mind?" Rafe murmured.

Mirlito wagged his finger. "Always a little crazy, but that little woman has pushed him over. And you, stupid *cabrón*. You saved her."

"So I did."

Mirlito leaned closer. "My Molly wants revenge. She bargains, saying she will be mine if I take the skinny little woman from Cooper and break his heart." He nodded, leaning back.

"Take her how?"

He shrugged and grinned, lying back on his twisted sheets. "This she leaves to me."

A sudden chill took Rafe's breath. Mirlito was a violent man. He forced his cold lips into a smile. "Mirlito, my friend. Can't you see that's all she wants from you? Are you truly going to kill for her?"

"Kill? Have I not killed for less?" He shrugged and yawned. "I do not like to kill a woman, even a skinny one. My knives are silent, but they are bloody. So probably I will not." He rubbed his eyes like a sleepy child and curled up, his hands tucked between his legs. "I will take the woman and turn her loose somewhere and tell Molly, yes, tell her the skinny woman is dead." He chuckled. "Tell her I made Cooper watch. Maybe I will kill Cooper instead. This I would like better. Pull him from Molly's mind, like pulling a snake from a hole, yes? And is he not a snake?" Mirlito rose up, then fell limp and began to snore, drooling.

Rafe slammed out the door and ran back down the path, battling the wind. He'd get her away, from Mirlito and that madman, both. A sudden gust whistled fiercely from the sea. It blew him against the rocks alongside the path. The sky opened and a torrent drenched him. He slipped on the soaked gravel and went down hard, his head striking a rock. He shook away pain and pushed onto his hands, then fell back. Spitting gravel, he got one knee under him but fell again, fell into darkness deeper than true night.

CHAPTER TWENTY-FIVE

The key in the lock was long and heavy. It would take both hands to turn it. Thank heaven her searching fingers had found it before anyone came. Alida let the quilt slip from her shoulders and worked the key until the front door blew open. Rain rattled on the roof of the portico above her, running off in torrents. Wind slanted sideways, molding her skirt to her legs and blowing her unbuttoned bodice wide. She turned to grab the quilt, but it pooled just out of reach. Dizzy, she stared ahead into darkness and wind-whipped oleanders.

Better to drown in the rain than stay a moment longer. She took a deep breath, ready to plunge down the steps, but then pulled her scattered thoughts together. She couldn't leave William. His father was more than brooding and cold—he was cruel. He had drugged her, given her what she hated, what she fought against, or was it more? Was something in the tea? That would be Cora, but maybe only Cora's potion. Mr. Cooper would have poured it in the tea and—she took another breath.

A scurrying step and forlorn cry came from behind her. She spun. "Seth?" Of course not, was she going mad too? It was William. He stood just inside the open door, his nightshirt flapping around bare legs.

Before she could say a word, he stumbled out the door and burrowed into her skirts. She lifted him high and he wound his arms and legs around her like Seth had done in that other storm. This time she would save the child who trusted her.

"Don't cry, William. We have to leave, but we'll go together. I won't leave you. Never." She stumbled across the veranda with William clinging tight, his face hidden against her throat.

A hand gripped her arm. An ululating cry shrieked from behind her. Alida struggled to wrench away but Cora's fingers dug into her arm like talons. The old woman opened her fearsome mouth and tipped her head back, howling again in that horrible way. Alida twisted, throwing Cora's frail-boned body side to side, but the old woman held on.

"Let go, Cora! You want me gone, let me go!"

"You can't be leavin' in the dark of a storm, taking the boy." She panted. "No peace comin' like that. You got to go upright in the light. He got to see you clear."

Alida pulled Cora's fingers away one by one. Martin Cooper ran through the door, shouting curses. Alida screamed, enraged, as he snatched William from her. William shrieked too, but his father only thrust him into Cora's arms and then jerked Alida against him, lifting her high and tight to his chest.

Cora backed into the house, dragging William. The boy struggled. "Let me go, Cora!" he shouted. "Miss Alida! Father, don't. Don't hurt her!"

"It's all right, William. Don't fight," Alida said, breathing hard. "Go with Cora. I'm not hurt."

"Of course you're not hurt," Cooper said. "Hurt? I would never hurt you."

"Then put me down." Alida's heart raced, and her mouth felt fuzzy with fear. She shoved against his chest with both hands but he didn't seem to notice.

"Hush now," he whispered in her ear. "You're safe. I saved you. You and William both." He buried his face in her hair, nuzzling her neck.

Alida tried to twist away from his harsh, hot breath. He only held her tighter, carrying her into the house and up the stairs.

"I can walk, Mr. Cooper."

He stared down at her as if in a trance. A flash of lightning showed dead eyes in a slack face. "I knew it was possible," he murmured. "Knew you could return. The storm took you, but gives you back, just as it does so many treasures."

Terror made her struggle harder. He tightened his hold, whispering endearments, staggering a little as he moved up the stairs. She smelled brandy on his breath, brandy and the drug he had forced on her, the bitter-sweet syrup of poppy she hated so much, the source of her husband's delusions and mania.

She fisted her right hand, pulled it back and hit Cooper in the face as hard as she could. The blow glanced off his cheekbone, but startled him. He stopped at the top of the stairs and shook his head, leaning back on the railing as recognition flooded his eyes.

Alida swallowed her fear. "Mr. Cooper," she said quietly. "Please, sir. Put me down. You are not yourself."

"Not myself?" He smiled grimly. "Really?"

"Confused by the storm, no doubt, you thought I was your wife."

He shook his head. "I know exactly who you are," he whispered.

"Then you should know I do not wish to be held like this. Put me down."

"Since I first saw you at the old woman's house, I knew you were for me. How could I have left you there? That fool shopkeeper pumped seawater from your lungs. He touched your breasts, your face, your frozen limbs." He brushed each place as he named it.

Alida struggled. He gripped her tighter.

"Destiny brought you home. I knew I'd have the chance to make you understand." His voice thickened, growling from his throat. "You didn't give me a chance, but now . . ." The dark look of anguished desire returned.

Alida understood little of love, yet knew his expression had nothing to do with it. "Mr. Cooper. This is not the way to win my affection. You are not seeing me clearly. I am here only for William."

"Time. It will take time. And I shall see we have it."

So reason would not help. She fell limp in his arms, hoping to fool him, but he pulled her closer, kissing her throat. She shuddered, waiting for a chance to break free.

As he moved toward his room, he moaned against her ear. "Don't be afraid," he whispered. "Don't ever be afraid."

Alida stiffened and wrenched her head around. "Someone's coming, Mr. Cooper. Look! You have so much to tell me. We should be alone."

He lifted his head and turned, scowling. His grip loosened just enough for her to squirm away and tumble from his arms. She scrambled up from the floor and sprinted for her room.

He strained toward the light that moved from the other direction along the landing. "It's no one," he said. "Only Cora." He turned and screamed a name, not hers. Alida slammed her door, leaned against it and threw the flimsy bolt.

Rafe raised himself up onto one forearm. Pain slashed at his skull. The wind had whistled off somewhere. Still dark, but the sky hinted at dawn. He'd soon be able to see, if he hadn't struck himself blind, falling on those rain-slick rocks like the clumsy fool he pretended to be. He staggered to his feet, but fell to his knees again and retched up last night's meal.

He sat in the muddy path, wiping his mouth with the back of his hand. Lucky he hadn't ended down the cliff like Lacey. He watched the sea roll in, its surface calm now, but the sun was slow to rise, as if waiting to spring morning on him like a joke. He blinked a few times, fingering a place high up on his forehead. His hair had matted there. He brought his fingers close and smelled blood.

Turning his head carefully, he looked back up the path to Mirlito's shack. No sign of the man. He pulled one knee under him and pushed up, holding onto a boulder, then threw up again. He blinked himself from a gray blur and stumbled down the path to town.

It took him three times longer than it should have to make it there. He had to warn Alida about Cooper, make her understand. He had to keep Mirlito from her, save her. As he made his way through the streets, dizzy and stumbling, he imagined he saw the little man behind every wall, in every shadow—Mirlito with a knife, grinning. Near the *cantina* he met Twyla tossing out last night's garbage, offal not even fit for the preacher's hogs.

"Lord, shopkeeper, you look like five kinds of hell," she said.

Rafe winced and touched his head.

"You look worse than Mirlito."

"What? You saw him?"

"You best stay away from him. He'll bring trouble down on you."

"When did you see him?" The words echoed in his skull. "Which way was he going?"

Twyla shrunk from him. "No need yelling at me. He come riding by a while ago on a horse he must've stole. Never known him to have such a fine horse. He was packed up and heading out of town, weaving in the saddle. Likely fall off before he's done. I say good riddance."

"Not to Cooper's?"

"The other way, I said. Maybe going to where his fancy woman is stashed, the one what was Cooper's for a time." She shook her head. "That's one desperate woman, has a poor man, gets a rich man who treats her mean, and ends up with a little

217

bastard like Mirlito—both mean and poor. She just don't seem to get it right."

Her words drilled into his brain. He held his head, feeling like it would fall off. He nearly laughed, relieved Mirlito had gone.

"Hey, if you don't want to listen to me, why'd you ask?" Twyla smoothed her skirt as if it were ruffled feathers. "Take your sorry ass home before you fall over."

"He's gone. That's good." He turned, stumbled against a wall and held to it. More walls and a fence helped him find his way as far as the store. He had time now. He could go to Cooper's and get Alida. He would—but he couldn't think of what he would do. *She's safe. Safe for now.* This was his last thought. Then he fell.

CHAPTER TWENTY-SIX

William slammed through the shop door, his small boots pounding the floor like thunder. "Mr. Bishop! That was a big storm last night, wasn't it?"

Rafe winced. The boy's voice felt like knives in his brain.

"Miss Alida was scared."

"Was she? Because of the storm?" Rafe stepped around the counter and laid a hand on William's shoulder. "What happened?"

"She fell down at dinner and Father gave her medicine, but she didn't want it. Then she tried to run away. Today she said the medicine gave her nightmares." William shook his head. "I was scared she was leaving me so I ran after her. Ol' Cora came and then Father. I guess he helped Miss Alida. But . . ." He caught his breath after the long speech. "Later I thought I heard her crying." He frowned, then brightened. "She says she's all right today." He turned. "She's here."

Rafe looked past the boy. Alida stood framed in the doorway. As she walked in, Rafe stepped past William, who skipped to the door. "Miss Alida? That man outside has puppies in a crate. Can I go see?"

She nodded.

As William ran out, Alida moved closer to Rafe. "I told Mr. Cooper I had to come, for I needed thread and needles." She took a breath. "Mr. Cooper has given me dresses, but . . ." She spread her skirt wide between her hands, looking down at it.

"His wife was evidently taller, so not really like me, not the way everyone says."

Rafe stepped up next to her, shocked at her pale face and shadowed eyes. "William said you were ill?"

"No, not ill." She frowned up into his face. "But look at you. What happened? That's a cut on your forehead." She reached toward his hair.

"I'm all right." He ducked aside. "I slipped in the rain and fell. On my way to see you, matter of fact."

"Oh, no! No, you mustn't!" Fear flared in her eyes. "Don't come to the house. Nothing must interfere with—with William's education."

Rafe couldn't make sense of that. "William said something about medicine?"

She shook her head. "You know how I dislike laudanum."

"I surely do recall how you fought us over it."

"Well, Mr. Cooper didn't understand. He was trying to be helpful, I'm sure, and . . ." She shot an uneasy glance toward the door.

What was she afraid of—Cooper? "So you weren't ill?"

"Confused in the night. I hadn't eaten, you see, and the storm, or maybe a dream, made me afraid for a few moments."

"And Mr. Cooper helped you?"

"He brought me back, out of the rain. Perhaps he was dreaming as well. I smelled brandy and recognized the other, the tonic he takes for his headaches when he doesn't wait for Cora to help." Her lips twitched, not quite a smile. "My husband used it for pain. It's why I hate it so." She shook her head. "It can make a man confused. I believe Mr. Cooper mistook me for William's mother. He said things best forgotten." She turned away, her back rigid. "He has apologized. William saw me distraught and disheveled and was frightened. Mr. Cooper assures me everything will be forgotten and William will remain safe."

"I don't understand. Why would William be in any danger?"

"He's not. No, he's not. But everything must remain as it is." She tore her gaze from the door and searched his eyes. "At least for now. But if I have a chance, if I can find a way—"

The sound of buggy wheels reached them from outside. "He's here," Alida murmured. She rushed toward the door.

"Miss Alida!" William called.

"A way for what?" Rafe said. "What can I do?"

She halted. "Do? Do nothing. We can do nothing just now." She took a tremulous breath. "I need better timing." She sighed. "I will not fail this child."

Rafe touched her arm. "Of course not." When she didn't pull away he moved his hand to her shoulder and pressed gently. "And I will not fail you."

"Well, you saved me before," she whispered.

"I simply chose to lurch down that side of the rock rather than the other. An unlikely hero."

She closed her eyes. "Mine, though. I thank God for you."

"Now that's not something I've ever heard."

She smiled, but sobered quickly. "There's a mystery surrounding you, isn't there? You're more than you seem. Tell me why you have chosen this tiny place in which to put down roots. Do you hide away because of the tale you told me? Because of guilt?"

"I'm making up for my failing with what I do here."

She cocked her head. "Really? By keeping a little store? How can that make up for it?"

"That's part of what I must tell you. I've also come to realize my being here has even more meaning."

She raised her eyebrows, waiting.

"I'm here—to find you."

She closed her eyes and shook her head. Not sure what that meant, he floundered on. "I can clear the mystery up with some conversation. But tell me, is something strange going on in that house?"

"Strange? Not for *that* house." She forced a laugh.

"Danger?"

She squinted and drew her hand across a furrowed brow. "No, not to me. Don't worry about me. But be alert when a storm comes. Be alert for lights. I can't explain now, but . . ."

"Is that the danger you mean? You don't mean William?"

"William? He's calling me. I don't have liberty to stay. I must go home with William." She laid a hand on the doorknob. "And stay with him. Do you understand?"

Boot heels thudded up the path outside. "He's coming," she whispered. "Mr. Cooper is coming."

"Alida, wait."

"No, I *must* go. I promised." She opened the door.

Rafe scowled past her. Cooper was striding toward the porch, William hurrying after him. As he passed his father the man grasped his shoulder, clamping down hard. The boy winced and wriggled but didn't cry. Either very brave or very frightened.

Fueled by frustration, Rafe grasped Alida's shoulders and pulled her against him. She shrugged him off and he let her go, abashed, but she spun and lifted her face, giving his cheek a quick kiss. He forgot Cooper, forgot everything but her lips, warm against him.

Cooper rushed up the steps and through the doorway. He shoved Rafe hard, but Rafe set his feet and didn't fall. Alida cried out and stepped aside. William scurried in, and she clutched the boy to her.

Rafe favored Cooper with a hard smile. The man stared, stone-faced as fury stormed in his eyes. "We're leaving, Mrs. Garrison," Cooper said, his voice thick and low. He turned and grabbed William's arm. The boy began to cry. Cooper pulled him along, walking stiff-legged back outside toward the buggy. Rafe and Alida followed.

"Maybe the lady doesn't want to go just yet. Maybe she likes the company." Rafe turned to her, the smirk he'd formed for Cooper still in place. "Do you?"

Alida stood stiff-backed, her chin high. Anger clouded her eyes. He flinched from it, ruing his stupid smile and flippant words.

She shook her head. "You gentlemen are frightening William with whatever . . . contest you're engaged in. I believe I'll leave you to it."

Rafe's tongue twisted. He felt too clumsy to speak. He forgot Martin Cooper, thinking only of the hurt in Alida's eyes. It had come so soon after her sweet kiss. As she slipped by, he leaned down, his lips near the curve of her ear. "This isn't what you think," he whispered.

She raised her eyebrows as she pulled away from where his lips nearly touched her skin, her eyes ice-blue. "Oh? And what do I think? Once you told me how to feel. Now what to think?"

"Alida," he began.

She raised her chin higher.

"Let me explain."

"Can you?"

Cooper held out his hand. "Madam?" he called. "William is upset. He needs you. We are waiting. Come now."

Alida's face paled to ash, just two spots of color burning on her cheeks. "Yes, I'm coming." She raised her voice. "I'm coming, William." She picked up her skirts and ran to the buggy before Rafe could say or do more.

Cooper handed her up, then stalked back toward Rafe, his face closed like a fist. "You! Stay away from what is mine." He whispered the words, a choked, hoarse sound, spittle flying.

Rafe held his ground. "Is Alida Garrison yours?"

A flush began at Cooper's tight collar and colored his face a dull red. "I employ her. Yes, by God, mine. Stay away."

"I don't believe the lady is in any danger from me and I doubt she regrets any of our encounters."

"Yankee bastard," Cooper snarled and raised a fist. He was trembling with rage. "By God, you won't talk so bold when we beat you back, when the Confederacy is again set right and all is as it should be."

Satisfaction filled Rafe, sizzled like lightning. He forgot himself and straightened his shoulders, stood tall with fists clenched. "Mr. Cooper, the war is over. Though your cause is lost, you have life and limb and wealth. All your parts functioning, at least those I see. If I were you I'd not waste what's left of my days licking wounds."

Slowly, Cooper dropped his hand and splayed his fingers wide. "Who and what are you, Bishop?" he whispered.

Rafe shrugged, ducked his head and thrust it forward again, falling into his round-shouldered stance. "I've been asked twice within ten minutes." He limped a few steps, glancing sidelong at Cooper. "A struggling merchant, sir. But I might ask you the same." He gave a little salute and glanced toward the buggy. Alida held William close and threw Rafe a questioning gaze.

"She's waiting, Cooper. She and the boy are waiting."

"She?" Cooper whispered. He turned and staggered a step, then gawped in every direction. "She?"

"In the buggy, Cooper." What was wrong with the man? Was it the opium, or had he lost his mind?

"Yes, of course," Cooper whispered. "I see. She is waiting." He stretched tall, then seemed to shrink. "No. You're talking about . . ." He squinted. "The other one." He struck his temple with his fist. "That's Mrs. Garrison." His voice trailed away, sounding like a child opening a much anticipated gift to find nothing. He gazed at the ground like he'd lost something. "I tried to explain, but she wouldn't listen. Just like before."

"I mean to call on Mrs. Garrison. I trust there will be no trouble."

"Trouble?" Cooper looked to be struggling from sleep.

"I'd like to bring Mrs. Rivera. I'm sure Mrs. Garrison misses her and it's her right to have friends. You do not own her. Living as you do, undoubtedly you've forgotten. Owning people is all over now." Rafe gave a twisted smile, waiting for an explosion. But Cooper only sneered and strode to the buggy.

Rafe stared after him. For a moment Cooper had seemed a haunted man, pitiable. But Mirlito was right, he was mad, likely using threats to his own son to keep Alida close. Getting her away had become much more complicated.

He touched his check where Alida kissed him. A fever burned in him to end this. End it and begin again.

CHAPTER TWENTY-SEVEN

Alida stepped out through the French doors. A man she'd never seen straightened quickly from where he'd been lounging on a short wall. He didn't speak, but tipped his hat. She went back inside, where she lingered in the middle of the room. After a moment, she walked to the nearest window and tried it. Locked. So was the next one she attempted to open, and the next. All the downstairs windows were locked, as well as the two outside doors.

Mr. Cooper had kept to his room for the four days since the exchange with Rafe Bishop. Cora said he was sick and she had to brew up medicine for his pain. That bitter smell spread from the kitchen to the rest of the house. Alida asked Cora about it, but the old woman said it was "a little of this and that. What you smellin' is mostly the Devil's Cherries. Just a bit. Lets him see better times ahead."

Since the downstairs windows were locked, Alida opened every window upstairs she could, hoping to air out the house. Longing for a breath of freedom.

She had promised to take William to the village for a gathering. A *fiesta*, William had called it. Once there, she might slip away with him to *Señora* Rivera, then contact Rafe. She would see Rafe. But the locked doors and windows and the man outside—would she be able to leave? She fretted as she sat taking up the hem of a rose-pink linen dress. Any delight she might have felt over such a lovely garment had been buried in dismay over the situation she was in. She'd sent a note to Mr. Cooper with Cora and waited for an answer.

Alida was surprised at how strong her feelings for Rafe had grown. His infirmities no longer repelled her. She saw past them to the man, just as he must have put aside his prejudices about her Southern upbringing. None of that mattered to either of them anymore. They might start anew. Go away and—but William, yes, what of William?

Mr. Cooper had apologized for his behavior on the night of the storm, saying he'd had too much brandy, but he'd also insisted she had imagined much of it. She knew she hadn't, but she was quick to agree. It had been more than brandy, more than the opium tincture, for now he strongly hinted that her presence was tied somehow to William's well-being. Fear had clutched her heart at those words. Perhaps she'd read too much into it, but she feared to risk it.

"I hope I didn't startle you." Cooper's voice jolted her, and she dropped her needle. She hadn't expected him to be able to rise from his bed. He smiled, as if pleased by her distress. "I came to tell you that yes, you can go. And I'll be watching."

She searched for the needle on the carpet. When she found it, she straightened up, giving him a smile. "My, my. Watching? Are we prisoners, William and I?"

His eyes glittered, feverish. He stepped closer. "Whenever you're away from the house, look up," he whispered. "I'll be there."

She turned quickly to the window and saw her reflection with his behind her. Neither of them said more. Finally he left the room. She began work again, trembling as she thought it all through.

The man was ill. Perhaps he could be helped, but this was not her concern. William was. She would protect William.

★ ★ ★ ★ ★

The next afternoon she and William walked through the village and up the hill to the *Señora*'s house. Alida glanced back over her shoulder, expecting to see Martin Cooper galloping after them on his leggy horse, or maybe coming in the buggy as he had when she'd visited Rafe Bishop's shop. If he followed her this time, he was being extraordinarily clever. She did spot the man who had loitered outside the house. He was at a distance, watching.

So, if they ran they would be chased. If they hid they'd be found and innocent villagers might be hurt. She would wait, though patience had never been one of her virtues.

Señora Rivera welcomed them with hugs and kisses, and exclamations about how thin she'd become, though Alida doubted the truth of that. They walked to the graveyard to lay flowers at the headstones of the old woman's family and on the three newest wooden crosses. Alida touched Seth's cross as she would have stroked his hair, lightly, lovingly, then looked up quickly to be sure William was near. He lingered, watching children rolling hoops. "Stay close, William," Alida called.

The boy nodded and trotted behind her to the paved plaza outside the church. Heat still rose from the bricks, the air shimmered and the scent of flowers on the churchyard graves and the spicy smell of cooking wafted on the wind. A violin's melody floated to Alida over the heads of the smiling crowd. Rafe's violin.

The old woman took Alida's hand, smoothing it with her thumb. "Such music. A man who plays so sweetly cannot be bad, I think. But I worry, fearing he will fall in with bad men. Sometimes he seems reckless."

"Reckless?" She felt heat in her face. She'd like to see him reckless.

"He is always asking, wanting to know things that are best

left unknown." *Señora* Rivera looked up. "Ah, but listen to his music."

The violin's haunting voice soared over the heads of the crowd and found its way to Alida. She could imagine he played only for her. When the piece ended, the crowd sighed as one, then broke into applause. *Señora* Rivera pushed through to speak to him, but Alida held back, her throat aching with unshed tears. The poignant melody echoed in her mind. She wiped her eyes with a handkerchief she had in the pocket of her dress.

"You're crying?" Rafe's voice. He stood close, smiling, but with hesitant concern. She hadn't heard him approach.

She regained her composure. "I was moved by your music, Rafe. I envy your ability to make that violin sing so sweetly."

"Is Beethoven a favorite of yours?"

"I haven't heard enough of such music to have a favorite. I often played piano at my mother's house—hymns and dirges, patriotic songs at the start of the war, then as the years went on, even the thought of music, well . . ." She closed her eyes against memories.

He took her hand and pressed it. "That was the Adagio from a Beethoven violin sonata." He cleared his throat and gazed into the distance. "So in another place and time you'll know what to request. It sounds much better with piano accompaniment." He turned back to her, arching one eyebrow. "Maybe someday we might play it together?"

"Do you have a piano at your store?"

He smiled. "What? You don't think Mr. Cooper would encourage our musical collaboration?"

The joke startled her into laughing. Everything had been so serious lately.

He cleared his throat. "I'm sorry about that day."

"Which day?"

"Outside the store when I let the situation grow into more

than it should have been."

"You had some sharp words with Mr. Cooper. Is that what you mean?"

"I hated that it upset you."

"Confused me, yes. You don't need to apologize, though. After all, *I* kissed *you*. And that was not more than it should have been, it was just what it was."

He gave her a quizzical smile. "Hmm. Well. Before you came among us, I had only seen Martin Cooper once in the year I've been here. That one time I felt he sized me up, trying to decide if I was something other than I appeared. If I was harmless."

"Are you?"

He frowned. "Am I what?"

"Harmless."

He edged a step closer. "It depends on the definition of harm."

A sudden wind gusted through the crowd, whipping skirts and shawls, teasing Alida's hair from its fastening and into her eyes and tousling Rafe's hair. Carefully, slowly, she caught a strand of his hair between two fingers and smiled as she tucked it behind his ear.

"Well, thank you," he whispered. He leaned close and breathed in, then stepped back. "You smell of the sea. Like the first time I saw and touched you."

"The sea?" Her laugh sounded forced even to her. "So I smell of fish?"

"Like a breeze blowing off the sea from somewhere far away."

She tore her gaze from him, wondering where Cooper's watchman was.

His voice dropped lower. "Tell me quickly and plainly. Something is wrong, isn't it?"

She looked back over her shoulder. No sign of the hired watcher, but she did see William with his little group of new friends. "It's William," she whispered. "I imagine William needs me to save him." She sighed. "But then I tell myself it's more likely my guilt over failing Seth." She tried to smile, but fell short. "Do you see?"

He nodded. "More clearly every day." His eyes caressed her while his hands caressed his violin.

"Sometimes I'm with William, reading with him, watching him soak up affection and thrive, and I wonder if I'm imagining threats, making too much of what Mr. Cooper says, twisting his meaning. He's a complicated man. Then at other times—and I found lanterns, Rafe. So many. Too many . . . That little man with the hard dark eyes, and maybe Mr. Cooper, has something to do with the lights I saw. The lights on the rocks, just before the ship foundered. Or am I imagining that too?"

"No, you're not." Rafe handed her his violin. "It's warm out here. Too warm for this coat." He shrugged out of his jacket and changed before her eyes. Without his jacket he stood straighter, taller. His shoulders straightened without his seeming to notice, stretching his broadcloth shirt. "Trust your instincts, Alida. Sometimes intuition is all we have."

He rolled up his sleeves, showing the tanned and muscled forearms that had once held her. Without the coat and his shopkeeper's apron he was a different man. He took back the instrument and gazed into her eyes, smiling. "Who *are* you?" she whispered. "I've asked before. You say you'll tell me, but never do."

"I told you of my failure, shirking my duty when it mattered so much."

She nodded. "Of course, too sad a tale to forget."

He took a breath like he might be preparing to leap off a cliff. "I work for the army like I did back then. I'm here to dig out evidence of traitorous men planning renewed insurrection."

Stunned, for a moment she couldn't think of what to say. "So

231

you're not a storekeeper at all?"

He shook his head. "Good thing, for I'm poor at it."

"I should have known by the state of your accounting."

"This gimpy leg and crooked back is a disguise. Damned uncomfortable, I can tell you. Someone thought it best if no one saw me as a threat." He grinned. "But the man with that idea didn't have to twist himself into a knot to pull it off, did he?"

She assessed his scar.

"The scar is real, and my need to make up for my failure? That's certainly real."

"Why haven't you told me before? I believed us friends. You didn't trust me?"

"Not at first. I pray you forgive me." He swallowed. "The cadence of your speech took me too far back, back to when a woman I trusted, a woman I was going to marry, a Southerner, chose her home in Georgia over me. I understood her loyalty to family, and when she returned to Washington after the war, I was happy to see her. I chose to be with her rather than do my duty that night." He looked away. "That part was not her fault, but what sealed my loathing of everything about her was how she laughed at me. She applauded Lincoln's death and laughed at my pain. Ever since, the sound of a Southern woman's drawl has filled me with contempt. Yes, it's petty, but there you have it." He stared into her eyes. "I've shaken off such nonsense, but feared to tell you and put you in more danger. Now I fear I can't keep you from harm, even if I had the right to try."

"You saved my life," she said. "You can't give up on me now." Her heart hammered in her chest, suspended. Should she laugh and lighten these sober words? She feared to sound like the very type of woman he had just described.

"Do you forgive me my prejudice?" He caught her hand, studied it a moment and rubbed her palm gently with his thumb before tucking her hand around his arm.

She nodded, loving the touch of his smooth warm skin beneath her fingers. She felt a moment of calm, a sense of safety, a hint of what might be possible. "Of course. I'm not without blame. I judged you too. Thinking you'd be as hateful and abusive as my husband became before he passed, I wanted nothing to do with you. But I grew to know you and saw you as someone who rose above his suffering. A brave man."

"And all the time I was a liar."

She laughed. "Well, aren't we a pair?"

Their mutual confessions spun away with a dust-devil wind swirling down an alley. Alida, still smiling, scanned the street around them. Still no sign of Cooper's hireling. "Will Mr. Cooper be arrested? If so, can you help us? I'll keep William with me here and . . ." She lost her smile abruptly. "Rafe! Where's William? He was right here." She took three quick steps one way, then spun and went the other. "William!" she called.

"He went down this way following some children." Rafe ran to the end of the street. "There," he called, pointing. "There he is." He paused and reached back toward her. "Wait. Too late."

Alida ran to catch up, her hand at her mouth. The boy waved at them from where he sat on a spirited horse, leaning back against his father.

"He doesn't seem afraid," Rafe said.

"Why would he be? He loves any attention he can get from his father. He hungers for it." Alida clenched one hand at her breast.

"Come with me to the *señora*'s house. Don't go back there."

"I can't! The threat is too great. What if he means his not-so-veiled threats to William? I don't know what Cooper might do if I break my word."

"Surely he won't hurt his own son."

"I have no idea, but even if he wouldn't, I can't abandon the boy. You should have seen his face the night he thought I was leaving. His cries nearly broke my heart. It wasn't that he's afraid of his father, for he hasn't heard the threats." She sighed, shuddering. "He fears the loss of love. I won't take that away. If you would help me, Rafe, you must find another way." She nodded once, biting back words and swallowing tears, then strode toward Cooper's horse.

As she neared, Cooper twisted his mouth into a sneering smile, letting William down into her arms. He dismounted and walked with them, leading the horse. Alida felt him behind her and her skin crawled. She took William's hand, smiling into his upturned face, listening to his happy account of the day's fun.

CHAPTER TWENTY-EIGHT

William had been overjoyed when his father took him up on the spirited horse, but now? What words could Alida find to explain his father's return to being such a cold and distant man? Martin Cooper sat at his desk in the study, gripping his knees with white-knuckled hands, ignoring William, his scowl for Alida alone.

She drew the boy close. He snaked his arms around her neck, pressing his head to her shoulder. "Why is Father angry?" he whispered, tears soaking into her dress.

"William! Sit up and quit sniveling." Cooper glared at them, like a man who ached to give the speech he had prepared.

Alida was just as determined. She would not leave William, but she must get away. Therefore, he must come too. There could be no compromise. She tightened her hold on the boy and took a breath to speak.

Before she could say a word, Cooper spoke in a sneering tone. "What do you have to cry about, William? Did you know a little boy in the village died a few days ago? Yes, a little boy like you. It's easy for a little boy to die."

"Mr. Cooper!"

"You can't keep him wrapped in cotton, madam." He turned his sneer on Alida. "You must understand the world and its peril, William. Now sit up."

William leaned away from Alida and hung his head. "I—I didn't know little boys died. Only old people die."

235

Before Alida might console him and explain, Cooper gripped the arms of his chair so hard he nearly raised himself off the seat. "Your mother wasn't old." His voice was a harsh whisper. "Your mother died. Having a baby drove her mad, William. It killed her, having you."

William sucked in a breath and gaped at his father. For a moment they looked alike, both whey-faced and still, blue eyes staring. Then William's eyes softened and filled with tears while his father's hardened like blue marbles.

"Sir! I must protest." Alida drew William close again, but his body stayed rigid.

Cooper raised one hand, palm toward her, then clenched it. "Not one word from you, madam."

She bit her lip, burning to give him more than "one word." Much more. "Then I will take William to his room."

"Excellent idea." He stood when she did, but turned his back.

She refused to show she noticed when he slammed the study door behind them. The key clicked as it turned in the lock. As if she would ever want to enter that room again. As they passed a front window, Alida glanced out. The man she'd seen before was there. "Well, William," she said. "We'll have a quiet evening, shall we?"

He took her hand, nodding, but withdrawn. They climbed the stairs. In his room, William took out painted toy soldiers like the ones Seth had treasured. William only stared at them. Alida pretended to read, watching the boy. Every page could be blank for all she understood. Would Mr. Cooper burst in or call her out? What would she do? What *could* she do? As the hours wore on, she grew increasingly anxious at hearing nothing from him.

Dinner time came and Cora brought them a tray, though William only picked at the food and Alida ate nothing. When Cora returned at bedtime, Alida sent her away. "I'll ready him for bed, Cora. William and I still have things to talk about."

Cora fixed a probing stare on Alida, who did her best to ignore the old woman. After a few moments, Cora left. William shrugged into his nightshirt, crawled beneath the covers and turned his back.

Alida sat on the edge of his bed. "William, let me explain what your father said. He's not well, and we must not take to heart what he says just now."

"No, Miss. I know he hates me. It's all right." His voice was dull and years too old. "Goodnight."

Alida stayed a few minutes more, but in spite of her pleas, William would not turn to her. Finally she stood and made her way to her own room. There, she curled up in her bed, shivering, knees tucked inside her nightdress, tight to her belly. She drew up quilts, for the wind again blustered in off the sea, howled at her window and rattled the shutters, but its roar was not as fearsome as Cooper's scowl and icy smile. Any reasonable word she hoped to say to him bubbled inside, unsaid, fermenting into a sour mash of growing fear.

She thought of Rafe and how she had believed him a lonely, damaged man who somehow got on with life without punishing everyone around him like her husband had done. He was wary of love, but no more than she. She hoped they might find their way. If only she could get word to him. Cooper's mood had twisted into deeper madness today. For William and herself, she had to get them away.

She calmed, thinking of rescue. Stretching, fingertips touching her lips, the other hand palming her belly, she recalled the change in Rafe the few times they were together, how sure of himself he had been. Had she truly believed it was some mystical "power of a woman's love" giving him strength to straighten his twisted spine and the ability to boldly confront a man like Martin Cooper?

Love? Was it love? The word had slipped easily into her thoughts. It must be love. Finally, sweeter musings lulled her to sleep in spite of the raging storm outside the house as well as in her mind.

A thunderous noise and sizzling flash woke her, but faded, leaving murky darkness. Her heart pounded in the sudden silence. She had been dreaming of angry seas and rows of angelic lights showing her a path to safety. In the dream she ran to the lights, glancing over her shoulder. Rafe Bishop stood on the rocks and called to her but she could neither follow the lights nor return to him. She stood mired in the middle, sand sucking her under.

She shook herself more awake. Only a dream. She managed to calm her breathing. A shutter had blown open outside her window and banged at the wall. She burrowed into her pillows, covering her head with a blanket, but the predatory wind howled, crashing the shutter again. She threw off the covers and vaulted from the bed, dashed to the window to unlatch it, and stretched out to grasp the shutter. Its hook had been torn away. Alida leaned out further, her belly balanced on the sill, fumbling for the shutter. Lightning flashed, illuminating the sky and sea below.

A ship tossed in the waves beyond the rocks. She drew in breath when she saw it, but exhaled, relieved, when she realized it was headed safely out to sea. From out along the rocks came a steady glow. A row of lights? They burned more brightly, showing a way. The wrong way. The ship changed course, battling the wind, heading for the lights. "No," she breathed. "Go back." The lights blinked out. Another lightning flash showed the ship heading for the rocks, merciless wind driving it in.

"No, please no," she whispered, backing away, leaving the shutter to slam at the wall. The crew, the passengers—she imagined their horror when they understood it was too late to run to safer seas. Another flash lured her back to the window. The wind ripped the ship's sails apart, but it turned in spite of the torn canvas flapping around the mast. It wallowed, yet moved out to sea.

She spun, her nightdress billowing around her, and sprinted to the door. She would fetch William from his room and keep him with her. In the storm they might be able to slip away. Seeing a ship escape from lights where no lights should be opened her to the possibility of escape and flooded her with courage.

The latch wouldn't open. She shouted, pounded and kicked it, then leaned in and pressed her forehead to the sturdy oak. Like the last time she tried to escape this house in a storm, but this time no one had left a key in the lock.

Alida backed away, trembling and chilled. Her limbs were ice. She knelt and built up the fire, then pulled a knitted shawl from the arm of the chair and wrapped it around her shoulders, gripping it beneath her chin. She stared into the dancing flames, rocking and shivering, knees to chest.

Was this a dream, too? The room was real enough. The fire burned hot; the pine logs oozed pitch, sizzled in the flames and gave off smoke. She inhaled it like healing incense. The floor felt solid beneath her. The soft shawl brushed her face and smelled of roses, and though her hands and feet would not thaw—this was no dream.

Eventually the lightning and thunder ceased. The wind stopped moaning and the shutter stopped its angry, uneven drumming. Alida lay curled by the fire, falling into half-sleep. Rafe had once asked her about lights, asked her to be wary and keep watch. She had wondered what he meant, wondered if he was simply jealous of poor, misunderstood Martin Cooper. Now, alone, locked in and kept from William, she knew better. She'd found the lanterns, and Rafe hadn't seemed at all surprised when she mentioned them. Would they still be under the kitchen table, if she could go down there now? Or had they been carried outside, by men determined to condemn a ship full of people to death?

She let herself drift into sleep. She would not go to the window. What if the ship had *not* escaped? She feared to see what she was powerless to stop.

Sunlight streamed through the open window and kissed her awake. Her limbs ached so, but why? Why was she lying on the floor before a dead fire? In the morning sunshine, last night's terror seemed a nightmare. She dressed hurriedly, twisting her hair into a careless knot and slipping on her stoutest shoes. Then she went to the door. Was it locked, or was that part of the dream? She turned the handle.

The door opened. She took a breath and edged down the landing to William's room. His door was unlocked, but he wasn't there. She turned and rushed down the stairs, pausing at the open doorway to the dining room to look for William, praying Martin Cooper's back would be turned. Cooper would be there. He was always up before dawn. But if she could find William, and somehow get out of the house . . .

"Where you off to, so skittery-like?"

Alida took a breath and stepped in. The dining room was empty but for Cora. Ham, sausage, eggs and freshly baked biscuits on the sideboard gave off an aroma that set Alida's mouth watering. Cora had just carried in a coffee urn.

Alida's gaze jumped from corner to corner.

"Mr. Coop ain't here." Cora waved a serving spoon toward Alida. "You lookin' like ol' devil wrung you out and throwed you back. Storm keep you wakeful?"

Alida nodded and crossed to the sideboard. She steadied her hand enough to pour a cup of coffee, inhaling the bracing aroma before taking a sip.

So Wild the Wind

Cora jabbed the spoon at her again and chuckled. "Which storm? The one what was outside, or the one blowin' around inside you? I heard how you was a-kissin' on the gimpy shopkeeper. Mr. Coop mighty put out over that, yes, ma'am. I hear him rantin' about it most of the night."

Alida rattled her cup into its saucer and set it on the table. Her face flushed hot, fueled by anger, not embarrassment. "It's no business of his—nor yours."

"Oh?" Cora pursed her lips. "Lots of things be ol' Cora's business. This is my last chance for peace. I ain't leavin' here 'cept I be dead. Mr. Coop needs what I give him for his pain." She grinned with sly humor. "Can give you something too, make life easier here seeing how you ain't run off yet."

"I won't leave William."

"Oh, William, is it? Then you best get used to his papa. Won't be so bad. Ol' Cora help you ease into it."

Alida took a sip of her cooling coffee.

"He give you your first kiss?"

"Who do you mean?"

"Who we talkin' about?" Cora slitted her eyes. "Me, I never had no kissin'. What man be brave enough to kiss this mouth?" She grinned.

"I'm a widow, Cora, not an innocent maiden. And our kiss was between friends."

Cora raised her eyebrows and pursed her lips.

Alida would not let this old woman destroy a memory of sweetness with her cynical smirks. She nodded toward the window. "Did the storm do much damage?"

Cora shrugged, scowling. Likely irritated the conversation had turned.

Alida gripped the handle of the cup. "And the ship? Was it saved?"

Cora froze. "Ain't been no ship."

241

"I saw it. It headed for lights along the rocks."

Cora tilted her head. "Ain't no lights there. Guess you had you some bad dreams."

"I saw it. I saw the lights and saw them disappear. Those lanterns. You know what I mean."

"You see such a thing, why not come down and yell about it?"

"I yelled and screamed, especially after I found my door locked."

Cora's face went ashy gray. "No," she whispered. "You hear me, gal? Wasn't nothing but a dream."

Alida gripped the edge of the table. "I mean to see for myself."

Cora's hand snaked out and snatched at Alida's. "Don't go stirring things up past fixing. You push him past what he can bear and he'll not see you no more. He'll see *her*. Then I can't do nothing and . . ." She took a breath, wincing and pushing the heel of her hand against her breastbone. "I can't stop what's bound to be. Didn't I say I see death in a flame? Maybe somebody's death be the only way peace can come for Cora."

William clattered in through the open door. "Miss Alida! I was in the attic room looking out the window. Did you hear the thunder? And that lightning! Wasn't it grand?"

Alida hugged him, laughing. "You aren't ever frightened by storms, William? I'm pleased you're feeling better."

He ducked his head and blushed. "I don't mind storms. I like mornings after they move on 'cause Father is nicer after a storm."

"Yes'm," Cora muttered, smirking as she moved around the table, lifting lids on dishes growing cold. "His papa do like him a wild night."

"Grab a biscuit, William. We'll walk down along the shore, maybe farther," Alida said, keeping her gaze on Cora. The old woman seemed indifferent now, as if she'd given up. Alida's pulse beat faster. They could get away. She and William, far away.

"Father doesn't usually let me go right after a storm, but days later all kinds of things wash up."

"Yes, they do," Alida whispered, shuddering. "But let's go right now. There may be danger, so you must stay by me and not go running off."

William hopped from foot to foot, his eyes bright, laughing. "There's no danger, Miss. We're not going *in* the water. That would be silly." He grabbed a sausage and a biscuit.

"Yes. That would be silly, but you never know what we'll find." Alida glanced again at Cora, but she looked pointedly away.

Martin Cooper yanked a sweat-soaked shirt off over his head and splashed tepid water on his face, neck and forearms. He toweled dry, shrugged into a clean shirt and waist-coat, then slumped in a chair. Last night's work was invigorating yet exhausting. Only a small ship, but a good cargo. No weapons, but tools were easy to sell, and there were no troublesome survivors.

He glowered into the mirror across the room. He looked like the devil himself. When did his eyes take on such a haunted look? And his hair—when did it go so gray? He drew the back of his hand across his chin. He needed a shave.

He closed his eyes, desperate to get past memories that plagued him whenever he had to venture to the rocks. Mirlito was gone. Where, he couldn't guess. The other two had to be kept near the house, kept watchful, so he'd gone himself. He feared to see *her* there, running from him, accusing him with horror-filled eyes. He lowered his head into his hands and squeezed, hard, harder. She hadn't been there last night. Perhaps because she was here in the house. Maybe it was truly her, returned to him. He massaged his temples and the blinding pain receded, though he knew he needed Cora's special brew. So much better than the opium he sometimes had to take.

Yes, the woman was—but she tormented him now, just like then. His work had always been so important, to keep money flowing for weapons and supplies. Even now he'd heard of men active in Canada. During the war they had proudly worn the head of liberty cut from copper pennies on their lapels. Copperheads. Like deadly snakes. What a grand name. He would find them when he had enough guns. He'd join them to march south from Canada, or maybe north from here. All the way to Washington. Or maybe he'd buy a ship. He'd sail into New Orleans with the Stars and Bars flying proudly again.

His head throbbed dully, like a hammer smashing into sand. It came on him like this whenever he thought of the past. He imagined the pain came to fill the emptiness. Yes, he was empty of his true self. That creature haunted the Carolinas, wandered along the Ashley River. He'd never meant to live here forever. He'd been trapped here. His heart could not truly beat here. Was that why his wife called him heartless? She didn't understand his love of home. She liked it here. She rejoiced at the news of surrender, not caring who won, just thankful he didn't have to fight.

He pulled himself out of the past. The woman in his house now was not his wife. She was Alida Garrison. She was more practical, less emotional, but she was still a true Southern lady. She would understand how he missed that way of life once he had a chance to describe it to her.

Her name was Alida. But was it? Might it not be a ruse to confuse him, punish him?

He jammed a fist against his temple. The sharp, throbbing pain had begun again. He pushed up from the chair, swayed to a night table and braced himself against it. He couldn't wait to find Cora. She was so slow sometimes. Just now he couldn't tolerate her dithering ways, so he poured a generous dose of his own medicine and waited until he could blink away the pain. When he felt the opium take hold, he pushed his arms into his coat, brushing at a speck of lint. Finally he tugged open the night table drawer, took out his derringer, and slipped the pistol into his coat pocket, as was his habit. He was usually the first down to breakfast, then William, then the woman. The order was wrong this morning. He wouldn't allow it to happen again. Structure had to be maintained.

He eased down the stairs, the polished banister smooth beneath his hand, and gazed at his paintings of sailing ships and his tapestries showing battles at sea. He took in the gleaming teak and rosewood furniture, nearly as grand as the pieces gracing his home outside Charleston. News had come to him about the plantation house being burned by the rabble led by the monstrous Sherman on his march through the Carolinas, but Cooper would not believe it. His home waited for him. He knew it did.

He closed his eyes and visualized the stately, moss-bearded oaks guarding the lane, the fragrant flower-laden vines twining across the veranda to shade cultured men in fawn-colored linen coats and women dressed like flowers themselves, skirts swaying like bells to accompany their lilting laughter. And from the slave cabins came the soft singing, the moving, poignant melodies.

Indignation suddenly burned in his belly, rising to his throat. He nearly stumbled on the bottom step. *His* people never spoke of freedom. He'd used a firm hand, of course. A man had to be stern. But he was always fair. They were like his children. The North could never understand. Just look at Cora, so old, but wasn't she a child?

He pulled himself back from reverie. Men like Rafe Bishop had stolen his life, stolen his people. They likely died in misery and chaos, for how could they survive without him? He blinked away tears. How he missed them, grieved for them. They were all so dear.

He entered the dining room and spied Cora. She was all he had of the old days. One wizened hag. No butler, no maids, no smiling little boys waiting to run messages. Only Cora and a cook and a few people from the village coming in to clean and garden now and then. He poured his coffee and speared a sausage from a silver chafing dish, eating it off the fork. "Where's William?"

"With her. She come and had her some coffee, then take William off. He didn't eat hardly nothing."

"That's his loss, isn't it? He'll just have to wait until lunch."

Cora shook her head. "She knows."

"Knows what?" He grimaced at eggs gone cold, and filled his plate with biscuits and ham before sitting down.

"Saw a ship. Saw lights burn and flicker out. She's asking."

Cooper sprang from his chair. "Where is she?"

"She with William, I say. Why you so worked up? You think your evil ways gonna last forever?"

Cooper strode toward the door.

Her rasping voice followed him. "You got to let her go."

He turned to glare. "I'll do what I like."

"What, you thinking she another chance?"

"Don't go too far, Cora."

"Won't do no better with her. She high-minded too."

"High-minded? So what am I, a pirate? I am fighting for our way of life."

"Our? Ain't *my* way." She spat the words.

"Yes, as you have often reminded me, you are free. Yet you stay in my house, eat my food." He sneered at her.

"You promise me peaceful days. The end of me is comin' fast. I don't care about nothing in this world but peace."

He left her muttering, strode from the room and took the stairs two at a time. He glanced into William's room, the woman's room, then headed down again and looked in the library before returning to the dining room. Cora stood as he'd left her, her head high.

"Where is she?"

"Like I say. With William."

"Not in the house?"

"They go lookin' at the water."

"Damn you." Cooper strode to the window and jerked back the lace curtain. There they were, striding across the sand, the wind whipping her skirts and hair, snagging William's hat and obliging him to chase it. Were they laughing? William retrieved his hat and ran back to her. She took his hand. They ran, ran to the sea. Horror filled him. No, not again. Where was the guard he'd set to watch the house? If that idiot had dozed off . . .

He slammed out the front door and down the steps to the path, passing the hired guard on the way. The useless oaf was tying up his pants, had gone off to relieve himself at the worst possible moment. "Why didn't you stop them, you fool?" Cooper growled, on his way toward the latched gate. He kicked it open. It splintered with a satisfying crack. He sprinted across sand that sucked at his boots, slowing him, leaving water-filled holes. Anguish twisted his mind, his heart. Just as it did when he'd run after them before, screaming her name. This time he saved his breath.

Waves whispered against the sand, gulls squawked as they took flight, his boots crunched shells and rocks. The wind swirled, covering the sound of his pursuit. She didn't know he was close until he grabbed her arm and swung her around. He clutched her to his chest. "You," he stammered. "You—you can't do this again. By God, not again."

She leaned away, her fists wedged between them, and glared

up at him. "William and I are going past the rocks and into town."

"I forbid it." He gripped her tighter against him. His body stirred from pressing her so close. Ah, she must be feeling how he throbbed. Her eyes, blue pools in a sky of white, opened wide and fear crept into them as she struggled. He smiled to see the fear and held her closer.

"Father, stop!" William wedged himself between them. "Father, don't. You're hurting her."

Cooper let her go. She stumbled, nearly falling. William steadied her, his head at the level of her ribs, his little-boy's arms tightening around her waist as he twisted his head to glare at his father. Cooper blinked and then turned his back, closing his coat to hide his desire, until it drained away. How ridiculous to want a woman so much, how crude to show it.

"I saw a ship last night," she said.

He shrugged, his back still to her. "Cora told me what you dreamed."

"It was no dream. I saw a ship and lights where no lights should be. Like the ones we saw from our ship, the ones leading us to destruction. The lanterns from your kitchen."

"Go to the house." Cooper spoke quietly, then turned his head and glared at William over one shoulder. "Go now!"

The boy let go of the woman and stepped forward. He raised his chin defiantly, standing in front of her, shielding her. "No, Father. I won't."

The two of them, so alike, mother and son. He blinked and shook his head. No. He had to remember, she was not the other. He faced her, fisting both hands and stepping closer. "Return to the house, or by God!" He pulled her away from the boy and showed her the little derringer. "It only holds two shots," he whispered. "But I won't need more. I'll carry you if I must." He smiled. "But only you." He flicked his gaze to William, then back to her. "You understand? If you come now, William comes with you. Once you're home, if you leave, William *never* will. Never."

She sucked in a breath, her eyes like great blue pools, brimming with tears. Wind grabbed her hair, tangling it around her face. She pulled a long strand from across her eyes, nodding. The blue pools had iced over. "We'll both come." She hugged the boy to her side and he buried his face against her. "But I know," she whispered.

"What? What did you say?"

"I know what you've done, what you do. I once pitied you, thinking of how you grieved for your wife and your lost home, a ruined man. I imagined you and I might somehow be the same in our grief." She covered her mouth with one hand and he had to lean close to hear her muffled words. "My child. My sister and all the others." She pushed William a little ahead, as if to get him far away. "You killed them," she whispered. "Murderer."

She strode past him then and caught up to William, took his hand and ran with him all the way to the house.

Murderer? She called me murderer. Just as before. Cooper stood shivering in the wind, his head pounding again. He needed Cora after all, but would she help him now? Cora was angry too. The sea beyond the rocks heaved and roared, as if with laughter.

CHAPTER TWENTY-NINE

Rafe picked his way down a crumbling path. Near the rocks along the shore, he could turn and stare up at Cooper's house, but Cooper could stare down at him just as easily. He wouldn't be able to get Alida and William away from this direction.

He scrambled back up the path to *Señora* Rivera's house and caught his breath, then hurried to where she was working in the garden. "I need your horse, *Señora*."

She laughed. "Well, he's not much of a horse."

"He'll do."

She raised an eyebrow, still working on the herbs. "Bring him home by dark. Unless he takes me visiting, he wants only his stall for sleeping."

"Is there a saddle?"

"Can you see me astride? No, we both prefer his cart."

Rafe hitched the grumbling horse to the cart. Better anyway. He could more easily get Alida and William away. Cooper's house loomed gray and dismal in a rolling fog. Rafe managed to get within six feet of the steps to the veranda, but no farther, for the horse was disinclined to move a step more. The beast let its head droop, asleep as soon as Rafe stepped down. At least he had no fear of the animal wandering away. He bounded up the steps and knocked at the heavy door, forgetting to limp, forgetting everything but Alida.

The door eased open on well-oiled hinges. Lamplight flickered from behind Cooper's old servant, though night had not yet fallen. She grinned. Was showing those hideous teeth a ploy meant to scare intruders? Rafe pretended he didn't notice she looked like a shark and smiled politely. "I've come to call on Mrs. Garrison," he said.

The old woman scowled and closed the door quietly in his face, as if she'd looked but found no one there. He raised his fist to knock again, then had another thought. He turned and trotted down the steps, backing up to scan the second-story windows. Which room was Alida's? Would he be able to access it?

The front door opened again. This time Martin Cooper stood in the light.

Rafe ran up the steps. "I've come to see . . ."

"Yes, I was told." Cooper smiled, an affable host. "You appear spry today. A miracle cure, perhaps?"

"Something like that. Please tell her I'm here."

"The lady is, alas, unwell. Cora's caring for her, likely why the poor old thing was so rude just now. She's of an age when she can't do two things at once." He gave an icy smile. "I suppose I should find a better servant and turn Cora out to fend for herself, since I'm not obliged to keep her until she dies as was my practice in the old days. As you once pointed out, things have changed."

"Indeed. Now she's free, you wouldn't be able to get any kind of price for her."

Cooper's smile faded.

"Mrs. Garrison is ill? I'll fetch *Señora* Rivera."

"No need. An attack of nerves brought on by the storm last night. Memories of her ordeal have triggered a host of imagined fears."

"I'd not thought the lady so fanciful."

"Ah, she shows strangers a brave front."

"I still wish to see her."

"Of course. But first I'd like a word. Come in. We'll have a brandy against what will likely soon again be foul weather." Cooper shuddered. "I sense the wind brings us another storm. I am usually right about such things." He clapped his hands together. "I don't often have a guest." He gestured for Rafe to follow him.

The library was impressive. Books lined every wall. High-backed chairs, deeply cushioned, claimed the corners, each with its own lamp, lit and glowing. The ornately carved marble mantelpiece gleamed with pearl-like luster. Everything spoke of cultured richness, the room of the reasonable man now standing before him, not the wild-eyed tyrant Rafe had last seen. "A bit early in the afternoon for brandy," Rafe said.

"Come now, sir." Cooper gave a broad wink. "Surely any time is appropriate for good brandy. Think of it as a shield against the coming storm."

Rafe nodded.

"Good, good." Cooper rubbed his hands together and reached for a decanter.

Rafe, wary, took the glass but didn't drink until Cooper poured his own from the same decanter and drank.

"It *is* pleasant, isn't it?" Cooper said.

Rafe sipped and couldn't help a sigh. "I haven't tasted finer since before the war."

Cooper glanced around the room. "I have many fine things." He smiled. "No doubt you would like a house like this."

"Wouldn't any man?"

Cooper's face paled and his eyes glittered like ice. "Most don't have the wit or fortitude to build the life they want. They just take from those of us who do." He grasped at the air and made a fist, then cocked his head and smiled. "I know what I want and how to get it. What kind of man are you, sir?"

Rafe made his expression blank. "Why do you care?" He gave

Cooper a thin smile. "None of our dealings have been pleasant."

"Oh, misunderstandings only, don't you think?" Cooper's loud laugh rang false. He quickly sobered. "The way you look at my library and hold your brandy glass, I see you envy me. You have been damaged. That scar, the limp. Your government failed you, didn't it? You should have some reward for your loss, am I right?" He waved his hand as if erasing what Rafe might say. "No need to answer. A man who works for me once spoke of you. He said you wanted to rise in the world. He thought you might be useful. And since he seems to have disappeared . . ."

Rafe's heart pounded. *What had Mirlito said?* He tore his gaze away from Cooper, for the man might read truth in his eyes. He turned to face an opposite wall, gathering his words. A portrait hung there between two bookcases. Startled, he stepped closer. "But that's, she's . . ."

"Yes, my wife," Cooper said from just behind him. "How I miss her." He cleared his throat. "So, Mr. Bishop, we should talk again soon. You could make a better life for yourself with my help."

Rafe turned, thrown off-balance by how much Alida resembled Cooper's wife and confused by this affable version of the man. "Perhaps." He put down his glass. "Now could you please tell Mrs. Garrison . . ."

"I'll tell her you stopped by." He turned and headed for the hall, a clear sign that the visit was over.

Rafe followed him. "I mean now, sir. I have a message for her." The swish of a skirt on the landing above made him look up. Alida stood there, leaning slightly over the railing. She didn't look ill, yet something was wrong. She was holding a lantern. Not a lamp or a candle, as was usual for indoors. She lifted it and gazed at the flame, then at him. He shook his head, puzzled.

"Mrs. Garrison," Cooper called up to her. "You should be in

bed. Cora never should have let you up."

"Alida," Rafe said. "Are you ill?"

She gripped the railing with one hand, holding her lantern high with the other, and drew in a deep breath.

Cooper strode partway up the steps and halted, slipping a hand into his coat pocket. "Now, madam, remember our agreement? You promised to rest." He stared at Alida like a snake with a spellbound mouse.

"I have the cart, Alida. Come for a drive. It's still a nice evening. The storm's holding off." Rafe set a foot on the staircase, Cooper just ahead of him. "A short drive. Maybe William could come."

"I can't. William is—he's resting. Please go, Rafe." Alida's mouth trembled and she shook her head, though her expression pleaded for help, asking him to understand, to do something.

"Why don't you come down and we can talk."

"No! I can't. Something might happen." She pressed her fingers to her lips and turned her gaze to Cooper, then backed away. One last time within Rafe's sight, she raised the lantern high, then lowered it and rushed away down the hall.

Cooper backed down the stairs. Rafe glanced sidelong at him.

"See how upset she is?" Cooper said with a vulture's smile. "I fear it's the return of fever. Your visit was no comfort, so I ask you not to come again for a while."

"I'll be back later today with *Señora* Rivera. She can care for Mrs. Garrison like she did before."

"Mrs. Garrison is in no state for visitors."

"She'll see us." Further conversation with this man would lead nowhere, so Rafe walked slowly out the door and down the front steps and climbed into the cart. The sleepy horse was slow to move, but after a prodding with a switch, it sorted itself into a shambling walk. Rafe clenched his hands around the reins, thinking. That lantern—a signal? He turned the horse toward shore. The animal balked, wanting to get home to fodder and a warm stall, but Rafe flicked his switch and forced it into a trot. After a few minutes he pulled up by the rocks and watched the surf roll in, the sun setting behind him.

He looked back at the house on the bluff. One light burned in an upstairs window, showing the silhouette of a woman who likely thought herself forsaken.

CHAPTER THIRTY

Martin Cooper's threat echoed in Alida's head. "I'll kill him," he had said. "I'll kill anyone to keep you. You won't leave me again." Minutes before Rafe's visit, he had shown Alida the pistol in his pocket, while madness flickered in his red-rimmed eyes and spittle webbed the corners of his mouth.

"If you leave, or try to get a message to anyone, I'll hide William. Yes, that's what I'll do. Hah! If someone comes, or I'm killed, William will never be found." Cooper smiled then, ice-cold. "He'll die."

"But he's your son," Alida said, horror straining her voice.

Cooper shrugged. "If I hadn't grasped him five years ago, I might have saved—saved her." He closed his eyes, nodding slowly. "I'll not mind losing him. The sea is where he was meant to go. Do what I say, or I might simply drown him." He nodded. "Do you understand? You have returned to me and nothing else matters."

The conviction in his crazed eyes sickened her. When she heard Rafe's voice she'd felt a blaze of hope, but she'd had to demand he go. The loss of that hope still hollowed her.

Now Cooper pushed into her room, sneering. "What was that silly business with the lantern? The man is too stupid to understand such a cryptic message, my dear. Like most men of his class, he's greedy. You should have seen the way he sipped my brandy." Cooper rubbed his hands together. "He has no idea what I'm really doing."

"Nor do you, sir. You have surely lost your mind."

He raised a fist. She braced for the blow, but he stopped, gave a guttural curse and abruptly left the room. His heavy tread pounded down the stairs. A moment later, the front door slammed.

Gone. He had gone. Alida rushed to William's room but he wasn't there. She called to him, but no one answered. She stood motionless, fighting a desire to scream. Where was William? How frightened he must be. Perhaps Cora would help. She'd raised William, after all. Surely she wouldn't want him harmed. Alida paced the room, thinking. Rafe had said he would return. Now she feared for his safety as well as William's, while praying he'd find a way.

From outside the house came the sound of hammering. It jarred her from her thoughts. She looked up just as William appeared in the doorway. "Miss Alida?"

Relief surged through her. "William!" She started toward him, arms held out.

"Father says—he says to go in the library." William shuddered. "We've got to have lessons, he says. But, Miss? It's almost time for bed." The boy rubbed his eyes. "I don't understand, but that's what he said."

"You've been crying." She knelt and hugged him close.

"A little. The noises kinda scared me."

"Me too, William." She stood and took his hand. "Let's go see what that's about, shall we?"

They made their way downstairs to the library. The shutters were closed across the windows and the French doors. Alida drew a shaky breath. Now she knew what the hammering was. The shutters had been nailed in place.

William stared at them, wide-eyed. "I can't go outside anymore, Miss Alida, not even with you?"

Alida felt her face drain of color as she clutched William's hand tighter. "Not just now."

"Is another storm coming? Is that why Father closed us up? I wish he didn't, 'cause I found some big, jaggedy rocks and brought 'em to show you. They're on the veranda."

Alida drew him close again. "Yes, William. I'm sure that's why. We'll look at those rocks just as soon as we can. I'm happy we're together, though, aren't you?"

He nodded and stayed near, subdued.

By late evening wind roared in from the sea and rain drummed on the veranda outside. William leaned against the nearest window. "I wish we could see outside, don't you?"

"It's so loud we know it's raining. We don't need to see. It's a good thing we didn't go out." Her gaiety sounded false even to her.

"Father said—he said I couldn't ever go out." The boy recited the next words as if rehearsing a speech. "He said he for—forbidded it."

Alida kissed the top of his head. "Forbade, William. The word is forbade."

"And he said if I was bad, he'd make you go away." He swiped at his nose.

"Then we'll both be good. I'm not leaving you, William." She held him at arm's length, bending at the knees to look into his eyes. "Not ever. Now listen carefully. A time may come when you must do what *I* say, not your father. Only me. Can you do that?"

William's eyes widened. He nodded. "Yes, Miss. Miss? Cora calls ghosts haints. She says Mama is one. Are you a haint, Miss? Are you—are you—*her*?" He whispered the last word.

Alida brushed hair from his forehead. "No, sweetheart. But I would be proud to be your mama, as she would be proud seeing how brave and clever you are."

"Why is Father mean to us?"

"He is very ill. We have to get away and get help for him."

William nodded. "His head hurts bad."

Alida blew out a breath. "Yes. I know it does. Let's turn up the lamp. Maybe you could draw something for me? A sailing ship?"

"I can draw a clipper, Miss Alida. It has five masts. Father used to have one and he has a painting of it. I can draw it without looking." The boy fetched paper and pencil and went to work, his tongue caught between his teeth.

Alida sat nearby, smiling, hoping to appear calm while her insides roiled and shuddered. How to escape? Who would believe such threats to a child? And if Rafe believed them, what might he do? She must have seemed insane to him, with her lantern and little pantomime, yet how to make him understand? He couldn't simply rush in and take them. What if Cooper used that pistol on Rafe?

The storm howled outside, a little less strongly, it seemed to her. The waning of its power, slight as that was, steadied her. *In real life, heroes don't charge in and sweep the princess away from the ogre in the tower. Especially not a kind and gentle hero.* Rafe Bishop was supposed to uncover plots, not single-handedly put them down. His gentle nature was what drew her to him, for she'd had her fill of angry warriors. If she could only find a way to fight free of this nightmarish house. Once she and William escaped, she would happily fall into Rafe's arms, but she couldn't simply wait for rescue. There must be a way out.

Cora brought dinner on a tray, but neither spoke nor looked Alida in the eye. By bedtime, Alida's brave front faltered. She tossed cushions on the floor and arranged a drowsy William there, his head in her lap. Were they to be locked in the library all night? What could they use for a chamber pot? She couldn't help a smile at such a practical turn of mind. Princesses in towers likely never needed chamber pots.

She was nearly dozing off when the door flew open and Cooper strode in. He snatched William up and without a word, carried him away. The boy flailed and kicked but Cooper ignored him and Alida's pleas.

He left the door ajar. She ran across the hall after them. "Where are you going? Mr. Cooper, stop! Please."

"Miss Alida!" William screamed, pushing at his father, fighting him. "No, Father. I don't *want* to go."

Alida started up the stairs just behind the struggling pair. "Please, sir. Please wait. Let him go. I'll take him up to bed. *I* will, please."

Mr. Cooper turned to her, his face like granite, his eyes coldly determined. Determined to do what?

Alida stepped closer and touched his arm. Beneath his sleeve the muscles flexed, rock-hard. "Yes," she said with as much calm as she could muster. "That's it. I'll get William settled and you and I can talk." She moved her hand to William's sweaty head. He was sucking in hitching breaths and swiping at his streaming eyes. "It's all right, sweetheart. Let's just—"

Cooper spun away and pushed her with a swipe of his elbow. Not hard, but enough to knock her against the banister. She pulled up and started forward again, fists raised.

"Miss!" William wailed. "Father, you hurt her!"

Before she could reach them, hands clutched Alida around the waist. Cora's earthy scent enveloped her. "Tell him you is all right. Tell him and leave him be." She hissed the words in Alida's ear. "Think of that boy. Don't do him no good being so scared."

Alida struggled. "No, Cora. Let me go."

"William? Your Miss Alida? She fine, child," Cora sang out. "Jus' fine. You go with your papa now."

"He'll hurt him, Cora. He'll do worse than hurt him."

Cora dragged her back and down the two steps to the hallway.

"He gonna lock up that boy but ain't gonna do nothin' more long as you stay here."

"How do you know?" Alida sagged against the wall as Cora released her, rage and fear receding, leaving weary resignation in their wake. The old woman patted her arm, tugging her sleeve, putting it right.

"I knows it 'cause the kind of crazy he is—it like fox crazy. I won't promise he won't do more if you push him to it, but he is lost in his own dream-time. You are it and William is the key."

"But William is so frightened."

"Don't do no good makin' him worse. You got to be stronger for the boy." Cora huffed an impatient sigh like she'd had enough of all of them. "Don't I know it? Don't do the little ones no good seein' their mamas carryin' on about something they can't fix. Yes, Lord, don't I know it." Cora limped away, shaking her head.

Alida held to the wall as she stumbled to the front door. She threw it open and stared out into the rain. Yes, here was a way out, but she wouldn't go, not without William and Cooper knew it. She plodded up the stairs to her room, covering her ears against William's muffled cries for her to come. She stood outside Cooper's door and tried the knob but knew it would be locked. Gradually the boy's cries quieted. His father's voice quieted too until he sounded like any other man gentling a frightened son.

She wiped tears away and loosened her bodice, removed her shoes and fell across the bed. For a while she drifted in and out of sleep. She hadn't eaten the food Cora brought them. Now the old woman came in with a fresh carafe of water. Fearing to be drugged, she asked Cora to sip from the pitcher. The old woman smirked and sipped. "Didn't I say be gone from here? Tol' you long time back. Now look." Cora shook her head. "You thinkin' to come to ol' Cora for help, but ain't no help. You make ever'body in this house love you. See where it lead?"

"Everybody, Cora? You?"

"I don't love nobody. Ever'body I ever love been took away. No ma'am, ol' Cora don't love nobody, don't want to love nobody. You on your own."

The old woman shuffled out. Alida thought over Cora's words, recalling similar feelings after the shipwreck. But those feelings had changed. She had plenty of love.

She breathed in deeply and coughed at the reek of cigar smoke. It wafted from beneath her door, as if the smoker stood just outside. She'd shot the bolt, but doubted it would keep even Cora out if she took a notion to break through. She pushed every bit of furniture she could move against the door while outside, the rain rattled against her window and pooled on the sill. She had to think, had to—but she'd had so little to eat, so little rest.

She heard something. Was that Rafe's voice? Was he downstairs again? Her heart burst into a wild rhythm, but no more words came. She turned up her lamp and then went to the window. Was someone standing on the shore? She waved, but the figure turned and trudged away through the rain. Chilled, she climbed into bed and turned on her side to face the door.

A key clicked in the lock. The door rattled, but the bolt held. She sat up, clutching the quilt to her chest. The door opened as far as the piled furniture allowed. She watched in terror as her improvised barricade shifted until space opened enough for an arm, a leg, then the rest of a man to slip inside.

She scrambled out of bed and backed away, searching for something to throw.

"Nice touch," Cooper said. "A melodrama. The virgin bride, fearful of her lord and master." His breath rasped and the stink of brandy and sweat wafted from him.

"I'm no one's bride and you're certainly not my master," she said, hating the way her voice trembled.

"Oh, but you'd like to be someone's bride. Bishop's? That mewling peddler. He wouldn't know what to do with a woman."

"You're drunk. Leave my room."

"Leave—my—room." He mimicked her in a nasal whine. "Call yourself Alida if that pleases you," he whispered, inching closer. "I know who you are." His voice changed to a whine. "I had wanted to win your love. To win back your heart. I tried so hard."

"Mr. Cooper, I am not your wife. Your wife is dead."

He took two quick steps forward, then stumbled sideways. He scrubbed at his face with both hands. "Why can't you love me? I've been kind."

"Kind? You threatened to kill your child!"

"What does that have to do with us? Well, no matter. It's too late." He lowered his hands, leaped forward with a growl, and grasped her around the waist.

She screamed, not for help, but in outrage. There was no help in this house.

He pawed her dress apart. She twisted away. He snagged a handful of hair and jerked her backward, throwing her to the floor. He sank to his knees and straddled her, staring into her face, then lay full length on her, pinning her to the floor, grinding his hips against her, muttering nonsense. She worked her fingers between them, aiming for his eyes.

A shadowy figure pushed through the half-open door, the head no higher than her dresser. *William?* "William, run! Run for help. For the love of God—"

"You think I am the child? You funny woman. And for the love of God? I do not recall God doing much for me, for love or hate."

Alida kept struggling. She could see the smaller figure clearly now. "Mirlito! Help me."

He stepped closer. "I am supposed to help you into your grave, little woman."

Cooper rolled off her and stumbled to his feet. He grabbed Alida's wrist, jerked her upright and threw her on the bed. Then he spun to face Mirlito. The little man widened his stance. With great care, he set his bowler hat on the night table and folded his arms across his chest.

"Get out, Mirlito!" Cooper shouted.

Alida got to her feet and edged around the bed.

"Ah, *Señor,* you are drunk," Mirlito sneered. "I see now how you want this woman." He pointed at Cooper's groin. "That snake pushes from your trousers, wanting her." He laughed, bending over, his hands on his knees. "You are crazy, thinking she is the wife, in truth?" He shook his head. "That one would not stand by you. She chose death. But this one would live, I think. She is strong and would more likely kill *you.*"

Cooper advanced on him, swaying. "Don't you dare speak of—"

"If this one goes away, your heart will break, so Molly said." Mirlito shook his head. "I was going to take her from you, but did not think to see you in her room." He shrugged. "No matter. Now I may choose who dies. Now my knife can do its work."

Alida seized her moment and dashed past Cooper. Mirlito jumped between her and the door. "Oh, *Patrón.* Molly will laugh when I tell her how the woman ran, hating you more than fearing me."

Alida stumbled against the wall, slipped down and covered her head with her arms as Cooper rushed forward, giving the little man's face a smashing blow. Mirlito yelped, but stayed upright. He laughed and scrambled across the piled furniture and out onto the landing. Cooper followed, roaring.

Using the wall for balance, Alida pushed to her feet. Let the animals fight. She would find William and get them both away.

CHAPTER THIRTY-ONE

Rafe pawed through *Señora* Rivera's trunk. It should be here, wrapped in oil cloth, covered with a scrap of blanket. He dug down and deep, past his landlady's extra clothes, beneath tarnished candlesticks and cracked dishes. He heard scuffling at the doorway and spun, still in a crouch.

"You look for the pistol?" the *señora* said.

"You've seen it?"

"When I looked for something of my own. No mistaking a pistol, I think."

He turned back and resumed his search. "I can't find it."

"It is hidden."

He let his shoulders sag, then stood and turned slowly. He rubbed his hands down the seams of his trousers. "Please, good lady," he said quietly. "With respect, I ask you. I need the pistol."

She glared at him. "Why?" She stepped close and clasped her hands, shaking them as if in fervent prayer. "You have caught the greed for money like that evil little man? I curse the day I said his name to you."

He shook his head. "There are things I couldn't tell you then. I'm . . ." He gripped her clasped hands. "I beg you to trust me. I have a job to do. It has nothing to do with money. Alida is in danger. I have to get her and the boy away from Cooper."

She opened her eyes wide. "Then go! Go now. Why do you

wait? Always I have known that house held evil. *Señor* Cooper showing kindness to her was only a way of tricking us." She swept toward the butter churn. "The pistol is here. I have no goat, no cow, so I knew it would not be found." She tore off the top and fished out the pistol, holding it out to him on her palms like a holy offering. "I will go to Father Sebastian. I will go even to the *cantina* and find help for you."

Rafe took the pistol and kissed her forehead. "I knew I could count on you." He ran out of the house toward the *señora*'s patient horse. As he slipped the beast's bridle back on, he imagined the old woman rallying the men and Twyla at the *cantina*. Now that would be a sight. He urged the horse into a stumbling lope, ignoring the pain from the animal's blade-like backbone, and was at the house in a few minutes.

Leaving the horse frothing and spraddle-legged in the downpour, he kept to shadows, slipping unseen past a miserable-looking man huddled by the door. Wrapped in a rain-soaked coat, his hat pulled low, the man was not an enthusiastic guard. Rafe crept around to the back of the house. Near the locked back door, a lower window had been left ajar. Rafe slipped inside, head first. He fell against a rocking chair, but managed to avoid knocking over a small table. A lamp had been left on, turned low, and showed a simple room, likely Cora's. It smelled of herbs and the drying flowers he brushed against as he moved across to another door. This one opened to the kitchen. In the darkness he edged past a long work table, his pistol ready.

Sounds of struggle and running feet came from upstairs. He shoved through a swinging door, charged up the staircase and paused on the landing. A door creaked open. Cora peered out, holding a candle. She raised it high, squinting at him. He crouched less than four feet from her, his arms out straight, the gun pointed at her.

She grimaced like someone had just told her a bad joke.

"Death," she whispered. "She bring death jus' like I say."

"Where is she?"

"Seems death ride them waves and crawl up on shore with her." She chuckled and shook her head. "Time was, devil never trick me, but ever'thing too much nowadays." She blew out the candle, backed into the room and gently closed the door.

Rafe took a few more steps, then flattened his back against the wall as a child-sized figure darted from a nearby doorway. The figure disappeared around a corner into the dark.

"William?" Rafe hissed. "William, wait!"

Seconds later Cooper stumbled out, cursing, oblivious to Rafe. He rushed off in the opposite direction from where the small figure had gone.

Before Rafe could start after the boy, Alida shouted from the room. "Rafe? You've come. Do you have William?"

Relieved, he stepped away from the wall. "No, I . . ."

She screamed. Rafe charged forward, pushed through a half-open door and stumbled into a pile of furniture.

He looked up. Alida stood a few feet away, gripping fireplace tongs high over her head. Out of her reach, near a dark gap in the wall, stood Emiliano Mirlito, grinning. Blood ran from his nose and lip as he tossed a knife from hand to hand. "Ah, little woman," he said. "Cooper runs the wrong way, crazy man. He forgets the hidden door, a door to paradise, for many times I slipped through it when Molly lived in this room. I promised her to take you from him. So let us go now." He held his right hand over his heart. "Our bargain has been sealed." He kissed the air and moved the knife back to his right hand, holding his left out toward her. "You do not have to die. I will leave you somewhere in the hills. It will be our secret." He touched his lips with one finger.

Alida didn't move. "What about Mr. Cooper?"

"Later maybe I will kill him. He is no good to anyone. Probably he now runs all the way to my house." Mirlito laughed. "Come."

She shook her head. "I won't leave William. We have to find him."

"Ah, you ask too much. The boy?" He shook his head. "A boy is trouble."

Rafe eased up behind Mirlito. Alida saw him, but Mirlito was too full of words to notice her deep breath or her eyes flicking to Rafe and then away. Rafe brought the pistol down hard. The little man was so much shorter, the blow took him to his knees. His eyes rolled back and he dropped the knife as he crumpled to the floor.

Rafe kicked the knife across the room. Alida swallowed hard and lowered the tongs. She fumbled at tugging her torn dress together, then gave up and rubbed her hands down her skirt. "That—that was a big knife," she said. Her shaking hands rattled the fire tongs back into the stand.

She pushed at wildly tangled hair. Her chin trembled, her eyes glistened, and Rafe wanted to rush to her and take her in his arms, but he feared to upset what seemed a delicate balance.

"Wasn't that a big knife for such a little man to carry?" She spoke calmly, as if they discussed the weather.

"Yes, it was. Brought in for a special job, you might say."

"Murder?"

"Murder or protection from being murdered, I suppose. Not good for much else." Rafe watched her, his apprehension growing.

She edged around Mirlito's crumpled form and shook her head. "I don't know him. I've only seen him once or twice."

"He promised to take you from Cooper. Promised a woman named Molly." Rafe stepped closer to her. She seemed so vague. Would she faint?

"Cora mentioned Molly, but I don't know her."

"Well, Cooper used to. He wanted her and took her. Now he wants you."

She shook her head hard. "No—his wife. He thinks I am his wife." Alida leaned closer, but didn't touch him.

He reached out one hand slowly, palm up.

She frowned at it, then took it.

He drew her into his arms, holding her gaze. He touched her face with his fingertips. "I doubt we can understand what he's thinking." He kissed her cheek, gently, his lips lingering near her mouth. "We'll get William and I'll take you both to *Señora* Rivera. Then I'll go after Cooper. He's likely wandering out there in the storm, confused. We'll sort all this out later."

She stood straighter and puffed out a breath.

He kissed her mouth as tenderly as he knew how. "I love you," he whispered.

"Is that what we need to sort out?" She spoke the words against his mouth. He wrapped both arms around her and pulled her closer again. "I think that's the simplest part." He broke away. "Now." He handed her the pistol, curving her fingers around the grip. "Take this. It's mine from the war, a Navy Colt. It's hard to cock. You'll have to pull back hard."

"I could never use it."

"From what I saw of you and the fireplace tongs, I suspect you might. Until I find Cooper, we're in danger. Would you use it to protect William?"

"Of course."

He nodded. "Then protect yourself as well, for without you, William will have no one." He squatted down by Mirlito and shook the man's shoulder. Mirlito breathed deep but too fast. "This fellow is in a bad way."

She tucked the gun in her skirt pocket. Its handle protruded awkwardly. "What can we do for him?"

"Not much. We'll leave him for now." He spread a blanket over Mirlito.

"Rafe? Mr. Cooper said he would hide William. We have to search the house."

"I imagine he's with Cora."

They scrambled over the furniture and into the hall. Rafe went to the room next door, where he'd seen Cora, and shoved his way in. William cowered by the bed. Cora was nowhere to be seen.

"Here he is. Here!"

Alida pushed in and gathered the boy close. "Then hiding him was a lie to frighten me. It worked well." She took a breath and forced it out. "Find Cooper. Finish this."

Disheveled and fierce, she stood with the boy in her arms. Rafe hoped he could match her ferocity. He nodded once. "I will. Now go. I'll meet you at the *señora*'s house."

CHAPTER THIRTY-TWO

William whimpered and burrowed into Alida, his face against her throat. Had Cora given him something to keep him quiet? He smelled a little like the tonic Cora brewed. His arms and legs dangled limp as an armful of twine. She'd have to carry him.

"I was scared," he said. "People yelled and . . ." He yawned wide.

Alida breathed in the clean, soapy scent of his hair. His mouth was sticky with peppermint. Cora must have given him candy with the tonic. The scent consoled her, for she needed to believe in innocence, even as she possessed a gun and was told she had to be ready to shoot someone. She settled William against her shoulder, heading for the door, away from this grand house filled with reminders of a woman long dead. "If you are haunting here, rest easy," she whispered. "I will protect your child."

"Who are you talking to, Miss?"

"To myself, sweetheart." She stepped on her hem and realized her feet were bare. She would need shoes to make it down the graveled carriage road. She turned back through the hidden door that connected this room with hers and set William on a cushion while she found both shoes. She eyed the little man on the floor nervously. He hadn't even twitched since he fell, though he breathed slower now. Blood still seeped from his scalp and pooled around his head. Then, as she stared, he pushed to his knees and swayed. He climbed to his feet, scowling.

Alida cursed the stupidity of getting so far from William. The three of them now made a triangle. Mirlito might lunge either way.

The little man touched the back of his head, wincing. "How did you hit me? You were in front, yes?" He stared at the floor. "*Mi cuchillo?* Where is my knife?"

Alida's palm was slick with sweat. She drew the pistol from her pocket. "William, come here. You! Go while you can. Help is coming."

"Help?" He grinned and shuffled closer to William. The boy, who had inched toward Alida, froze.

Mirlito reached into his boot and brought out a long, slim blade. "This one here, she sometimes likes to work." He kissed the blade. "So often kept in the dark of my boot. She is patient, as am I." He gestured toward William. "Molly did not speak of this boy. I think I will not kill him." He grinned. "What do you think?"

William whimpered.

"Don't be afraid," Alida said. "This man is joking and will leave now so I don't hurt him."

Mirlito laughed, then winced and pressed one hand against the back of his head. He stared at the blood on his fingers. He jabbed his knife at her. "I am happy I have decided only to steal you. Though you are too skinny, it would be shameful to kill a woman with such sharp wit."

"I'm surprised you recognize wit."

He thrust out his bottom lip. "You wound me, *Señora.*" He narrowed his eyes. "Enough talk. Maybe I *will* kill you both after all." He took a step toward her.

Alida forced back the pistol's hammer. Rafe had been right. It took both thumbs and all her strength.

The door slammed open against the piled furniture as if the wind had blown it. Mirlito turned and Alida pointed the pistol at the floor. "Rafe? Thank God. I—"

She broke off. Cooper stood in the doorway, weaving from side to side. He leaned on the frame, his face bloody, madness flickering in his eyes.

"Where's Rafe?" Alida shouted. "What have you done to him?"

"Someone attacked me, but I will not be kept from you. So it was Bishop? He fought well for a cripple."

Mirlito grinned. "Now this little woman does not know who to shoot with her big pistol."

Cooper staggered into the room, glaring. "Mirlito, you are a roach, skittering around in the dark."

"Ah, but *la cucaracha* lives forever," Mirlito said, grinning wider.

William reached for Alida. Before she could grab him, Mirlito grasped the boy's nightshirt and hugged him close, the knife to his throat. A drop of blood welled around the point. Alida raised the pistol.

"Put that down, little woman." Mirlito grinned and pushed the point harder against William's skin. William yowled, his eyes shut tight. "You would shoot this boy?"

"No! I'm putting it down, see?" She placed the pistol on the chair, her hands trembling, then stretched her arms out to William.

Mirlito nodded at Cooper. "Now you step back or I will gut this boy. Who better than you to know what I can do."

William rolled his eyes, staring from Alida to his father.

"William, be brave," Alida said. She longed to scream, refused to cry.

"Oh, *sí*. Be brave. All will be well," Mirlito sneered. "Your papa has no choice."

273

"Slit him ear to ear for all I care," Cooper said. "It's the woman I want. He's nothing to me."

"Father?" William wailed. He closed his eyes and shrank from the blade at his throat.

Alida inched closer. "He doesn't mean that, William."

Mirlito shook his head slowly, his mouth turned down. "No, *Señora*." He threw Cooper a disgusted glance. "Even I am not so cold as this man. I have never before met such a man. His own son?"

Alida took a deep breath. "I care for William, but Cooper cares about *me*. Let the boy go. I am the better hostage."

"You are trying a trick?"

"Look at him!" Alida yelled, then lowered her voice. "He's out of his mind. Take me. Let William go."

Mirlito's eyes were slits. He nodded. "Come closer."

Alida edged slowly toward him, her eyes on the glinting sliver of steel at William's throat. Her heart hammered in her chest even as she took slow, deep breaths, moving within an arm's length, calculating how fast she might pull William away from the blade.

Mirlito moved it an inch from William's throat. Alida reached out. "Shh, William. Everything will be all right," she whispered.

Mirlito laughed. Cooper bellowed and launched himself forward. As he slammed into her, Alida grasped William's arm, jerked the child against her, and pulled him to the floor. William screamed, but Alida hauled him up and spun toward the door.

The men fell in her path. They rolled, both grappling for Mirlito's knife, twisting and grunting, holding each other in a violent embrace. Mirlito, so much smaller, wriggled away and jumped up again, still holding his blade, thrusting and slashing. He bared bloody teeth as he backed against the splintered door, then moved toward the side door.

Alida retreated. The men's fighting had toppled the chair

where she'd left the gun. The weapon was gone. "William," she said, lips against his ear. "Hide. Hide there between the dresser and the wall." She pried his hands away and set him on his feet. "Now, William."

Tears washed his face. He shook his head and gripped her skirts.

"I won't leave you. I have to find the gun." She gave him a push toward the hiding place.

Mirlito laughed, teasing Cooper with the knife. He lunged and danced close, then away, still blocking Alida's escape. William scooted to the wall and crouched, covering his face with his hands and peeking out from between his fingers.

Alida dropped to her knees, searching around the chair. She pushed thoughts of Rafe away. She would not grieve, not before she knew for sure she had lost him. Behind her, the men faced each other exchanging insults. Disgust for them both warred with her fear.

"Such a crazy fellow," Mirlito said, circling and feinting forward, jabbing at Cooper's belly.

Cooper jumped back, stumbled, but stayed on his feet. "And you, an animal."

Mirlito tapped his forehead with one finger. "You are so crazy. Molly, once *your* Molly, told me to kill, not you, but the skinny little *woman*. Molly wanted you to live and suffer." He smiled a grim smile. "It is *I* who want you dead."

"I saw a ship on the horizon, Mirlito." Cooper pointed toward the window. "Get your men. There's work to do."

Mirlito drew his head back. "Work? I told the men to go. Only one remains, the lazy one, sleeping in the rain. All that is over, crazy man. There is no ship. This here is my job."

The men's words were like the squawking of crows. Alida thought only of getting away. Rafe might be alive. He needed her. She eased onto her belly. There. The pistol was beneath the bed. She couldn't reach far enough, so inched back out. "William," she whispered, beckoning to him.

The boy crab-walked to her.

"Try to crawl under the bed. Bring the gun to me, can you?"

William swiped at his nose. "Under—under the bed?"

"Be brave, sweetheart." Both men had crouched and were staring into each other's eyes as deeply as lovers. "We must stop your father and that little man," she whispered. "I need to scare them with the gun."

William nodded and gulped. He slithered beneath the bed.

From behind her came the slap of flesh on flesh, then a wet, tearing sound and a deep-voiced scream. Alida sucked back a scream of her own and turned to look, keeping one hand around William's ankle.

The men were locked together, Mirlito's face pressed to Cooper's belly. Blood gushed from between them. Alida couldn't tell whose, yet what did it really matter? Mirlito would be unlikely to let her live now.

"Hurry, William! Hurry." She turned back toward him.

Hands grasped her shoulders and jerked her up and away from the bed. She screamed and let go of William's ankle.

"Miss Alida!" William yelled, his voice muffled.

"Stay there!" she shouted. "No matter what you hear, William. Don't come out."

CHAPTER THIRTY-THREE

Cooper crushed her to his chest. The coppery stench of his blood-soaked shirt and the acrid smell of his sweat sickened her. She steeled herself against his plundering hands. Once he'd satisfied himself or realized she wasn't his wife reborn, would he kill her? And what of William? She had to stay alive for William, whatever it took.

If Cooper had killed Rafe, she would stay alive for vengeance.

"Mr. Cooper," she said, inching her hands between them and shoving both palms against his chest. "Please. Stop. Stop and think."

He'd been holding her high, her bare toes grazing the floor, but now he let her slide down enough to stand. He mashed her against him, covering her face and neck with wet, sucking kisses, trying to reach her lips. She twisted her face side to side away as he pawed her breasts with one hand.

"Say my name." His hoarse voice cracked. His teeth nipped her ear like a mad, ravenous beast. "Say it like you used to. Say *I love you, Martin.*"

"Martin. Yes, Martin. You must stop. Think."

"Why did you leave me?"

She tried to wrench away. He kept his grip on her shoulders. "Look at me," she shouted. "Who am I?"

He stared wide-eyed and slack-jawed for a few heartbeats, then blinked and slumped. A sad smile crossed his face. "Alida Garrison." He took a deep breath and ran his hands down her arms until he gripped her wrists.

She stood as still as she could, fearing to jar him from this lucid moment.

"But I want you nevertheless. By God, I shall have you. I hoped you could love me. I wanted to win you, but you are incapable of love, it seems. I shall have you just the same. You will live with it the best you can." He sneered and loosened his grip. "You can tell yourself it's for William."

She twisted from his grasp and stumbled back. "I will fight you every time."

He smiled grimly. "A fight can be as arousing as true passion."

She shook her head. "You will live every hour of the day and night knowing you disgust me and that I plot your end."

His smiled faded. He shrugged. "So be it." He turned and walked to the door where he paused, head down, shoulders sagging, the picture of a defeated man. Then, with a roar, he raised his arms and swept the furniture aside. Spent, he turned to her, breathing hard. "I must first find your gallant shopkeeper."

"He's alive?" She stepped forward.

"Hiding somewhere, most likely. Not much of a hero, my dear."

"Rafe is more than you think . . ."

"That name!" he shouted. "I'm sick of it. He dies tonight."

Alida lifted her chin high. "He's been sent to bring you to justice."

His eyes opened wide. "What?"

"Yes. *And* the one before him."

Cooper snorted. "Lacey? I never thought much of him, either."

"What about when you saw me kiss Rafe, when you knew I loved his touch? You thought something of him then, didn't you?"

He strode toward her, fists raised. Alida stood her ground.

Cooper stopped and spoke slowly, quietly. "You will never mention him again. You never kissed him. He never touched you. It never happened, do you understand?"

"I understand nothing about you."

He gave her a hard glare and left. She stared at the empty doorway, then shakily knelt by the bed. "William, come out now. It's all right."

"I haven't—I can't reach—you know."

He backed out slowly from beneath the bed. As soon as she saw his ankles, Alida pulled him out and lifted him onto his feet. She brushed cobwebs from his hair and clasped him close. "It doesn't matter now. We're going."

A light on the rocks? Could that be Bishop? Cooper had seen him with a lantern before. A long time ago, it seemed. So, Bishop was investigating him all this time. How inept. Cooper scanned the shoreline again, blinking, one fist against his temple to hold back sudden pounding. Everything had gone so wrong. How? No matter what she called herself, no matter what she said or did or felt, he would have her, take her far away and show her how a woman can be loved.

He shook his head faster. The shake became a shudder. His obsession with her was ruling him, obstructing the return of his cultured life in the Carolinas and revenge for the insults heaped on his beloved South. All that had fallen away when she returned, cast from the sea.

She had never understood him. Did she return only to thwart his pursuit of the sacred cause? Her fear for the boy's life would keep her in line, though she'd not seemed so concerned before. That day, she'd meant to take him with her. He shook his head. He would work this out later. He peered down the beach and saw a running man. Mirlito was dead, but the other two? Mirlito said he'd sent them away, so who—? He stepped forward, squinting through the drizzle.

Abruptly he turned and ran back toward his house, ignoring shouts to stop. The commands only spurred him on. He must get to her. Only *she* mattered. He bounded up the back steps, kicked the door open and crossed the kitchen at a run, racing into his library. He'd put the little two-shot derringer safely in the drawer. It should be waiting for him there, but he couldn't find it. He ripped the drawer out, fighting down panic. No gun. He darted from the room and scrambled up the stairs, hardly feeling his boots touch the treads. Never mind the pistol. He wouldn't need it, why would he? This was his home, his fortress. No one here but Cora and she was nothing, nothing . . . there she was, crouched in front of the splintered bedroom door. "Get out of the way," he yelled.

Cora peered up at him. "Couldn't make you bring us peace." She shrugged. "Gettin' too old. Saw how that gal brung death with her, but couldn't stop it nohow."

"Get away from the door, Cora."

She felt above and behind her for the doorknob, grasped it and pulled herself to standing. "Go on in, then. The gal ain't there. Ain't nobody here but haints." Cora stood as tall as she was able and lifted her chin, glaring at him. For a moment the scars on her face seemed to pulse as she bared her teeth. She looked young and strong.

Cooper shook the illusion from his mind. "Go," he snarled. "I don't care where, just go!"

She slumped, then hobbled along the landing and down the stairs, holding to the wall.

"Savage," Cooper muttered as he reached for the knob. "I'll sell you off, Cora," he shouted. "You hear?" He paused and his hand shook on the knob. He remembered something, what was it? Yes, the day the waves disgorged the little woman. Cora spoke of death in a candle flame. Cooper took a breath and pulled back his hand.

But Cora had just said *she* wasn't there. Then where? He pushed open the door and looked in. The stench of death rolled toward him. Mirlito's death. Otherwise the room was empty. He backed away and ran downstairs and out the front door.

There they were, on the veranda. But what had happened? The woman lay with her head cradled in William's lap, her tousled black hair spread across the boy like a storm cloud. William's tears rained on her face.

"What is this?" Cooper was at William's side in two long strides.

"She tripped. She—she was running and fell. She opened her eyes one time, though. She'll be all right, won't she, Father?"

Cooper knelt and gathered the woman from William, holding her, kissing her face.

"Father, no." The boy grasped his leg and held on like a leech as he stood and started toward the door into the house, clasping the woman to his chest. Cooper kicked to shake him loose, but the boy hung on. "No, Father. She doesn't like you. She's afraid."

With a roar, Cooper kicked out harder. William rolled off and hit a pillar where it met the floor, hit with a loud thump and a little squeal, then flopped like a rag doll. Had he killed the boy? Cooper shook off the nagging thought. No time for regrets. Nothing mattered now but getting away.

He wanted her even as danger pressed on all sides, wanted her even as she lay weak and confused in his arms. How wonderful the way desire rose from the mere touch of her flesh, the scent of her hair and skin. "I could have you now. You'd only know it in dreams," he whispered, his lips to her ear. "Your skin would tingle, your mouth would be swollen from my kisses." He laughed. "You'd wonder why. You wouldn't know."

"But I would." Rafe Bishop stood on the bottom step, breathing hard.

"Bishop," Cooper whispered, backing away into shadows.

"Put her down."

"I can't. She's—she's hurt. She can't stand."

"So help me, Cooper—if you've hurt her—let her down."

"I'd never hurt her." Cooper's mind raced. Was Bishop armed? His hands were empty. All this thought took so much effort. Weariness crept over him, cloying and heavy, weariness and a pounding pain. "I can't think, Bishop. I have failed. My work is lost." He closed his eyes. "But I have my woman. I won't give her up, not again." As he eased her down, he nodded toward William. "I fear my boy is badly hurt."

Bishop flicked his gaze from woman to child. Cooper was on him with a roar. His weight knocked Bishop backward into a pillar. The man shook his head, dazed.

Cooper smiled and shoved him on his belly. He straddled the shopkeeper, pinning his arms. Bishop bucked and twisted as Cooper searched him. No weapon. He smiled at the fellow's stupidity. "Good God, man, what would make you rush up here unarmed? What would make a man so stupid?"

"You should know. You call it love."

Bishop twisted himself to one side, then to his back. Cooper was too strong for him. He'd not be thrown off. Rage burst inside him and he wrapped his hands around Bishop's throat. "Love? You equate what you feel with true passion?" He would choke the life from this loathsome man, who bucked and twisted to no avail. "Finally to be rid of you."

A scrabbling noise behind him. William? He turned partway, surprised into loosening his grip. The woman stood there, holding a large, heavy stone. Beneath him, Bishop drew in breath, coughed and struggled harder.

"Let him up." Her voice hardly trembled at all and her hand

was remarkably steady.

Cooper smiled. "Look how brave you are. I never knew you could be so resolute."

"Move away," she said.

"You are like an avenging angel," he whispered. "A goddess of ancient Rome. No, a Celtic queen." He glanced back down at Bishop, tightening his grip around the man's throat. "But, my dear, we must be rid of him." He lifted Bishop by the neck and slammed his head against the pillar.

"Get off him," she shouted.

"Such stern commands." He chuckled. "I will happily give over to you in our intimate moments, but . . ." The thought excited him. "You were never like this when you were William's mother. Always sweet and willing, but . . ." He shrugged and stood, then stepped over Bishop and approached her with arms outstretched.

She backed away. "Don't touch me."

"Do you think I mean to harm you?" He shook his head, trying to catch and keep her gaze. "I'd never hurt you." He took another step toward her.

"You've hurt William," she said, blinking away tears.

"Oh, well. We can make another. A better one."

"Alida," Bishop spoke from behind him, his voice rasping. "Take William and run!"

So the man still lived. Cooper chuckled. "You won't do what Bishop says. You don't belong to him. You belong to me, and always will."

She backed further away. "Don't come any closer. I will strike you down. I will."

He kept moving toward her. The little pile of rocks, from which she must have claimed her weapon, was within reach now. William had likely collected them to show his governess. *Thank you, William.* "I'm so proud of you, my love. Your hand, so steady." He opened his eyes wide and drank her in. "Your eyes flash, as cold as ice. You have become a fierce warrior. The kind of woman our new South will need." He shook his head, blinking in wonder. "So fierce. How did you get to be so strong? Remember before, how you jumped from the rocks? You submitted to the sea. You let it take you. You'd never do that now, would you?"

Something rustled behind him? Bishop again? He huffed out a breath and snatched up a jagged stone. He should have finished the man. Rage spiked, making his head throb as he turned with the stone in his hand.

Bishop was on his knees, shaking his head. Cooper stepped closer and raised the heavy stone high with both hands, then glanced over his shoulder. He wanted to see her face, hoping she understood the significance of what he was about to do. "I'll rid us of him." He gazed into her beautiful blue eyes as he swung the stone in a downward arc.

A gun barked. Something stung his chest. It burned. She gaped at him. She had no gun. He dropped the stone and looked down to see what had hit him. But he couldn't. So dark on this windswept night. Then what little light there was winked out.

CHAPTER THIRTY-FOUR

Alida threw the stone away. She slipped to her knees, then looked up.

Cora lowered her hand. A little pistol clattered to the floor. "Peace," she whispered. "Yes, Lord. Don't seem like so much to ask, here at the end of days. Ever'thing else been took away from ol' Cora. Had me two men, both gone. All my babies, gone. All I ask of him now was peace." She backed into the house and vanished in the shadows.

Alida crawled to William. He stirred and whimpered. She lifted him into her lap as Rafe staggered over to them. He knelt and reached for her. She burrowed into his arms, William between them. Rafe held them close, rocking and taking whistling breaths in through his bruised throat.

"Is he dead?" she asked, her face against his shoulder, afraid to look.

"His chest is bloody, but I see him breathing. I suspect he's past hurting anyone."

Alida tucked William's face against her, not wanting him to see. "Why would Cora do it?"

Rafe swallowed and winced. "She likely had more reasons than most for wanting him gone. Especially since he broke his last promise."

Alida looked at Cooper, determined to see him helpless so any lingering fear would leave her. "He's trying to speak," she said.

285

"I don't know what he'd say that I want to hear."

Alida pulled gently away from him, leaving William in his arms. She crawled to Cooper's side. The man turned his head and stared through her. He let out a breath and blood frothed his silently moving lips.

Alida leaned closer.

"Alice," he said, closing his eyes. "Alice, my darling, how could you leave me?" He opened his eyes again, his gaze boring into her. The confusion in him cleared for a moment. "Ah," he said, and at the end of a long exhalation, the light in his eyes faded to emptiness.

Alida shuddered, then turned to Rafe and William. She pulled the boy onto her lap.

"I couldn't help you," William said.

"You did fine, William. Just fine." She felt his limbs for injury, fingering the bump on the back of his head. The boy tucked his face beneath her chin.

She tipped her head so she faced Rafe, taking in his bruised throat and his bloodied face, grateful he was alive. "Some time ago I believe I heard you say you love me."

He nodded.

"I imagine that's for the best, for I have become uncommonly fond of you as well." She sighed, stood and helped William up. Rafe staggered to his feet. She turned and sagged into his arms. They leaned into each other like two halves of an arch, strong and whole with William between them.

Rafe lifted the boy.

"Mr. Bishop," William said. "You won't let Father hurt Miss Alida anymore?" He rubbed his eyes.

"No, William. She's safe. Your father can't hurt anyone again."

Alida touched William's face.

"My head hurts a little," he said.

"Looks like we all have bumps and bruises to spare, son," Rafe said.

"I couldn't get the gun for you, Miss Alida."

"We didn't need the gun, William."

"Is Father gone? I mean gone like my mama is gone?"

"Yes. I'm sorry, William."

"Father did bad things."

"Maybe he's gone to be with your mother and she can help him be better. He can rest."

William nestled against Rafe's side. "Father was sad without Mama." He straightened again. "Where will I live, Miss Alida?"

Alida blinked, taken aback by such a practical question. "I—well, I don't know."

"Don't make me live with Cora. She doesn't like me very much anymore."

Alida took the boy's hand, looking at Rafe.

"How about staying with me at *Señora* Rivera's house," Rafe said. "Until we get things sorted out?" He caught Alida's gaze and held it.

The longing in his eyes was like William's. It took away her breath. She answered the unspoken question. "I'll be staying there, too, William," she said. "For a while."

Rafe cleared his throat. When he spoke, his voice stayed whispery. "Later—maybe not so much later, maybe very soon," he said. "I could take you with me to a place north of here, William. I have a ranch. It needs work." His gaze still held Alida's. "But maybe we can visit Father Sebastian first, and he can say some words for us so Miss Alida can come too, if she wants." He glanced away abruptly, looking stunned, as if his words had jumped from his mouth without permission.

Though it was likely the oddest proposal any woman could hear, she smiled. The confusion in his face didn't frighten her.

It only meant surprises lay ahead. "I'd like that very much, Mr. Bishop."

Confusion melted from his face. He grinned and nodded like a satisfied man. "Let's leave this house," he said. "This big, cold and lonely house. We'll ask *Señora* Rivera to make us chocolate. She would love to feed a brave boy chocolate." He hoisted William up against his shoulder and took Alida's hand.

As they stepped down, Alida paused and turned, tugging him to a stop. "Cora," she said. "We can't leave Cora. She saved your life, maybe all our lives."

They made their way inside and through the kitchen to Cora's little room. Alida knocked, but no one answered. She eased the door open. The old woman sat in her rocker by a dying fire. She was staring into it, as if trying to read another message. Alida moved closer and touched her face, then her skeletal wrist. No blood pulsed beneath that chilled, leathery skin. She closed Cora's eyes. "I could never understand her. Couldn't decide if she was trying to help or hurt me. She wanted peace. That's all she ever said. Peace. I hope she's found it. She talked in circles so often, spoke of spells and forewarnings. I was never sure she was serious."

"Did she cast love spells? I believe they worked, for I surely am bewitched."

Alida cocked her head at him. "Well, she's gone. Has the spell lifted?"

Rafe hitched William up higher in one arm and reached to touch Alida's face, shaking his head. "What's come over me must have come from somewhere else." He leaned down and kissed her cheek, the corner of her smiling mouth, and then her forehead. "Must be a different kind of spell, the kind a mermaid casts on a man who finds her washed ashore."

She opened her eyes and took his arm. "Love is a big risk. I believe your mermaid said exactly that? Well, it's a risk I'll take."

She smiled up at him, then at William.

William's expression softened as he melted into the curve of Rafe's arm, his head on Rafe's shoulder as they walked away. Up the hill came *Señora* Rivera, Father Sebastian, and some others led by a large-bosomed blonde woman. Rafe murmured explanations to the priest while the women of the village gathered around Alida and William.

"I had to shame these into coming," *Señora* Rivera said. "This took too long, but you are all right. All of you," she sighed. "All right."

Alida closed her eyes. She had saved William, been strong enough this time to save a child who depended on her. She would let herself love William, love Rafe, and be unafraid of loss.

She let the cadence of Rafe's voice and the murmurs of the village women flow over her, not trying to understand the words, letting the sensation of peace fill her. Every other emotion, everything but love drifted away on what was, at least for now, a calm and gentle wind.

ABOUT THE AUTHOR

Bonnie Hobbs grew up outside a small town along the central coast of California, always reading, inheriting her father's love of stories of the Old West and her mother's passion for mystery and romance. She's carved out a career as an RN, most recently caring for hospice patients. She began writing seriously some years ago and has won and/or been a finalist in various contests. Her story "Nugget" was awarded the First Place LAURA award for short fiction (2014) by Women Writing the West. She and her husband live in southern Oregon.

The employees of Five Star Publishing hope you have enjoyed this book.

Our Five Star novels explore little-known chapters from America's history, stories told from unique perspectives that will entertain a broad range of readers.

Other Five Star books are available at your local library, bookstore, all major book distributors, and directly from Five Star/Gale.

Connect with Five Star Publishing

Visit us on Facebook:
https://www.facebook.com/FiveStarCengage

Email:
FiveStar@cengage.com

For information about titles and placing orders:
(800) 223-1244
gale.orders@cengage.com

To share your comments, write to us:
Five Star Publishing
Attn: Publisher
10 Water St., Suite 310
Waterville, ME 04901